I0533411

PRAISE FOR

THE PRICE OF FREEDOM

BOOK 1: Unlikely Allies

Judith Gelberger writes this novel as much from personal experience as a Hungarian émigré from the failed 1956 Hungarian Revolution, as from her imagination. Fiction, yes, but so plausible that it could easily be mistaken for fact. Everything has a price, as "Speedy," the daughter of the head of Hungary's brutally ruthless Secret Service, discovers. Everything comes with strings attached. Trust no one, for the tentacles of Hungary's Secret Service are long, unforgetting and merciless.

— **Michael Joll**—

Author of two collections of short stories. *Perfect Execution and other Stories and Persons of Interest,* and several novels. *Hacker* is his latest.

Gelberger has brilliantly described the plight of Hungarians in the post Hungarian revolution era and the obstacles faced by new immigrants to Toronto in her intriguing, fast-paced novel, *The Price of Freedom.* It is a spellbinding tale…full of intrigue.

— **Dr. Kennard Ramphal**—

Author of *Slippery Ochro,* 3r Prize Winner Guyana Prize for Literature (Fiction 2023).

Perfect timing for Gelberger's book. Today, we, in North America, are in a battle for freedom every bit as great as her characters faced. She shows us how people fought to be free. Her tight writing and a well-crafted, exciting story lead us to today and how we got here in the battle for freedom. Every day we lose a bit of it and she shows how painful it was to obtain. She entertains and educates through her strong, complicated characters.

— **Jennifer Footman**—

Poet, editor, fiction writer and journalist

A sprawling trilogy inspired by the remarkable life of the author.

— **Eric Choy**—

Writer, editor, and aerospace engineer. Author: *Just Like Being There: A Collection of Science Fiction Short Stories*

i

ALSO BY JUDITH KOPÁSCI GELBERGER

Heroes Don't Cry

Ruthless Rhythms

THE PRICE OF FREEDOM
Book 1: Unlikely Allies
A Novel

Judith Kopácsi Gelberger

MiddleRoad | Publishers

www.middleroadpublishers.ca

Making Literature See The Light Of Day

Library and Archives Canada Cataloguing in Publication

Judith Kopácsi Gelberger

The Price Of Freedom, Book 1: Unlikely Allies

Editor Ken Puddicombe

ISBN 978-1-990765-43-8 (soft cover)

Front cover photo courtesy: pexels-pixabay-47227

Back Cover: Ken Puddicombe

Front Cover design: Kathryn Lagerquist

Kathryn.lagerquist@gmail.com

The charm of Hungary is that it is not perfect. It's a village that has gone through hell, a country destroyed and reborn.

—Gyorgy Konrad—

(1933-2019)

Hungarian novelist, Pundit, essayist. Author: *A Guest In My Own Country*

DEDICATED

To those who have ever sought freedom against all odds, and to my family, whose love and support made this journey possible.

Table of Contents

ACKNOWLEDGMENTS

I can't thank enough Ken Puddicombe, my Publisher/ editor/ fellow writer/ friend, for his infinite patience and dedication to guide me to the final English version of my novel.

It would have been impossible to complete this work, without the tremendous help of the archivists at the Historical Archives of the Hungarian State Security Services, who managed to gather close to 2000 pages of documentation regarding my father, Dr. Sandor Kopacsi, the former Police Chief of Budapest, who sided with the revolution, consequently imprisoned and tried in secret by members of the Soviet army. Serving seven years of his life sentence, he managed to escape, with the help of his daughter, and many others, to Canada in 1975. The novel loosely follows his life and experiences.

And I can't thank enough my husband and partner in life and crime, Peter Gelberger, to stand by me all through the years, encouraging, and supporting me, no matter the setbacks, he never lost faith in me. I also thank my daughter, Eva Gelberger and her husband, Steven Brown for their insight and their positive outlook to carry on.

Had our son, Leslie Joseph Gelberger survived, I'm certain he too would have contributed, as he did, editing my memoir, HEROES DON'T CRY, in 2009. May he live in our heart forever.

Chapter 1

*T*he train departing from platform nine makes stops in Eger, Miskolc, and Satoraljaujhely. Please take your seat and mind the door!

Kira heard the announcement, followed by the steam engine letting out a sharp whistle, and the train rolled away from the station. Listening to the monotonous drone of the wheels on the tracks, Kira was pleased to have the booth for herself for the time being. Partially covering her face with her scarf, she promptly fell into a deep sleep.

The ticket agent, knocking on the window of the compartment to get her attention, slid the door open and said, "Tickets, please."

With a nervous smile, she reached into her coat pocket, pulled out her ticket, and handed it to the agent.

He took the ticket, clipped one corner and passed it back. Then, reaching out towards the other person in the compartment, he did the same thing to his ticket. His job done, he shut the compartment door and moved on.

Kira stared at the person across from her, shocked. It was Peter Gorgey, a former high school classmate, known as Rocky. He must have arrived after she fell asleep. Her sudden motion made him look up from his book, and she saw the recognition in his eyes. For a long minute, they could only stare at each other mutely.

Kira broke the silence. "What's the matter? Don't look at me like that. I am not a ghost, you know."

Rocky said, "No, you don't look like a ghost. But it is a surprise to find you here, of all places. Where are you going?"

"To Eger."

"I didn't know you had any relatives there?"

"Why should you know that? You never asked?" Kira replied tersely.

"That's true," Rocky admitted, then stared at her for a while, contemplating his next question. "How are you? I haven't seen you for almost three years."

Kira suspected Rocky had always found her attractive, but she had no intention of letting him penetrate the wall she'd created between them many years ago. His usual friendly manner towards everyone, including Speedy, Kira's childhood friend and now her arch-enemy, made her conscious enough to avoid him.

"How's your family?" Rocky enquired.

She snapped, "Just fine, thank you. Couldn't be better."

Rocky, feeling snubbed, shrugged and picked up Kira's newspaper from the side table. He blurted out, "Kira, are you going to university?"

Kira looked at him and shook her head. "I didn't even apply. What's the use? Comrade Winter, our high school principal, told me clearly enough that he would prevent it. Don't you remember how he used to say," —Kira imitated the unusually high-pitched voice of the man— "*For people like you, I recommend the construction industry? Mixing mortar and pushing heavy wheelbarrows would at least make you a useful citizen of the Dictatorship of the Proletariat.*"

The train came to the first stop. The sign over the station read *Eger*. Rocky picked up Kira's bag, but she snatched it from him as they headed for the platform.

Rocky said, "Kira, how long would you be staying? Look, why don't you come for dinner tonight?" He reached into his pocket, retrieved a piece of paper to jot something down, and passed it over to her. Kira took the paper and looked at him with a frown.

"It is my father's address," he explained.

"Thank you," she replied, still in a daze. "I might." Then she picked up her bag and walked away.

**

When Kira told her mother she would visit Charlie in Eger, she had told the truth. Well, that is almost the truth, as her destination wasn't really Charlie. But it wasn't a fib either, as it *was* in the same neighborhood. She didn't want to avoid seeing Charlie; she just wasn't sure she was up to his penetrating questions. The trouble with him was that he could always read Kira's mind by looking into her eyes. But then, he was a Gypsy, and Kira knew Gypsies saw beyond the material world.

Charlie still lived in the Gypsy Quarter by the Eger River. The place had changed since Grandpa first brought Kira as a small girl on a visit. By the late spring of 1967, the so-called Gypsy Quarter was just another part of the city, with large brick homes and all the amenities edging the neatly paved streets. Long gone were the narrow, muddy lanes of one-room huts of adobe bricks, with stove pipes sticking through one tiny window, except for the hut left as a relic—where the old blind woman lived by the very edge of the river.

Kira pulled her hood over her head as she walked down the street. Despite being in the middle of May, a stiff wind from the river chilled her. But it also kept people off the street. She missed the liveliness of the old days, when dirty little children chased one another, throwing mud and insults at passers-by, and through the open doors, one could hear shouting, crying, cursing, and laughter. She was half expecting a hand to appear, throwing a piece of bread to the children or emptying a potty in the middle of the lane.

She passed by Charlie's new house. Five years ago, Kira came with her grandparents to attend the housewarming celebrations. The cosmic event included the usual bonfire in the garden and the mouth-watering smell of the roasting bacon and sauteed onion. They opened many bottles of the famous red wine named after the *Bullsblood of Eger*, dancing into the night to Hungarian folk music provided by the local gypsy band.

But this time, Kira was not in the mood to hear Charlie's reminisces about the time when the Romanian army in August 1919 captured him along with Grandpa near Budapest, barely dodging being shot by the officers. Their platoon decimated—a punishment for being members of the Red Army during the reign of the months of the Hungarian Soviet Republic trying to defend Hungary from the invading international armies of the Allies. Kira had to live with the aftermath, as even decades later Grandpa still had disturbing nightmares recalling that event, when through sheer luck, Grandpa and Charlie were the ninth and eleventh persons in the line, both standing by either side of the unfortunate man being chosen to be shot.

There was a time in Kira's life when she was eager to hear the stories of Charlie's exploits, especially the one when the Nazis caught Charlie in the winter of 1944.

"They wanted me to tell them where the Chopakys were hiding. *Look at the old castle of Dédes,* I told them. Of course, the only thing they could find besides a few remaining walls was an old, not too deep dry well. But then, they wanted me to take them directly to their hiding place." Charlie lamented. "When I refused, the bastards chained me to the well and left me with one guard while they searched the area." At this point in the story, he usually winked at Kira. "It took me only seconds to untie my hands from the chain. Then I just grabbed the guard and dropped him into the old well. And ran like the devil was chasing me in the opposite direction! I would not wait around for the other soldiers to come back and beat me to death for misleading them," and his famous uproarious laughter shook the entire house.

Kira knew it wasn't one of his tall tales, as Charlie was big and strong enough to pick up a large cage with ten rabbits and carry it as if it were a sack of feathers. He had done just that during those winter months of the German occupation when the Chopaky family, with seven others, thirteen people altogether, were hiding in Bukk Mountain. "Somebody had to feed them," Charlie explained, and he did that.

Full of her reminiscences, Kira smiled as she walked toward Blind Maria's house. Despite the stiff wind, the old woman was sitting on a wooden bench by her door. Kira hesitated as she recalled Aunt Panna, Uncle Charlie's wife, pointing at Blind Maria's house, scaring the boisterous children to behave. "The Old Witch will transform naughty kids into cats!"

By now, Kira knew better—Blind Maria was a harmless old woman with the reputation of being able to predict the future. Her customers were mostly desperate women and girls who wanted to learn about the fate of husbands, sons, fathers, and lovers, swallowed up by the wars or languishing in prison.

For years, Kira could only pity those who made the trip and wished to look into the future. It was when her life had been secure, her family widely respected, and everyone loved and protected her. A cataclysmic upheaval, like a revolution, followed by many years of uncertainty about her father's fate, had sent her to get answers to her questions from the blind woman today. She knew that even her mother visited the old woman before her father's trial and returned home reassured.

She stopped a few feet away from the old woman, whose dark blue eyes seemed to penetrate Kira's soul.

Maria tilting her head toward Kira, called out, "Bless you, my child. I was expecting you." Pointing out with her right hand, she said, "Careful, there is a step-down, see?" The old woman patted the place next to her on an old couch covered with a large, slightly yellowing blanket made of goat hair. "There, sit here beside me."

The voice resonated like beautiful music made by a cello. It came from somewhere with no pain. It echoed as one's voice does in a deep valley, and soothed like a cool breeze on hot summer nights. Hearing it made all of Kira's reservations melt away, and sitting down, she tried to think of what to say.

"Give me your hand," Maria requested.

She took Kira's hand firmly, her fingers traveling around Kira's palm, following the lines. "You are lonely and scared. You lost someone very special recently. The loss drained your strength and hope away." The voice traveled through time and came back with an echo. "You had a happy and secure childhood. Something happened to you at eleven that changed everything. I can see a struggle, then a crash. Then, after many long years of waiting, your wish came true, but not as you had hoped. God gave someone back to you but took away another one."

Rationality seemed to return, and in a sudden panic, Kira tried to free her hand from the woman's grip. She suddenly didn't wish to know what the future held for her and would rather just melt into a dark, painless void, before she heard something she couldn't handle.

The soothing voice reached her again. "Relax, child. There is nothing for you to be afraid of—not here." She released Kira's hand.

Kira sat, as if hypnotized and, it took a while before, still hesitantly, she placed her hand back in Maria's.

"The friends you had turned away from you. You're feeling so desperately lonely that you are contemplating the unthinkable."

Kira felt powerless to leave. The blind woman's voice bewitched her, motivating her to stay and listen. "You just turned twenty-one, yet you feel that you have had over one lifetime's share of bad luck. Don't fret. The past will give you the key to your future. You will travel across the ocean, and you will not go alone. You will find friends and happiness there. Don't lose faith."

Kira's scepticism returned, as a large part of her problem was the recent rejection of her visitor's visa to Canada.

She got up, and without saying goodbye, stumbled out in a daze. She walked for a long time. She kept hearing the old woman's voice reverberating in her ears, "Go across the ocean...Will not go alone...Bright future...future...future..."

Kira sat on the grass beside the Eger River, exhausted. Finally, the tears came, releasing all the pain kept inside for so long. She hadn't wept for the past four years, even at Grandpa's funeral. She had no tears when she faced the ache and humiliation of aborting Thomas' child at sixteen. She didn't cry either when Thomas rejected her. She had simply been walking around with a frozen heart for a long time now, just going through the motions of getting up in the early morning to catch the train to an office, surrounded by hateful colleagues, compiling reports with non-existent numbers that changed at the whims of their superiors. After work, they went home to a silent apartment, where each member tried to hide their pain from the others.

When Kira ran out of tears, she stood up and looked at her watch. It was five thirty in the afternoon, too early to set out for the cliff, and she was hungry. She knew she would not go to Uncle Charlie. He knew her too well and would want to stop her.

She reached into her coat pocket for a handkerchief. She could feel a piece of paper there, and, puzzled, she dragged it out. It was the note Rocky gave her at the train station, and she remembered the dinner invitation.

**

During the four years they attended the Madách Gymnasium, Kira and Rocky had few occasions to talk except for the two weeks they spent together during the summer of 1962 at a camp in the village of Szob by the east side of the bend of the Danube. On their first evening there, Kira, with a small group, walked beside the river Ipoly on a dirt road under a canopy of large beech trees. They were only fifty steps from the main road when soldiers with guns pointing, surrounded them.

"Where do you think you are going?" bellowed one of them.

"Just out for an evening stroll," Rocky said, calm and reassuring.

"Just stroll back to where you came from. This is not a public beach. Move it!" The soldiers aimed their guns and shoved them back off the road.

"Why? Where does this road lead?" Rocky said.

"This is the border between Czechoslovakia and Hungary. No civilians allowed within fifty meters of any border," one soldier answered, his rifle menacing.

They had no choice but to obey the order and return to the village. Barely outside the forbidden parameters, Rocky pulled out a map from his pocket and studied it. Then he turned to Kira and, pointing at the map, he mouthed: "Maria Nostra."

Horrified, Kira glanced at him. She recognized the name of a picturesque village nestled in the hills of the Börzsöny Mountains, the penitentiary hiding the most notorious criminals, mostly enemies of the state: former aristocrats, renegade communists, writers who supported the counter-revolution or others deemed to be incorrigibles. But, of course, its location was not public knowledge. Prisoners on release had to sign an oath of secrecy unless, of course, they wanted to return and suffer more hard labor, starvation diet, and daily beatings by the sadistic guards. She knew some of the former prisoners, friends of her father, who had never regained their physical and mental health after a few years of incarceration in that place. *As a prison, Maria Nostra was a hellhole compared to the others.*

**

On her way to the address Rocky gave her, Kira passed by the Teachers Academy of Eger. In the blistering stiff wind, few people dared to challenge the elements on the street. She spotted a tall, greying man with a chiseled face, wearing a grey overcoat and a large grey hat. Using the tall building for cover, the man stopped, reached into the large pocket of his greatcoat and pulled out a pack of cigarettes. He drew out one with two fingers and placed it between his lips. Then he reached into the other pocket, as if he had all the time in the world, and pulled out a silver lighter. With a smile, he nodded at Kira, flipped open the lighter, lit his cigarette and inhaled. And as if it were the most gratifying experience, he blew a couple of rings and followed them with his eyes as they floated away in the air. All this he did with such grace that Kira had the urge to clap, as if witnessing a virtuoso performance. This friendly pantomime made an instant connection between the white-haired man and Kira. Smiling, they parted company.

Chapter 2

It had been nearly a month since Rocky ran into Speedy in City Park. They had not seen each other since they finished high school. Although they used to be classmates, other than a few words, they barely spoke during those years. Rocky was studious, mostly keeping to himself, while Speedy was busy taking part in national and international sports events and running wild, partying heavily on the weekends.

Rocky was totally surprised when Speedy, seemingly on the spur of the moment, invited him to the Officers' Club of the Ministry of the Interior.

"Sorry, no time. Busy, as usual," Rocky said, trying his avoidance tactic. Grabbing the leash of his ugly pug, he was ready to turn and head home, trying to find an excuse to avoid being seen anywhere with the daughter of the *Grand Executioner*.

"Coward. You are afraid of me," Speedy teased. "Would you avoid me if my father was not what he is?"

Feeling challenged, Rocky was getting hot under his collar. It was degrading to be called a coward. ""So, what's so special about that club?" he asked, shocked when Speedy stuck her tongue out and roared.

"You should have seen your face when I suggested the place. But it is not at all what you imagine. Actually, every Friday night, they show movies that one can see nowhere in the country—fresh off the press, so to speak. I guarantee you will love them. It is usually a double feature. And strictly by invitation…"

Rocky's curiosity won over. "Do you know what's playing this Friday?"

"Let me see." Speedy dug into her bag. She triumphantly pulled out a typed page listing the monthly program. "Here it is. This Friday, they'll show *Ben Hur*, the newly released major film with

Charlton Heston. And I guarantee unless you go to London, you'll not see any of them soon."

**

The following Friday night, Rocky met Speedy at the club's front door. It was in the center of Budapest's business section, on Vaci Street. Speedy grabbed Rocky's right arm and led him inside. They stepped into a large room set up as a restaurant. The tables were all occupied, mostly with young university students. They saw only a few middle-aged couples, some wearing police uniforms.

"Hello, Speedy," one youngster called out from the corner, "come and join us, will you?"

"Later, guys, later. After the movies are over," Speedy said and directed Rocky towards the backstairs leading up to the theatre.

Rocky stopped for a moment, confused. "That guy who called out to you by any chance was Joshka? Is he an officer or what?"

"The one who used to be the secretary of our communist youth organization in high school? Aye, that was him. No, he is not an officer. He is just a fourth-year student at Marxist University. Mind you, he is still a busybody in the Communist Party, one of the few people volunteering to go to Vietnam to fight the American Imperialist aggression."

Rocky observed Speedy's hand gesture, pointing a finger at her head, showing her opinion of Joshka's ambition to join the fight on the side of the communist Vietnamese. "Do I detect a bit of sarcasm?"

Speedy puffed out her cheeks. "Let's just say that I find it totally insane that the only official opposition this regime is currently facing is coming from the far left. They are the so-called Maoists, who find the current Kadar regime—with even the little liberalizations and reforms by allowing some privately owned stores—moving away from the Communist ideals. They got as far as admitting that things Marx had inscribed in the original manifesto were not happening the same way or not fast enough. So, they turned toward Mao-Ze-Tung, or Fidel Castro, as their modern-day leaders to follow.

"And would you believe it? They are considering a peaceful march to show their support of the Communist Party? You care to guess how the powers will approve their enthusiasm for the cause? Judging by my father's reaction, instead of the expected pat on their shoulders, most will be kicked out of university, and some will even end up in prison. Do you know the irony of this? Faithful communists had brought up all of them!"

Rocky heard a commotion in one of the private booths. The light in the theatre was already low, so he could only observe the hazy smoke and the unpleasant smell. It was the pungent odour of a live cat's tail on fire, irritating the throat and the eyes.

Rocky wheezed, trying to catch his breath. "What the hell is that stink, Speedy?"

"Oh, just a few of them sharing a toke or two. Don't mind them! Nobody does. A few children of the Upper Echelons enjoying the fruit of dirty Capitalism. Eating the food, the average worker can't purchase, drinking foreign beers and wine, and watching foreign movies no one else in the country can access. Please note them flaunting the latest fashions, like blue jeans, that normally sell on the black market for the princely sum of a month's worth of salary of an average worker. Or admire their long hair that our police force would drag others on the street to the nearest barbers to give them a severe crew cut, besides being charged with hooliganism. And when arrested for using illegal substances, just one phone call from the parents to the Police Headquarters will release them and drive them home without leaving a trace of a police report."

"And why do you suppose the *Power* is prepared to tolerate this more than those over-enthusiastic leftists?"

"Because they are far from being a threat to the *Power*! As long as they have their daily booze and narcotics, they care nothing about politics, rights or wrongs, to question or overthrow the regime."

**

"So, what did you think of the movie?" Speedy asked as they walked out of the cinema.

"It would be difficult not to be impressed by such an epic historical drama film! With the largest budget and the largest sets built of any film produced. Over two hundred camels and two thousand, five hundred horses, with some ten thousand extras? Not to mention the

- 11 -

chariot race, one of cinema's most famous action sequences!" Rocky stopped briefly before he added shyly, "I must admit that I would love to see it a few more times. If I'm lucky, I might see it in London…sometime."

Speedy grabbed Rocky's arm and guided him toward the dining room.

"Speedy, I have no time to stay," he said, after realizing Speedy's intentions. "Please let me go home. Uncle Varga is waiting for me."

Speedy looked at Rocky, challenging him to admit the truth. "Rocky, that's a lie, and you know I know it. Uncle Varga still has a few more months to complete his sentence, right? So, what's the story? Are you still living there?"

**

Mr. Varga, a close friend of Rocky's father, was a high school teacher who provided room and board for Rocky since 1960 when he finally started at the high school where Mr. Varga was teaching in Budapest. Mr. Varga was a well-loved teacher in his early fifties, known to dress immaculately in a tweed suit, wearing a bow tie, and in the winter, a long trench coat and hat, always carrying a large black umbrella. With his wavy silver hair and hooded grey eyes, he looked like an old patrician, and his soft baritone voice demanded instant respect that he never abused, even with the rowdiest students. Without exception, he called everyone Mister or Miss, and it was normal enough for him to stop in mid-sentence to bring a noisy class to attention. He taught English, Russian, and German in high school but offered private lessons in Latin, Hebrew and Ancient Greek as well. Twice a week he had an open house in the early evening in the guise of language instructions for any of his students to participate in a lighthearted discussion about life. Aunty Margit, his aged housekeeper inherited from one of his long-lost relatives, kept preparing and serving free sandwiches and aromatic hot tea by the gallon while shaking her head, covered with the *widow's kerchief*.

"Where do they come from?" she grumbled, "this looks more like an orphanage than a private home of a linguist professor. Some of them look like they were just released from delinquent institutions." Aunty Margit rolled her eyes while spreading butter on thickly sliced bread for the current crowd of youths.

Rocky often attended these unprompted gatherings, enjoying the easy-going discussions, diverse opinions encouraged, as long as expressed respectfully. The only rule was that these discussions had to be conducted in the chosen language of the day.

One day, at the end of August 1964 at the ungodly hour of two o'clock in the morning, the professor along with Aunty Margit and Rocky were rudely woken up by a loud banging on the front door. The professor, usually a light sleeper, got up in a hurry, pulled his house coat over his pajamas, and, trying to find his other slipper, hopped around on one foot.

"There must be some drunken guys," he muttered and hurried toward the front door. "Sheesh, there's no need to wake up the entire building! Are you lost…" he said, before he realized he was facing four uniformed police officers.

"Is this the Varga resident?" the tallest one said.

"Yes, it is. What can I do for you, Gentlemen?"

"Are you Mr. Varga?"

"Yes, I am."

The men stepped in, grabbed Mr. Vargas's arms, twisted them behind and cuffed him roughly. Rocky stepped into the hallway, wondering what the commotion was all about.

"Who are you? And what do you want with the professor?" Rocky said.

"The question is, who are you? And what is your relation to Mr. Varga?"

By this time, Aunty Margit also showed up in her large flannel housecoat and warm pair of slippers, holding a large knife in her hand, ready to attack the drunken intruders.

They arrested the Professor for giving illegal Bible lessons in his home. During the subsequent house search, the officers stripped books from the shelves and scattered the Professor's carefully arranged research papers all over the floor. They considered the original Latin and ancient Greek manuscripts, including various editions of the Bible in different languages, as evidence of the audacious crime committed. Both Aunty Margit and Rocky were assigned as witnesses.

Rocky would never forget the professor's testimony during the trial.

When the Judge asked the professor why he opened his home to the youth, he, deep in thought, reached into his breast pocket and extracted his glasses. Then he pulled out a clean handkerchief from the other pocket and wiped the lenses clean before he placed it on his nose and faced the Judge.

"Honourable Judge, it was because, since the late winter of 1944, I've had no family left."

The Judge looked at him, thoroughly confused. "Why, how?" he stammered.

Patiently, as if addressing a class of students, Mr. Varga explained. "It happened in December nineteen forty-four, after the invading German forces put the fascist Arrow Cross party in power in Hungary. A couple of their punks, acting on information from the superintendent, raided my home while I was out searching for food. When I returned home, I found the front door broken and the contents ransacked. Signs of struggle everywhere. My wife, my aging mother, my two children, along with the dozen Jews we were hiding were all missing. My apartment is on the bank of the Danube, and on my way home, I heard the shots and saw the normally dirty grey river turn red and the corpses bobbing up and down, floating downstream. At that moment, I failed to make the connection."

Rocky looked on as Mr. Varga wiped his eyes and blew his nose in his handkerchief before the man found his voice again. "And from then on, only my faith in God kept me alive. I put all my energy into teaching teenagers' foreign languages in a high school in Budapest, even though I was qualified to teach at any university of my choosing."

"Why?" the Judge said.

"Because I believed the bullies, mostly teenage boys, who killed my family had no one to teach them any better. As an educator, I must teach the future generation the difference between right and wrong. And I chose languages and the Bible to do just that."

However, the word of God was seditious in the Proletariat's Dictatorship, and spreading it earned the good man three years in prison.

**

"I'm still staying in his place," Rocky admitted, "…keeping everything in order…like paying the rent, providing Aunty Margit with a home in his absence; feeding and walking the dog."

"Oh!" Speedy said.

"Why are you so shocked? What would you have done in my shoes? Leave them to their destiny?"

Speedy leaned closer. "Are you telling me, Rocky, that you're the sole provider for Mr. Varga's household presently? By the way, can you visit him?"

"Once a month."

"And how is he? I mean, his health and morale?"

"The last time, he requested that I get him Spanish and Italian language books so he could add to his repertoire of languages in the meantime."

Speedy shook her head. "But how can you do it? I mean, I just assumed, judging by your keen interest and excellent marks, that by now, you would be in your third year at the Electrical engineering faculty at Eötvös University. And everyone knows it is a very demanding course, so when do you find the time to make money for all that?"

Rocky raised an eyebrow. "What university? I keep applying, and they keep refusing to admit me."

"But why? You'd been one of the best students at the Gymnasium. You kept winning all the math and physics awards. What is their excuse for rejecting you?"

Rocky looked hard at Speedy. "What do you really think, Speedy? You can't be that naïve to think that one's family's background would not determine whether you'll get a higher education?"

"Are you suggesting that they still force the children to pay for their father's sins? Only the fascists did that…"

"Remember, Speedy, that we in Hungary currently are living under the dictatorship of the proletariat, which is not the same as a democracy? So, logically, it suggests that they would favor children of working-class background to achieve higher education while forcing the sons and daughters of the former aristocrats to taste the joy of hard physical labor."

Rocky was the grandnephew of legendary General Arthur Görgey, who gave the Hungarian Army the order to surrender on the Plain of Vilagos in the summer of 1849, thus ending the year of a bloody War of Independence against the Austrian Empire. An action that all at once was the termination of bloodshed and the end of hope for a sovereign, free Hungary. A name so deeply etched into every Hungarian's psyche that its mention, even a century later, could still provoke feelings of betrayal, anger, and shame.

"Mind you, they would never directly spell out the real reason for the rejection." Rocky added, "The excuse they use is that there are too many applicants. I also tried to apply for a passport to visit my aunt in London, England. No surprises there. They already rejected my application twice."

"So, how are you managing?"

"By working at a small television and radio repair shop owned by a close friend of my father. I'm the person who will make the house calls, pick up the item, take it to the shop, repair it there, and take it back to the customer. And since we are prompt and polite and do a good job, we get a lot of calls. And in my spare time, I give private English lessons. It all adds up."

Speedy looked at Rocky, as if contemplating something important. "So Rocky, tell me, if you had your wish, what would you really like to do?"

Rocky smiled. "Thank you for asking. It is good to know someone cares." He looked up squarely in Speedy's eyes and blurted out, "Go to England, attend University there, and live happily after. As I mentioned, I have an aunt living there, and she would be happy to have me. But without a passport, there is no chance."

Speedy's sudden smile radiated throughout her face. She reached out and grabbed Rocky's hand over the table. "Rocky, why don't you try again? Put in an application for your passport and the university of your choice in England. The only thing you risk is another rejection."

"Which is guaranteed. Why would it be any different this time?"

"But if I go with you, your chances of getting it will multiply," Speedy insisted.

Rocky looked at her suspiciously. "And you would accompany me in person and use your father's influence to get me the passport? Why the sudden interest in helping me now, Speedy?"

"Busted. All right, I admit it: I want to get into your pants. It is a long-time dream of mine, if you really want to know. Why else would I offer my help to an outcast?"

"Why indeed? Why the sudden change in your interest in me? Could you have really developed some social conscience and want to help the downtrodden? It would be easier for me to believe your sincerity, Speedy, if you had also offered your help to Kira Chopaky as well." He stopped there for a moment and added slowly, "Although I have to admit, I never really bought the sincerity of your monstrosity toward her. Without exception, it happened in front of the school when your father came to pick you up. Was that strictly for your father's benefit? Why? What did you get out of it? It was horrible, the way you tore into her and then left her heaving on the stairs!"

"Did you know I used to be best of friends with Kira before the Uprising?"

Rocky shook his head.

"I used to spend more time at her house than at mine. The Chopakys took pity on me, a motherless child. I remember we used to play in Alex's official car, driven by Frank during lunchtime, and Frank, being a childless widower, doted on both of us. He let us get away by turning on the sirens in the official police car and playing hide and seek with us in the park," she added wistfully. "Then the Uprising happened, and Alex was arrested. One day, I spotted Kira and her mother at the bus stop. We were in the car, by then driven by Frank. I shouted, *Stop, stop! There is Kira! Let me hug her!* Frank stopped, and I jumped out and ran toward Kira. My father was right behind me. Without a word, he grabbed me by the collar of my coat, turned me around, facing him, and slapped me on the face in public. Then he roared, *This will teach you to be friendly with the enemy! If I catch you again fraternizing with any, I'll skin you alive!*"

Speedy looked at Rocky, her eyes filled with tears. "So, what was I supposed to do? We were only eleven years old then! And since then, I could rarely go anywhere alone without a chaperone."

"And now?"

"Look, I already feel rotten about the whole thing, and believe me, I try to remedy it the best I can. I already arranged Kira's passport." She didn't elaborate on the reasons, circumstances, or how she achieved that. She said, "I believe they delivered it to her a few days ago. She will never guess my involvement, and it should remain a secret between us, Rocky."

Rocky, stunned, could only offer his hand in sympathy. Speedy grasped it with both hands and asked hoarsely, "And now, can I accompany you to get your passport?"

Chapter 3

André Görgey arrived home and let himself into the house using his own keys. He was smiling, reflecting on the young woman he had just passed on his way home. He liked her, although he couldn't quite pinpoint her appeal. Others noticed how people would stop and turn to look at the tall, slim girl with short black hair framing her oval face, sparkling hazel eyes and a perfectly framed mouth with a hint of a smile. However, he also observed that her eyes were red as if she had been crying recently. He restrained himself from stopping to inquire about her troubles.

He had barely reached his room when he heard the doorbell ring at the main entrance. He contemplated whether to open the door himself or let Betty handle it—he decided to let Betty handle the situation.

"Oh, oh!" he muttered, "Someone's in trouble! Whoever just arrived and rang the doorbell will face Betty's wrath! This will be entertaining!" He stood close to his door, eager not to miss the show. Within minutes, he heard Betty's slow shuffling behind the heavy oak door, along with the ensuing curses, for Betty despised anyone who rang the bell.

Betty suffered from a typical Eastern European ailment known as *Bell Phobia*. This affliction had its roots in the years between 1948 and 1956, when the secret police would ring the bell forcefully and conduct violent searches upon entry. It was never a social visit but a vulgar and systematic search followed by an arrest. The arrested individuals often vanished for life or many years without a trace. Betty couldn't help but associate the doorbell with those monsters who had shattered her world in the early summer of 1950. From that time on, she never stopped complaining about them.

"Never mind that those bastards woke me up from a pleasant dream," she said, "but they took away my employer, and they left a terrible mess behind." Betty deemed each crime a capital offense, deserving a punishment ranging from a single to a triple hanging, regardless of the logical implications. André understood her unique criminal code.

André heard her muttering as she attempted to turn the heavy iron key to open the door.

"How often must I tell you not to ring the bloody bell? I know you're there. We have a dog. He can smell you, and he can bark, too. Grrr. Woof, woof,"—she attempted to mimic a dog's bark in a lower voice.

She opened the door.

"Hello, Betty. That dog is getting old and wheezy," Rocky casually informed her.

André saw Betty raise her hand as if to smack his son's face lightly, and pretending to be angry, she scolded, "Do you want to kill me, boy? Who do you think you are, ringing the bell like the Secret Service?" She pulled him into the house by his sleeves. "You've grown again."

"No, Betty, you are shrinking," Rocky replied.

She stepped back and examined him from top to bottom, shaking her head. "You're too skinny. Is there no food in Budapest?"

"It's good to see you again," Rocky said, then he looked around the hallway, searching for lights shining beneath the doors. "Is Father at home?"

"Which one?" Betty asked casually, a twinkle in her eyes. "Father Tibor is in the study, and Mr. Görgey is out for a walk." She shouted, "Father Tibor, we have a visitor!"

Father Tibor arrived at the door, a small, balding man in his sixties with warm brown eyes that lit up when he saw Rocky. "Rocky, my boy! What a surprise! How are you? Welcome home. We didn't expect you so soon. I hope you have good news!"

Rocky, being careful not to crush the smaller man, hugged him tenderly. "Wait until Father comes home, and then I'll share my news."

Father Tibor walked to his chair and sat down, watching Rocky, whose face turned slightly red. "Son, is there anything you want to tell me before your father arrives? Did you do something you're ashamed of?"

Rocky, his eyes focused on the floor, swallowed hard. "I thought you gave up on confessions when you left the order."

They both laughed, though there was a hint of bitterness in their reaction.

Indeed, Father Tibor had left the order and everything associated with being a Jesuit when the Secret Service ordered him to break his oath of secrecy regarding the sacrament of confession. He had firmly refused, equating the officer's request with the actions of the Nazis during World War II. Indignantly, he had walked out of his office. Fortunately, the officer, a former inmate of a concentration camp, chose not to arrest the priest but instead arranged for him to become the official tour guide at the Fort of Eger, leveraging his expertise in sixteenth-century Hungarian history to continue educating the children.

André left the house using the side door and returned through the main door, pretending to have just returned from his walk. He caught Betty in the hallway, diligently dusting the spotless and perpetually shiny brass doorknob with her trusty dust cloth. With a serious expression, he asked, "What's going on, Betty?"

"The priest has a visitor. He said it's okay for you to go in," Betty replied, motioning her head towards the study.

André walked into the study, and his eyes brightened when he saw Rocky. He hugged the tall young man and jokingly scolded Betty, "Old woman, how dare you trick me like this? A visitor!"

Rocky called out, "Betty, come in. There's great news! I just received confirmation of my scholarship to England. I'm leaving in about a month. Isn't that exciting?" He hugged everyone and then turned to his father. "By the way, I hope you don't mind, but I invited a guest for dinner tonight."

They looked at him in surprise—Rocky rarely brought visitors home.

"Well, that's a surprise!" André whistled, looking at Rocky with astonishment. "I can't recall you ever bringing a guest for dinner here. Who might this be?"

Rocky cleared his throat. "Her name is Kira Chopaky, and we went to high school together. I met her on the train today, and I invited her over."

"Chopaky. Is she related to *that* Chopaky?" André inquired.

"Yes, she is. And she had a very rough time because of it in high school. Our beloved principal, Mr. Winter, that dirty son of a...well, I don't mean to curse, but every time I think of that monster, my blood boils. I could have throttled him those times when he called her out in front of the class just to humiliate her."

Both André Görgey and Father Tibor gasped.

André said, "Oh, my God! Poor girl! It must have been devastating for her!"

"Well, maybe she was dying inside, but each time, she stood there and boldly returned his stare. White as a sheet, she stood her ground. This silent exchange normally lasted a few minutes, always ending with Comrade Winter turning red and storming away. Anyway, I met Kira on the train today, and she looked like she could use a friend."

When the doorbell rang again, André Görgey opened the door. He smiled and, without thinking, reached out and grabbed Kira's hand. "Oh, it's you! I wondered who that great-looking girl on the street was that I passed by recently."

She stood at the door, clutching her bag with one hand, stunned by the warm welcome. "Hi, I'm Kira Chopaky," she added shyly, "I hope I'm not too early?"

André took her hand with both of his, covering it protectively. "No, no. You're right on time. Come in; we were waiting for you." He took her bag and placed it on a bench by the door, then gently guided her to the Great Room, which served as a study, a bedroom, and, on special occasions, a dining room.

Bookshelves covered three of the walls, while in one corner, cluttered with more books and papers, sat André's old desk. Against the fourth wall, a battered army cot covered with an old Turkish Kilim rug was his bed. Two armchairs faced his desk, with a small round table between them. On the other side of the room was a large wooden table from a local monastery, capable of accommodating close to ten people sitting on each side of the wooden benches. The room was an ideal place for lively discussions and a haven for daydreaming, working, and sleeping in the friendly company of lingering ghosts.

André pointed to the armchair across from the desk and he sat in the one opposite Kira. Rocky sat on his father's cot and the priest took the chair from behind the desk. André picked up a pack of cigarettes from the table and offered one to Kira.

She said, "No, thank you. I don't smoke."

"Good girl," André said as he lit his own cigarette. "I smoke a lot, partly out of gratitude. One of these sticks saved my life a few years ago." He winked mischievously at her.

"Isn't that a contradiction?" Kira asked.

"Father, another audience for your famous Chesterfield story," Rocky said. "Do you really want to hear it, Kira?"

"Of course I do."

André Görgey goaded his old friend, "A drink then? Father Tibor, would you mind sharing your secret stash of French cognac with us? It's a suitable occasion, you must admit."

Father Tibor obediently turned toward the desk and pulled a bottle of 21-year-old *Courvoisier Vintage Connoisseur Collection* from one drawer. He poured the precious liquid into the goblets on a round silver tray on the desk.

André Görgey slowly picked up his glass, swirling its contents for a moment before taking his first sip. He had a distant look in his eyes as if trying to recapture a memory. With a sigh, he placed the goblet on the table beside him and, focusing on Kira, began his story. "I assume you've heard about the László Rajk trial in Nineteen-forty-nine?"

"Yes, I have. I met his wife and son in the summer of Nineteen-fifty-six. I also spent a few days in the Yugoslav Embassy with them after the Russians returned."

"Well, it's no longer a secret that the László Rajk trial was a hoax. Everyone arrested during those times was accused of spying for the CIA and Tito. Tito, the secretary of the Yugoslav Communist Party, had fallen out of favor with the Soviet Union for daring to chart his own course instead of following Stalin's leadership."

André plunged into his story with gusto.

"Why they chose Rajk for the *honor* of purging the Hungarian Communist Party of its enemies in Hungary is still a mystery. Rajk was not only a perfect Communist, but at the time of his arrest, he was the newly appointed Minister of The Interior as well. I could never picture him collaborating with the Nazis, as they later accused him of doing. It must have been simple jealousy of our bald and short leader, Mathias Rákosi. Rajk, a hero of international reputation, was tall, good-looking, and had thick, wavy hair. But of course, to make the charge of treason stick, they needed reliable witnesses to prove direct contact between Rajk and the Western imperialists. I was perfect for that role. We fought together in the International Brigade during the Spanish Civil War in Nineteen-Thirty-Seven, and I met him again in Paris shortly before the Germans invaded before I left for England. And I came from an old aristocratic family. Knowing all this, I couldn't have been a more perfect partner for his crime, could I?"

André Görgey stared into his goblet. He lit another cigarette, inhaled deeply, and watched the ashes grow at the tip. "I was also the newly appointed Hungarian Cultural Attaché stationed in Rome from Nineteen-Forty-Six. I took myself seriously," he added self-mockingly. "Just after the war, there was an excitement in the air, filled with positive energy...making most of us believe we could rebuild this country and wipe away the bitter stain that Hungary was Hitler's last remaining ally. True, while in Rome, I heard about the election irregularities in Nineteen-Forty-Eight when the Communist Party came to power in Hungary by stuffing ballots using the names of dead people. But I just chalked it up to the growing pains in any new democracy. And Rajk's presence within this government put my mind at ease.

"So, I didn't hesitate to come back when they ordered me to return. I wanted to be the first one to congratulate him on his new appointment. Imagine my surprise when, within a few short months after returning, they arrested me and took me to prison. They informed me I would be in good company there, as I could share the cell with the gangster Rajk and his chief collaborators accused of overthrowing the Dictatorship of the Proletariat. Mind you, even that was a lie, as they had kept us in solitary confinement unless they had dragged us to *testify*.

"At first, of course, I denied I was an Imperialist Agent, sent back to Hungary in Nineteen-Forty-Six to blackmail Rajk for being an informer of Admiral Horthy's regime during the early forties. Why would I admit to such obvious and outrageous lies when there was no truth in them? I'll spare you the gory details of the daily tortures and how they forced us to learn our scripts. It was obvious we were being prepared for a Public Trial. I assume they had drugged all the others as well, each day varying the doses, evidently to assess how much to use when the big day came. During our dress rehearsals, we kept parroting our prepared answers to the wrong questions. The result was such crosstalk that it would have been hilarious under less macabre circumstances. We did not know when the trial would take place. All the rehearsals looked like the real thing.

"Then, one day, I got my lines perfect. To show appreciation for my excellent performance, my interrogator took me to his office and offered me a cup of espresso and a Chesterfield cigarette."

Rocky interjected, knowing the story too well, "Which he later regretted."

André nodded. "I was a chain smoker before my arrest, so my craving for nicotine was more overwhelming than hunger. But, besides continually being starved, they repeatedly drugged me as well. That cigarette, the first one in many months, caused such strong intoxication that I started yelling, *It is a lie! Nothing but a gigantic hoax! You dirty fascists, murderers...*I called them everything I could think of. It was very clear that in this state, I was useless as a witness in a public trial. Thus, they quietly put me in solitary confinement. They released me some months after Stalin's death in nineteen fifty-three. They executed all the others who confessed to their crimes."

André Görgey leaned back in his chair with a bitter smile and concluded his story. "So, this is how the Chesterfield cigarette saved my life."

Kira took a deep breath before breaking the silence following the revelation. "As far as I know, they had not tortured my father physically before or during his trial in Nineteen-Fifty-Eight."

"It would be quite interesting to know what really happened at the Imre Nagy trial. But of course, it will take some time before anyone would dare talk about it," commented André.

"I should say so," Kira replied sharply, "unless they have the urge to go back and complete their sentences...any survivors released by the general amnesty had to sign an oath of secrecy."

André Görgey nodded. "It was standard procedure in my time as well. However, I don't believe anyone cares about my story nowadays, and I'm pretty sure our walls have no ears here." He pointed at the thick walls in his study, not noticing Kira's skeptical smile.

Betty appeared with a large tureen, filling the room with the delicious aroma of steaming soup. They ate silently, with determination, concentrating on their dishes. After Betty served coffee, Kira got up, thanked them for the lovely dinner and left abruptly, leaving an uneasy silence behind her. Her hastiness took everybody by surprise.

Something was amiss and Rocky grabbed his jacket without his father's prompting and said, "I'll go after her."

Chapter 4

All day, the threatening rain had loomed, with dark, expectant clouds blanketing the mountains and valleys. As soon as Kira left the Görgey house, the sky opened up. A sharp northern wind seemed to target her, pelting her with raindrops.

It would take her at least an hour to reach the cliff tonight, a path she had traversed many times. The area was a well-known tourist attraction, so nobody paid much attention as she strode along the rail line used by visitors from Eger to Miskolc during the warmer months. People were accustomed to dedicated hikers enduring the elements. Since she planned to spend the night there, she had packed her backpack with food, a flashlight and a waterproof blanket.

She followed the railway along a winding road through the valley to Szarvaskő. From the station, it was about two hundred steps before she crossed the rails and turned left. A narrow and treacherous path led her up to the ruins of the Fortress of Szarvaskő. By the sixteenth century, its historical importance had faded, but its scenic location remained a favorite among tourists.

Kira struggled up the steep, rain-soaked hill, slipping and sliding, clinging to wet branches and crawling on her hands and knees to maintain balance. Darkness had already set in, and she retrieved her penlight. She clenched it between her teeth as she ascended, the beam wavering and flickering, affected by her labored breathing.

It felt like an eternity before she reached the plateau. Exhausted, she collapsed by a large oak tree, her back against it. Panting from the exertion, she felt a sharp pain in her chest. Compared to the paralyzing numbness she had endured for the past few years, the pain was a welcome sensation, though.

She illuminated her watch with her flashlight. It was already eleven o'clock, much later than she had anticipated. The clouds shrouded the night, casting the countryside into total darkness. But that didn't matter. In the darkness, she couldn't gauge the steepness of the cliff, though she knew it was a sharp drop of about one hundred meters. In daylight, many times she had seen the narrow highway, a serpentine ribbon through the mountains, with cars and trains looking like toys in the distance.

A few years ago, before turning seventeen, she believed she could soar like a hawk over her beloved Bükk mountains or make her dreams come true with the snap of her fingers. But lately, faceless entities haunted her at night, threatening to consume her and those she cared about.

She tilted her head, anticipating a familiar voice and reached out, hoping for a friendly touch. There was none. She recoiled, curling into a fetal position, moaning in pain. The prolonged absence of loving touches intensified her sense of loss.

She pondered why she felt so estranged from the very place that had always given her a strong sense of identity and belonging. She knew she descended from a long line of heroes, a source of immense pride throughout her life, and this should have sustained her.

Hungarian history wasn't just dates and names for Kira—it was her ancestors, generations risking their freedom and lives for their country, including her own grandparents and parents. She recalled Sunday afternoons when old friends gathered in their kitchen to reminisce about how her grandparents and parents had fought the Nazis and sheltered many people during World War II.

Kira had always regarded her father as a hero, even after he received a life sentence for opposing the brutal Soviet invasion during the 1956 counter-revolution. She firmly believed that history would eventually clear his name. She clung to this belief, fantasizing about how she and her classmates would rescue him. At the tender age of twelve, she had concocted elaborate scenarios of storming the prison and freeing her father.

But reality shattered those dreams. There were no throngs of friends storming the prisons. Most of them were imprisoned themselves, except for a fortunate few who had escaped to the West. Those who remained in Hungary stayed silent out of fear. Even old friends crossed the street, pretending not to know her. She remembered the incident when Speedy, her childhood friend, attempted to greet her on the street, only to face public humiliation and threats from her own father. Her brave plan to free her father with her classmates also amounted to nothing.

Kira had to confront the painful truth—her father's release in March 1963 did not align with her fantasies. In her grandfather's stories, heroes were always exonerated. Kira convinced herself that her father, once released, would reward his loyal followers and punish the treacherous.

Instead, her father's first taste of freedom after seven agonizing years led to a solemn march behind her beloved grandfather's coffin in the cemetery. Grandfather had passed away on March 25, 1963, just hours after hearing János Kádár, the Secretary of the Communist Party, announce a general amnesty on the radio. Kira suspected that her grandfather had died from the shame that the regime he once supported almost killed his only son.

Kira struggled to comprehend that her father's release did not equate to true freedom. His release was conditional, subjecting him to potential return to prison for the next ten years. It came with the suppression of his civil rights, including his voting privileges. His law degree relegated him to a factory as a lathe operator, performing grueling piecework for minimum wages.

With their apartment bugged, phone conversations monitored, and even friends from his prison days suspected of being informants, Kira felt that the walls of her father's prisons had only expanded, now encompassing every family member. The years of stifling secrecy, mistrust and uncertainty slowly drained their spirits.

Kira's only solace during this time had been Thomas Dióssy, a high school classmate who walked her home and helped with her studies. Thomas was a quiet, friendly boy, accepted by all cliques in their class. He had a passion for cars and while he rarely offered opinions, he could discuss cars endlessly. Their friendship deepened, and their relationship turned passionate over time.

After two years of gentle persuasion, Thomas convinced Kira that he truly loved her for who she was. His love and encouragement rekindled Kira's long-forgotten habit of singing and inspired her to dream of a normal life with a university education and a loving partner. She hoped to emulate the enduring relationship between her parents, understanding that her mother's love and support had been crucial to their survival.

Almost two years had passed since she last saw Thomas...

**

As he approached the statue of Anonymous near the Vajda-Hunyad Castle, something seemed amiss. It had been a shock when Thomas received his conscription, following their graduation.

Kira had always thought that Thomas would escape conscription, as most boys dreaded it, and some even took extreme measures to avoid it. During the year since Thomas had been stationed far from home, their interactions had been limited. Every time he returned in uniform, Kira expected to see changes, though she was not ready to acknowledge them.

Kira disliked seeing Thomas in a uniform which, to her, symbolized ruthless power. She often sat on their favorite bench where they had shared countless moments, holding hands, studying, and growing closer.

As Thomas approached, Kira sensed something was terribly wrong. The Thomas she knew, with his pleasant demeanor and smiling face, now seemed to bear a malevolent sneer, ready to unleash destruction. She instinctively moved away to create some distance between them.

"Why are you still in uniform?" she asked, her heart sinking.

Thomas said, "Sit down and listen. I owe you an explanation, not that you really deserve one." He paused, swallowed hard, and continued, "I've been given an ultimatum: either break up with you or forget about attending university."

Kira reached out to touch his face, but he pushed her hand away. She sat on the bench, trying to comprehend what had just transpired. Thomas's anger didn't seem genuine—it felt like a poorly acted scene. She wondered who was watching and orchestrating this public confrontation and why.

Thomas was now visibly agitated. "I can't take it anymore. I won't let my future be jeopardized because of you, Chopaky. You and your damn traitor, Jew-loving father!"

Kira stared, in shock. She couldn't believe her ears. It felt like a nightmare or hallucination. She tried to pinch herself, hoping to wake up, but the hurtful words kept coming.

"You always defend him, don't you? I stayed with you this long because Mister Winter told me to break your loyalty to your father. Are you really that blind, or do you just refuse to see the price you're paying for it? It doesn't matter anymore. You're hopeless, and you're in my way. My university education, my entire future, is on the line. So, Chopaky, get lost. Goodbye, so long, and all the rest."

Kira watched as Thomas walked away without looking back. She would never forget the numbness that enveloped her then, freezing her emotions. In the following nights, faceless figures pointed at her father, blaming him for all her misfortunes, including being rejected by universities and losing three jobs within a year. It felt like she was tied to her father's fate as long as she remained in Hungary.

**

She sat under the large oak tree by the ruins of the old castle, the very place that had prompted her to leave Budapest earlier that day. She had embarked on this journey seeking solitude and clarity, but now she confronted acute loneliness and the pain of losing Thomas, her closest friend and lover. She longed for his soothing words and affectionate touches.

Kira pondered if she could realistically expect a twenty-year-old boy to choose a girl with a seemingly hopeless future. Would she ever find a partner who genuinely cared for her without ulterior motives? After Thomas's rejection, how could she trust anyone's friendship to be based solely on her own merits and not be tainted by espionage for the state?

Her father had recognized her dilemma and tried to help by arranging for her to leave the country. He had asked his childhood friend, László Singer, during his visit from Canada in January 1967, to take Kira with him. The Singers had promptly sent an invitation letter and an airplane ticket. Kira had applied for a passport, doubting its usefulness, but was surprised to receive it in record time. She suspected her father still had friends in the passport office.

Encouraged by this progress, Kira applied in person for a Canadian visitor's visa. During the interview at the Canadian consulate, a tall blond man with drooping whiskers questioned her motives. Kira explained that she wanted to spend six months in Canada studying English while visiting close friends of her father. The interview appeared pleasant and relaxed, and she left with optimism.

However, her hopes were shattered when she received a rejection letter from the Canadian consulate. The bureaucrat believed Kira had lied about her intentions, deeming it unrealistic that she would only need six months to learn English. It closed the only escape route for Kira. Caught in a catch-22 situation, she couldn't leave Hungary without a visa, yet she needed to leave to apply as a refugee,.

Feeling trapped and hopeless, Kira sat on the ground, sliding further toward the precipice.

Chapter 5

Strong arms suddenly grabbed Kira from behind and pulled her from the cliff's edge.

"You...idiot," she heard a hoarse and agitated male voice and found herself shaken, then pulled from the precipice and thrown to the ground. "I knew you were going to do something stupid! I just knew it!"

The intruder's voice sounded familiar to Kira, but she was too stunned to respond. And in a blur, she recognized Rocky.

Rocky slapped her, and the force of it stung and left her in a daze.

"I followed you since you left the house. Why, tell me why did you want to jump? Answer me, Kira!" Without waiting for an answer, he grabbed her again and dragged her under the oak tree on the plateau, far from the cliff's edge. He slumped down beside her and pinned her arms down when she tried to free herself.

"Stay still, or I'll break your arms and legs, too, if I have to. Kira, answer me! Why did you want to jump?"

She wasn't sure whether to laugh or cry, but a hysterical laugh just burst out of her.

Rocky let her sit up, a puzzled look creasing his forehead. The next minute, with no warning, her laughter turned into a terrible raspy wailing.

Rocky pulled her close to him and rocked her gently as if she were a frightened child who needed comfort. She kept sobbing for a long time, her body shaken by tremors as she clung to him, digging her fingers into his back.

She didn't realize when their mouths met, but in one thunderous moment, the world ceased to exist, it seemed, for both. Their lovemaking was more than just two bodies uniting. For Kira, it was a combination of relief from over-tensed nerves, and for the time being, it didn't matter to her about Rocky's motivation. It could have been a simple gymnastic act, taking advantage of the situation, or a kind gesture reaching out to a lonely soul in torment.

Instead of words, they could only share passions, anger, understanding, taking and giving, roughness, and tenderness. Then, completely exhausted, they lay beside each other, holding hands, trying to catch their breath.

Not trusting the sensations, Kira finally broke the silence. "I believe it is time for me to leave." She stood up, put her backpack on her shoulder, and prepared to walk away.

Rocky grabbed her by her ankle and pulled her down beside him. He shouted, "The hell you will, Kira Chopaky! Do you realize that if I didn't stop you from jumping, by this time, you would be a much-splattered mess on the ground? Do you have any idea how steep the cliff is?"

"Of course I do," she said smugly. "I know this area very well. I chose this spot purposely, you know."

"You are a nut, you know. What made you want to jump? Does it have something to do with Thomas?"

"Oh, no!" She moaned, in despair. She simply was not in the right frame of mind to explain to Rocky that, at this moment, Thomas was just a small pebble, irritating to walk on, but not enough to end her life.

"Now that is just too funny!" She declared sarcastically while wiping her tears between the bursts. "I left home with a pretense of visiting a relative, came as far away as possible to be left alone, to think and decide on my life, and just when I thought I had come to the right conclusion to end the misery once and for all, you had to show up, Rocky, to interfere! And I believe you think you just did me a favor, don't you?" She sighed wearily, looking at Rocky accusingly.

"Look, this is not a police interrogation. Although you know very well how they would treat a suicide attempt."

"Sure, they would drag me to the hospital, pump my stomach, regardless of whether I swallowed any poison, just for the joy of it. Then, they would charge me for breaking the law. Makes perfect sense to me! They may make my life miserable, but I have no right to end it. That's why I came up here, so I could make my decision with no interference. But no, you had to follow me! I hope you don't expect gratitude now because none is coming," she screamed.

"But surely nothing can be really all that bad?"

She wanted her sarcasm to be clear. "How would you know? What earthly problems did you ever have to face, Rocky Görgey? Broke a nail or lost a valet?"

"Now, hold on for a minute Just because I don't keep walking around with a sour face doesn't mean I didn't have my share of difficulties.

"In case you're wondering, my mother was pregnant with my sister when they arrested my father in the early days of nineteen-fifty. She had no relatives, no friends here, except for old Betty. They forced my poor mother, in her condition, to work on a construction site, carrying cartloads of heavy bricks. She died of internal bleeding with my unborn sister."

"How old were you then?" Kira, ashamed, whispered.

"Four years old."

"Who took care of you?"

"I ended up in an orphanage. Remember Betty, the old woman at my father's house back in Eger? The one who served us dinner? She was our housekeeper before they arrested my father. It took her months to find me there, as I wasn't even registered under my name. When she finally found me, asking no one's permission, she grabbed me by my hand and walked out the door. We boarded the train to Eger because, by then, she was working there for Father Tibor as his housekeeper. When they finally released Father, he found me there, and we stayed on. That's how we became one happy family. Anyway, it was with Betty's help that my mother learned Hungarian."

"How come?" Kira said.

"My father met my mother in London during the Blitz. One night, he stumbled upon a nightclub where she was singing. Everybody was in love with her. I remember her as a petite, exquisitely proportioned red-haired beauty with the voice of a lark. Her green eyes were like a pair of emeralds. I used to think she was the most beautiful thing walking on earth. She stopped singing for the public when she became pregnant with me, but she never stopped singing for me. I was born in England. When we moved to Hungary, she could only say a few words in Hungarian. But being a singer, she had an extremely good ear for languages, and with Betty's help, she learned Hungarian within a few short months."

Rocky's eyes welled up, and he whispered, "Now you can see that I, too, may have enough reason to hate them... for destroying my family, killing my mother and sister. And believe it or not, I hate them for what they've been doing to your family and you, Kira."

She looked at him with raised brows, then pulled away from him.

"Now, what's the matter?" Rocky said.

"Well, considering it didn't stop you from being friendly with Speedy Bogár, did it? Do you know who her father is?"

"Croaky Colonel? Of course. Everybody knows who he is."

"Yeah, we all know his rank since he's flaunting it day and night in public. But do you know what he's really doing for a living?" Kira probed further. "He is the public executioner, you fool. He was the one who hanged Imre Nagy and all the others sentenced to death. And if I'm not mistaken, he actually volunteered for the job when some of the others called in sick that day."

"Kira, I think you're being unfair to Speedy. She hates what her father is doing as much as you do. And you, of all people, should know better than to dislike anyone based solely on who their parents are."

But Kira was beyond logic, and in her pain and frustration, she was ready to bolt. She pulled her arm away, picked up her backpack, and hurriedly descended the steep path to the valley.

Rocky caught up with her and landed on the slippery slope at her feet.

"What do you want from me?" Kira shouted.

"Kira," he said, after catching his breath, "I have a scholarship in England. I'm about to leave in a few weeks. Why don't you give me your address so I can write to you?"

Looking down at him, Kira thought giving her address would be harmless. Not that she expected to hear from him ever again. She'd learned by now that in the heat of the moment, people often promise things they don't mean. She shrugged, wrote her address on a small piece of paper and passed it to him, adding, "Look, just to clarify, what happened tonight may have saved my life, but remember, I didn't ask for it," and she picked up her bag and continued down the path that led her into the valley.

Chapter 6

Father Tibor was correct in assuming that if Rocky was not necessarily in trouble, he was at least in a very serious bind. The passport and his successful application to the University of London were expensive. Speedy, as promised, accompanied Rocky to the passport office, where she made sure he filled out the proper forms and let the officials know her personal interest in this case. Rocky soon received an official letter inviting him for a *friendly* chat. The conversation took place in a room in an unmarked office building. The two well-dressed, middle-aged men who greeted him were remarkably friendly. They shook his hand, congratulated him on his successful application to such a distinguished foreign university and offered him expensive foreign cigarettes and cognac. He thanked them but declined, wanting to keep his wits about him.

"But of course, being such a smart young man," one man, introducing himself as János Kovács said after he took a seat behind a big desk, "you must have realized already that this is a great privilege that not everybody can have. It must be earned." He winked at Rocky.

They offered Rocky a seat in an armchair on the other side of the desk, but he hesitantly looked from Mr. Kovács to the other man, who had taken a seat behind him in the corner. The man didn't bother introducing himself and Rocky could easily interpret his silence as ominous.

Sizing up the situation, Rocky swallowed before leaning forward in his chair. "Colonel,"—he was only guessing the man's rank— "What do you have in mind?"

The man, puffing at his cigarette, smiled amicably and corrected Rocky. "Just a major, but really, my boy, we must not stand on formality. Mr. Kovács will do nicely. We are here just to have a friendly chat and hope to reach a mutually pleasing agreement." He looked down at an opened file in front of him, pointed at something in it, and said, "I see you were born in London and that you applied to go to a university there."

Rocky nodded.

"And the reasons for it? Do you have family or friends there?"

"Yes, I have an aunt living there, my mother's younger sister. But I haven't seen her since I was three years old. She couldn't get a visa to visit us since nineteen forty-nine." Rocky thought they must already have this information in his file.

"Yes, yes, of course," Major János Kovács said. He drew out his gold-framed glasses and wiped them with a nicely folded white handkerchief he had pulled out of his breast pocket.

Rocky straightened his back as he observed the ritual intended to intimidate him. He took a deep breath and held it until his nerves settled down. He was sure of a few things: the man's name in front of him wearing an elegant civilian suit was not János Kovács and they did not call him in just to offer him a nice cup of coffee. He had no clue yet what they really wanted from him, but he was sure he would find out soon.

"Well, whether you can see your aunt in London, of course, depends on you, my dear young friend," the smooth-talking agent said. "After you complete a small task, we trust you with, you can, of course, come and go anywhere your heart desires." He inhaled his cigarette smoke deeply before he opened another file on his desk. "In the meantime, we request that you switch your destination from London, England, to Toronto in Canada. Here is your passport with the visas, plus your airplane tickets."

With a straight face, Rocky leaned forward and reached out to take the package.

The man hesitated. "Aren't you curious why we directed you to go overseas instead of England?"

"Of course, I'm curious. But I'm sure you'll tell me when the time is right." Rocky tried to appear calm.

The man nodded. "Speedy was right, as usual. You're a cool candidate. You'll do nicely."

Rocky swallowed and promised to question Speedy about her recommendation to involve him in any scheme. But he was also curious to find out what his assignment would be. He didn't have to wait long as the man pulled a photograph out of his folder and passed it over. An oval-faced man with a short crew cut in his early thirties was wearing a Hungarian military uniform. His face was familiar, even though Rocky could swear he had never laid eyes on him personally. He looked at the man sitting behind the desk with wonderment.

"You found him to be familiar?" The man smirked with great satisfaction. "But of course, you would. He is none other than Miklós Görgey, a distant cousin of yours, presently living in the United States of America. Mind you, this is not a current photo. We dated it a few years back, but I don't believe he has changed too much since then. Anyway, now that you plan to be so close to him in Canada, you should get together. And give this letter to him in person. Don't worry," —he raised his hand up to reassure Rocky— "it is a perfectly legitimate and humanitarian request. He is the only son of his widowed mother, who recently became hospitalized, and she is in such a sad state that she can no longer communicate. So, we are sending you to Toronto requesting that you contact the son via a postcard. That would inform him you have a very important message regarding a private matter that you can only tell him in person when he comes to see you in Toronto. Once he arrives in Toronto to receive your promised personal message, we'll take over and ensure his fast and safe return to Hungary to see his mother before it is too late."

Rocky, confused, protested. "I've never heard of this man before, and I have no clue where I could find him, either."

"No surprises there, my son," Mr. Kovács smiled. "As far as we know, there was a fallout between the cousins some time ago. You could easily check with your father. And we ask you to deliver the message because it would be more convincing coming from a relative, no matter how distant, than receiving it from a cold-hearted official."

Mr. Kovács got up from behind the desk, gently tapped Rocky's shoulder. "My friend, I hope you realize how lucky you are. Being offered a once-in-a-lifetime opportunity to go overseas, enter one of the best universities, and, in the meantime, do your cousin a big favor… Just think of all the other young men who are conscripted into the Hungarian army for three years instead of traveling worldwide! And I'm not saying it is not an honorable duty, but consider the treacherous training and exercises with live ammunition! You've heard enough rumors of deadly accidents in the fields…"

Rocky was smart enough to take the hint but was still unsure about his assignment.

**

"It's true," admitted André Görgey when Rocky asked him about his supposed distant cousin. "Our grandfathers were first cousins, and at the turn of the century, they had a huge fight."

"About what? Do you know?" Rocky asked.

"What did any Görgey fight about since the summer of Eighteen-Forty-Nine? Whether Arthur, our common ancestor, was a traitor or a hero." André shrugged. "Same old, same old," he added with a sad resignation. "Even though we never met, I knew about Miklós. He attended the military academy. I only heard rumors that he had a promising career ahead of him. But I lost sight of him after my incarceration in Nineteen-Forty-Nine."

"He must have escaped to the west since then. What about his mother? According to Mr. Kovács, she is in a terrible state in one of the state hospitals. Can we find out where?"

"I knew the Nazis executed his father in Nineteen-Forty-Four for his known opposition to Hitler, but I do not know what happened to his mother. She used to be a great beauty in her days—I saw her pictures on society pages of the newspapers in the thirties. My father referred to her as Duchess Irene. I suppose they had also deported her to the countryside after the war to starve and endure the bitter cold in a shack, like most people, deemed class aliens. I'm sorry, but having our own troubles, I lost sight of her. But maybe we can try to find her now and see if we can help her."

"By the way," Father Tibor pitched in, "how are you supposed to find your relative in the United States? Do you have his address?"

"Other than a mailbox number in a post office in Washington, DC? No. That is all I have."

"Well, I suppose you can also write him a letter and advise him about your existence and where he could find you," Father Tibor suggested. "But I thought you applied to the City University in London and intended to stay with your aunt, Lady Anna. How will you make your way to Canada from there, and when? Aren't you supposed to arrive in London by the end of August to register for the fall semester?"

"Mr. Kovács strongly urged me to transfer my studies to Canada at the University of Toronto and, once settled there, to contact my relative via a postcard." With a frown on his forehead, Rocky said, "But I think I can afford a brief visit with Lady Anna before I leave for Canada. Although, I still do not know why they insisted I go to Canada and try to connect with this guy from there."

"If you're looking for logic from this bunch, you can forget it," André Görgey said. "Think about the twisted reasoning for locking all typewriters and copy machines away a day before any National Holidays—just to ensure that the enemy couldn't access them to produce seditious literature."

"So, they assume the enemy to be so stupid that they would write their pamphlets a day before any national holidays? And use only the typewriters and copying machines in government offices and factories?"

Betty, bringing in coffee on a tray, pitched her opinion. "Did I hear you correctly that the Duchess is ill? Once you locate her, I'll be happy to recommend a good nursemaid to her who would also cook for her and do her laundry. Knowing the state of affairs in any of the hospitals," —she rolled her eyes in disgust— "she could starve to death and die of neglect there." She grabbed the empty tray and marched out to the kitchen. They could hear only her angry muttering and slamming of hard materials against the butcher block for a while.

"Execution à la Betty," Rocky finally commented. "But she is right; we should try to locate the dear old soul and see for ourselves."

**

When Speedy checked in with Rocky about his traveling details, she found a very icy reception. "What's with the sour face?" Speedy inquired, "Did anyone piss in your cup?"

"You might say that again!" Ready to throttle her, Rocky roared. "Speedy! Were you somehow involved in getting me to do something shady? Because it certainly came across as if they had not only your wholehearted approval but that it was your idea to begin with!"

"What the heck are you talking about now?" She got close enough to look directly into his eyes.

Rocky stepped back, and somewhat calmer, he asked, "So, you do not know that I'm supposed to get in touch with my cousin in the States from Toronto?...intending to get him back to Hungary to see his dying mother?"

"This is the first I hear about it! But I thought you wanted to go to England and attend university there!"

"That's right! However, for the privilege of allowing me to leave Hungary, I'm supposed to prove that I'm worthy of such an honor."

"Have you tried to find the poor woman, at least?" Speedy asked, with a serious frown.

"Of course we had! And got nowhere in a hurry."

"I bet you didn't think about checking prison hospitals," Speedy suggested smugly. "So let me try my magic." She flexed her shapely fingers.

"Speedy! Don't joke about it. Why would the poor soul be in a prison hospital?"

"Why? To make sure you would not find her easily. That's why. Someone thinks she is important enough to be kept under scrutiny. Let me try to find her and see if I can arrange for one of you to see her. I would suggest it be your father, as he is the only one who could identify her."

"I hope so too," Rocky replied, "as it was quite a long while before he could have been in touch with her. She could have aged beyond recognition or had a stroke wiping out her memory or the ability to communicate with him."

A week later, Speedy called Rocky with the news, "I think I found her in one hospital specializing in contagious diseases. This means that nobody may visit her."

"Did they at least tell you what the disease is exactly?"

"They will release information only to close relatives, definitely not over the telephone, but only in person," Speedy said angrily.

"My father is her closest relative here. Would they talk to him?"

"I asked, and I was told that since she has a son, he must be the one they would release any information to, but only if he shows up in person."

"You know, Speedy, the more I think about it, the less I like this business."

Speedy, equally mystified, just scratched her head and said, "Look at it on the bright side! You have a valid passport with the visas and have been admitted to a world-class university. Granted, they coaxed you into a rather shady deal, but knowing you, you will find a way out. But just in case, keep in touch."

Chapter 7

It was Grandma who greeted Kira at home. "How's Charlie?" she asked.

"He is fine," Kira replied. She averted her eyes, and hastily added, "He sends his regards."

"He must be a magician," Grandma replied testily, "if he could be in two places simultaneously. So, where were you?"

"What do you mean, two places at once?" Kira turned red.

"Because he was here, looking for you. It really surprised him to hear that you went to see him. So, what's going on?"

Kira broke down and confessed that she had gone to Eger, to the cliff, to think and reconnect with no one influencing her. Grandma nodded and, hugging Kira, whispered, "Why don't you visit Grandpa? You could also go to church."

Kira didn't dare to look at her grandmother. She could explain to her she hadn't been to the cemetery since the funeral, as it brought back too many painful memories. But when Grandma suggested she should go to church, Kira hesitated. A few years ago, Grandma had insisted that only people burdened by sins attended church regularly, like one of her sisters-in-law suspected of poisoning her husband. Grandma only changed her attitude about religion after her only son—Kira's father, was threatened with the noose.

**

Kira decided she had nothing to lose by following Grandma's advice. The following day, she called in sick at work after spending the morning waiting at the local Medical Clinic. Finally, armed with a note from the doctor proving she wasn't playing hooky, along with a new prescription for her constant allergy symptoms, she hopped on the streetcar to the cemetery. She bought a small bouquet of *Forget-me-nots* at the gate from a vendor. After placing it on her Grandpa's newly erected tombstone, she sat down on the bench facing it.

"Sorry, Grandpa, for not visiting earlier," she said. "I just couldn't admit that you were no longer with me. I was too angry—No, not with you," she added quickly. "With the powers, whoever they were, that allowed this atrocity to happen."

And that was the real problem. The subjects of her fear and anger had no face or name. They were dark substances, shifting shapes, circling around her, threatening to choke her. The swirling objects kept pleading, "Just admit it! Declare it! Your father is a traitor! He is the reason for all your miseries!" But as soon as Kira reached out to crush them or at least to ward them off, her fists entered only a soft block or warm butter, but when she withdrew them, they were covered with blood and her skin shredded to the bone. And she woke up hearing herself scream from real pain and terror. Trying to keep away the monsters, night after night, she kept herself awake, staring out the window, hugging her knees, waiting for the first light. Those sleepless, terror-filled nights drained her energy, making her unable to function and ready to give up.

She recalled how Grandpa lost his job after her father's arrest. As the Mayor of Rákospalota, a suburb of Budapest with combined agriculture and industrial areas, he had successfully governed the district for close to a decade. He never missed a day of work. But when his son was arrested and accused of crimes he never committed, Grandpa found himself unemployed at the age of fifty-eight, with a partial pension, unable to get even a part-time job as a lathe operator in any of the factories. And to add more insults to his humiliation, he had to endure people, once close associates, crossing the street to avoid him. Almost overnight, Kira observed her grandpa turn from the jovial, upright person into a bent down, bitter shadow of himself.

Blinded by her tears, Kira fumbled for her handkerchief in her coat pocket. She looked around and noticed the lack of visitors in the graveyard. She supposed it was in a middle of a working day and few people were free to spend time with their dead loved ones. She blew her nose and continued with her silent conversation. "Grandpa, please help me get the Canadian visa." Kira desperately wanted to believe that the dead could hear and achieve what a mere mortal could never do. Maybe creating miracles out of despair was all that religion was about!

On her way home from the cemetery, she stopped by a Calvinist church. It was still daylight, but she found the door to the church firmly locked. She thought it was odd, as the Catholic Church near her home seemed always open even when there was no mass conducted. She dropped by regularly with Thomas before, and she resumed even after they broke up, just to soak up the silent tranquillity the empty church provided. Kira believed that if God existed at all, her voice would reach him even in an empty church not dedicated to her own religion. Her desperation for Divine Intervention was so strong that she began her walk towards the church dedicated to Saint Teresa of Ávila, the majestic ornate building a few blocks away from her home. There were only a few old women sitting in the pews, silently meditating, when Kira entered through the main door. She slipped into the last pew at the back and, resting her head on her arms, began her silent conversation with God.

Dear God! Not being a practicing anything, please forgive me for addressing you so informally and directly. I know Catholics turn to their priests to confess their sins and ask for direction, but as I'm neither Catholic, nor Presbyterian, nor anything, I can't even seek a priest to burden him with my troubles. I was raised as an unbeliever, questioning everything not visible to me. And even now, I'm not convinced that I could trust a priest to be my interpreter between You and me, as I fear that the secret service has eyes and ears everywhere, including the confession booths. And that is only one of my problems, as I'm not even sure what exactly I should ask for! My biggest dilemma is: TO STAY OR TO LEAVE, as either of those would cause my life to turn upside down.

If I stayed, I see only misery and loneliness in my future. Subjected to humiliation, not knowing who to trust. But if I leave? Will I be able to handle an unknown future, surrounded by total strangers, separated from all my loved ones— probably forever? Both of them seem too frightening. I confess, even a few days ago I was much tempted to end it all! But Rocky put a stop to that. I still don't know whether to curse or thank him for that? So, God, it seems I have no choice but to trust you to make this decision for me.

Kira looked up at the elaborately painted ceiling of the church: *I hope you appreciate how difficult it is to give up my self-determination by placing my future into the hands of an unknown entity.* Strangely, she suddenly felt relieved. As if a heavy burden had been lifted off her shoulders.

When Kira arrived home, she informed Grandma that she had a long discussion with Grandpa at the cemetery, and after that she truly attempted to go to the Presbyterian church, but since she found it locked up, she went to the Catholic church. Before Grandma could berate her, she said quickly, "You told me that there was only one God, and that he doesn't discriminate which building anyone would use to talk to him." She only hoped that her sincere appeal would land in the willing ear of an omnipotent entity.

Two weeks later, an envelope from the Canadian Embassy arrived. With trembling hands, she opened it and pulled out a letter informing her she had received a non-renewable visitor's visa, limiting her stay for only three months. Within a few days, she also received a letter from her Aunt Paula, who explained that it was Rabbi Salamon in Toronto who took a risk of flying in the middle of an electrical storm to Ottawa to persuade the authorities to give Kira the special visitor's visa so that, as the only close relative of the bride, she could attend her cousin's wedding. Enclosed in the envelope was a return airline ticket.

This was the first time in Kira's life that she could claim to be the recipient of a *Divine Intervention*. But the irony of it was indisputable: it was not only definite proof of God's existence, but in addition, he had exhibited a sense of humour, when he chose a Rabbi of all people for her request.

The day for Kira leaving the country had arrived. Grandma woke her up. When she saw grandmother's tear-filled eyes, they hugged and rocked gently, quietly comforting each other. Kira dressed in a hurry and joined the family for a last breakfast in the kitchen— buttered toast and tea with sugar and a twist of lemon juice. When the taxi came to take them to the airport, they were waiting in the hallway by the front door. Father picked up Kira's suitcase, while Mother carried the handbag filled with carefully packed figurines from the China cabinet. Kira was to give them to friends and relatives as gifts, as no proper lady arrived visiting empty-handed. Grandma held Kira's hand in the taxi all the way to the airport.

Father tried to break the solemn mood by pointing at the clear blue sky. "Even the sun approves of your leaving today."

At the airport, her father disappeared for a brief time, returning with an armful of magazines under his arm. "Something for you to read on the plane," he explained, before handing them over. Two literary monthlies —one called *New Voice*—dedicated to new Hungarian writers, and the other *Words from the World*, dedicated to foreign literary talents. Kira tucked them away in her carry-on bag. He hugged Kira before he turned her over to her mother, who, after a light kiss, pushed her toward Grandma. Kira's heart went out to poor old Grandma, standing there with her lips trembling, busying her hands with her little white handkerchief. Kira kissed her tears away, then turned around and walked outside to the tarmac, ready to climb aboard the bus carrying passengers to the airplane. She turned around and saw her parents and Grandma, waving, smiling at her from the viewing platform.

"How could they smile?" Kira wondered, hardly able to keep her tears rolling.

Just at that moment, the air raid sirens unexpectantly, suddenly and abruptly became activated. It's ominous pulsating, shrieking penetrated everything, paralyzing everyone in the airport's vicinity, turning them into statues. Pilots, mechanics, baggage handlers, stewardesses, travelers waiting to disembark kept looking up towards the sky, searching for the appearance of mysterious airplanes threatening to drop the deadly bombs. There was no earthly logic behind it, because in the summer of 1967 Hungary was not at war, and no country threatened to send airplanes to bomb. But the old reflexes were still prepared to be activated and in a few seconds, it would have inevitably triggered a total mass of panic.

But just in the nick of time, the public announcement came through, loud and clear: "Ladies and gentlemen. Please don't panic, we are not under attack! It was only a faulty switch that had accidentally activated the siren! I repeat, there is no need to panic!"

The communal tension visibly relieved, Kira finally entered the plane. From her window seat, she saw her parents and grandmother embrace one another on the viewing platform. They threw kisses towards the plane as it slowly rolled toward the runway to take off.

Chapter 8

Kira changed planes in Zurich and as soon as they were airborne, the pilot requested all passengers to fasten their seat belts. Caught in air turbulence, high winds buffeted the plane. She welcomed the turbulence, almost wishing the plane to crash in the middle of the ocean while she was asleep. As this was her first trip outside of Hungary, suddenly separated from all that was dear to her, she had difficulty picturing what would await her in a strange land surrounded by unfamiliar people. The feeling of isolation and the longing for the familiar weighed heavily on her heart.

Remembering the old gypsy woman's prediction in Eger, that she would not be going alone, she looked around, desperately trying to find a familiar face on the plane. There were none. Her heart sank, realizing that she was truly alone in this journey. *So much for that*, she thought, turning her thoughts to the people she was going to see in a few hours, hoping they would bring her the comfort of familiarity.

She recalled the letter from Emily, the wife of Mr. Singer, her father's old friend, offering to help Kira leave Hungary. However, they could only offer their hospitality to Kira for a maximum of two nights in their one-bedroom apartment in Montreal. "You understand that owning three shoe stores in Montreal, we are very busy people. Furthermore, we believe Montreal wouldn't be the best place for a young lady in her early twenties."

After reading the letter, Rozi, Kira's mother, interpreted it as follows: "In other words, Emily, being a few years older than her husband, must be insanely jealous and tries to guard him from temptations. Lucky for you, you are to travel to Toronto within two days, where you would be in the tender loving care of my cousin Aunt Paula."

Kira was to go on to Toronto by train, and at least until the wedding, she would stay with Aunt Paula, the mother of her cousin Cathy. Kira was looking forward to the promising reunion, as the last time she had seen her cousin and aunt was in December 1956, just a few days before they crossed the border to Austria. They stayed in Vienna for two years before emigrating to Canada, where Cathy's father died of a heart attack within the year.

As Kira's mother and Aunt Paula exchanged letters regularly, the family was aware that little Cathy, at sixteen, got engaged to a man named Desmond Diamond, in his late twenties. They planned to get married as soon as Cathy turned eighteen. One picture Aunt Paula sent showed a big American car with at least a dozen people standing in front of it. She commented that Cathy would become part of this extended family. "Ever since I lost my dear beloved, unforgettable Charly. . . it was hard raising a child all by myself without close family and friends. . . and as you can see, Desmond is a man who loves his family."

Kira recalled when Mr. Diamond, Cathy's fiancé, dropped in to see them unexpectedly a year ago in Budapest. It was early evening and as far as they knew, they expected no visitors that day. Kira went to answer the bell at the front door. A short man with the reddest hair and an arrogant expression stood in the doorway, and with a thick foreign accent, he asked in Hungarian, "Is Mister Chopaky at home?"

Kira had difficulty keeping a straight face. In her lifetime, her father was called many things: colonel, comrade, later traitor, counter-revolutionary, but never a Mister.

"Who would like to know?" Kira said.

"My name is Desmond Diamond, your Cousin Cathy's fiancé from Canada. Since I was in Vienna on business, I dropped in to get acquainted with the new relatives." He pulled a business card out of his vest pocket and handed it to Kira.

Kira took the card as if it were a fragile object, and said in her most formal voice, "Just a moment, please. I'll see if Mister Chopaky is up for receiving visitors." She turned around in a great hurry to inform the family about the great fortune that had befallen them.

"Father, Mr. Desmond Diamond would love to get acquainted with Mr. Chopaky. Would you be kind enough to receive him?" she asked theatrically, emphasizing the Mister.

Sitting on the Chesterfield in the living room, her father looked up from his book and scrutinized her. "Are you feeling alright? What the dickens are you talking about? What is this *Mister* business?"

Her mother jumped from the chair and said, "Alex, you know who that is? Remember Paula wrote about Desmond Diamond, Cathy's fiancé. Let him in."

Desmond Diamond was there to impress his new relatives. The white Mercedes he rented in Vienna, blocking the large ornate gate to the apartment building, was supposed to show his expensive taste and deep pocket.

However, according to Rozi Chopaky, a stickler for formality, Mister Diamond could be loaded, but he still lacked proper manners. The proof was that he showed up unexpectedly, without bringing flowers for the lady of the house.

Desmond finally convinced Rozi that he could be a generous relative after he invited his aunt and her husband, along with the Chopakys, to an expensive restaurant. The Chopakys learned that throughout the years, after Desmond left for Canada during the uprising in December 1956, he kept sending his relative's money regularly in repayment for the four years of free room and board they provided him while he attended a technical high school in Budapest.

Desmond's visit was also a significant turning point in Rozi Chopaky's brother, Uncle Eugene's life. During that week, Eugene and Desmond became inseparable. As Desmond was there to register some of his inventions, it was natural that Eugene, employed as a clerk in a patenting office, offered his help to Desmond to battle the bureaucracies.

Shortly after Desmond returned to Canada, Eugene went to Vienna on business for a week. By 1967, getting a passport and an exit visa to Vienna was not so difficult if he left his wife and child behind. That was assurance enough for the authorities that he would return to Hungary upon completing his business. They couldn't have known that Uncle Eugene, registered in the same apartment as his wife and child, was no longer married. However, because of the housing shortage, necessity forced them to share a small bachelor apartment.

Once he arrived in Vienna, he quickly grabbed the opportunity and requested political asylum. Although he sent his former wife a telegram informing her about his intention, the Hungarian Secret Service intercepted it and took the job of hand-delivering it.

Imagine his wife's surprise when, instead of the mailman delivering the telegram, two robust men kicked in their apartment door in a rather foul mood and ignoring the fallen unhinged door on the floor, they searched the premises. They interrogated the family about the "dirty scum of the dissident."

"What's a dissident?" piped up Susan, his six-year-old daughter, staring at the strangers sacking her home. She was familiar with the words *dirty* and *scum*, hearing her father described by others prior to that.

One of them shoved the telegram to Eugene's wife, who read it aloud: *ON MY WAY TO CANADA. WISH ME GOOD LUCK*, Eugene.

"Thank you for delivering it so promptly," Aunt Mira said, but still puzzled, added, "But what, pray tell me, was the reason for kicking the front door off its hinges?"

"We're allowed to search the premises and confiscate the possessions of the lousy traitor who left the country illegally," the men informed Aunt Mira.

Considering that the bachelor apartment could only accommodate two daybeds, a table with four chairs, and a wardrobe, the search didn't take very long. Eugene's possessions only amounted to two suits he brought to Vienna, and a winter coat, which, as usual, was kept at the local pawn shop during the off-season.

Aunt Mira always had a bizarre sense of humor. She thanked the two men for such prompt delivery of the telegram and handed over the pawn ticket, just in case they wanted access to Eugene's winter coat. When the two men left in a grumpy mood, she followed them to the staircase with the mild comment, "You could have been a bit more careful about the door."

Shocking as it must have been to Aunt Mira, she still talked about the incident with a smirk. "My consolation was that they, too, had to climb up to the seventh floor, as the elevator, as usual, was again out of service. But judging by all the huffing and puffing, they needed some exercise."

A month later, Aunt Mira received a letter from Eugène, full of excitement about working at Desmond Diamond's factory in Toronto as a "foreman" and with the promise to make enough money to get his apartment, a car, and a television in a short time.

"Sure," Rozi Chopaky said sarcastically, "and the Eiffel Tower, not to mention Niagara Falls. I'll believe it when I see it," she waved impatiently.

Kira didn't share her mother's skepticism about her uncle. Where her mother saw an irresponsible younger brother full of broken promises, Kira only observed the man full of optimism and dreams, not to mention a cheerful manner, ready to lift her mood through the years.

She would see him again in less than three days, and that thought comforted her. She would not be all alone in the new world. She believed he would protect and guide her to become a proper young lady in a strange land.

Chapter 9

As Kira woke to the Montreal skyline, a tapestry of colorful lights spread before her, reminiscent of gemstones on black velvet. She longed to touch it, to feel its imagined texture against her skin.

At the airport, Emily Singer greeted Kira. After a cautious inspection, Emily expressed relief that Kira didn't embody the feared traits of a nihilistic hippy—an image middle-class families dreaded. Kira's short hair and lack of blue jeans were practical choices rather than statements—necessities dictated by the realities of life in Hungary, where such luxuries were unaffordable on her salary.

Kira's first night in Montreal was quite memorable for both her hosts and their circle of friends when Kira ordered a plate of Wiener schnitzels in a Hungarian restaurant off St. Catherine Street with the comment, "I never had veal in my whole life. It was simply not available to purchase in any of the stores."

Mrs. Molnar, one of Emily's friends, said, "How so? I just returned from Budapest, where I found the stores, some owned by private citizens, filled with luxury items. I saw well-dressed women on the streets and heard people telling daring political jokes everywhere."

"True," Kira admitted, "but what you observed is what we refer to in Hungary as a goulash communism, which is the equivalent of a velvet dictatorship."

They all looked at Kira with great curiosity, waiting for an explanation. She nodded and elaborated, "Maybe I can illustrate this with a current joke."

The mention of a joke perked everyone up. Budapest was famous for making fun of everyday political reality. Exchanged and eagerly passed around, these jokes were treated as precious commodities. There were times during the *rampant dark fifties*, between 1949 and 1956, when some of these were only repeated in strict confidence for fear of landing someone in prison for maligning the *great socialist system*, so the fact that nowadays these jokes were more liberally spoken and spread gave the illusion of greater political freedom. Kira thought the best way to bring reality to these nostalgic people in Montreal in the middle of June 1967 was to tell them a relevant one.

"Some of you left Hungary after the nineteen-fifty-six Revolution. So, you'll well remember the late-night visits from the dreaded Secret Service, the disappearances of people for many years, even for telling an innocent joke. It was during those dark times that a party chief, speaking at a communist party meeting, described the great strides the Socialist regime managed in Hungary within less than ten years: no more unemployment, no more homeless, and no more hungry people.

"Everybody clapped enthusiastically, but nobody dared to mention the chronic food shortages. At the end of the meeting, he asked the members if they had any questions.

"Comrade Smith stood up and dared to inquire, *Can you explain where the meat, the butter, and other staples disappeared from the stores?* A few weeks later, only Comrade Kiss stood up at the question period and asked, *I only have one question. Where did Comrade Smith disappear to?*"

Kira explained that times had changed, and the political atmosphere was lightened. She illustrated it with a fable:

"The Lion King of the forest called a meeting and announced with great pride: *We are introducing a great change in our policy. In our infinite wisdom, we have decided that from this day on, TWO-TIMES-TWO WILL EQUAL FIVE.*

"Everyone except the mule stood up, cheering and clapping with great enthusiasm. The Lion frowned at the mule and asked, *What's wrong, mule? Aren't you pleased with the sign of democratization?* The mule slowly lifted his head and quietly said, *Your Majesty, I admit, it is a significant step in the right direction. However, I would like to emphasize that since time immemorial, two-times-two has always equaled four.*

"Furrowing his eyebrows, the Lion snapped his fingers. Two wolves stepped forward. They dragged the mule into a lavishly furnished office. They sat him down in an armchair and offered him espresso coffee, French pastry, and expensive American cigarettes, trying to sway him to the same conclusion: *Would it really hurt you to accept the King's decision that from now on, two times two equals five?*

"*But, cried the mule, can't you see? Two-times-two has always been four; and no matter what, it will always remain four. Nothing and nobody can change that!*

"By now, truly annoyed, one of the wolves stood up, grabbed the mule by the throat, and hissed in his face, *Mule, you are a stubborn fool. Understand this. YOU HAD BETTER BELIEVE THAT TWO TIMES -TWO NOW EQUALS FIVE.* And ready to smash the mule's face, he lifted his other fist and snarled: *Or do you want it to be SIX again?*

"Before you accuse me of being paranoid, let me tell you about Mrs. Forgacs, who visited the doctor to complain about the crocodile living under her bed." Kira continued with a straight face. "*What if it came out and ate me?* Mrs. Forgacs asked the doctor.

"The doctor patiently explained that there was nothing to be afraid of, as in the middle of Budapest, it was unlikely that she would have a crocodile hiding under her bed. But to calm her anxiety, he prescribed her some tranquilizer and told her to come back in a month for a checkup.

"She returned two weeks later and insisted she still had the same crocodile under her bed, and she was afraid it would come out and eat her. The doctor gave her stronger medication this time and told her to come back to see him in a week.

"Mrs. Forgacs didn't return in a week, either in two weeks; the doctor smugly rang the bell at her apartment a month later, doing house calls in her neighborhood. He kept ringing, but there was no answer. Finally, a neighbor pops out and informs him, *Are you looking for Mrs. Forgacs? Doctor, you didn't hear it? Three weeks ago, the crocodile under her bed came out and ate her.*"

Time and wishful thinking can alter any reality. Those sitting around Kira in that Hungarian restaurant in Montreal acknowledged that the situation back in Hungary was still not perfect, but for them, the changes meant the majority could finally visit the country and families they had left behind without fear of being punished for leaving the country illegally after the *Unfortunate Event* in October 1956.

Even though Leslie Singer and two of his brothers built up a successful shoe business in Montreal in a relatively short time, he was so nostalgic for his beloved Budapest that he tried to recreate it in Montreal. Their life was centered around the few corners close to St. Catherine Street, where they could hear people speaking Hungarian, have their meals in Hungarian coffee houses, read only Hungarian newspapers, and see the occasional Hungarian amateur theatre group playing mostly Hungarian operettas. Like the rest of their friends, they, too, only talked about the good old days in Budapest, nostalgic about the smoky air in their beloved Budapest cafes. This finally happened in 1963, when the general amnesty not only meant freedom for Kira's father but also lifted the sanctions against all expatriates who left Hungary illegally after the 1956 uprising.

Sitting in the restaurant that first night, one of the Singers' friends, Mr. Molnar asked Kira, "What are your plans? Do you want to stay here?"

She shook her head and answered hesitantly, "I'm not sure if I can, even if I wanted to. My Canadian visa is valid for only three months and is not renewable."

"Why don't you claim refugee status?" Mr. Molnár suggested, "With your background, I'm sure it won't be a problem."

"I can't do that," Kira replied in a hurry. "That would hurt Dad, and he doesn't need more harassment from the Secret Service, especially because of me."

"Why would they bother your father if you claim refugee status here? After all, you're an adult, aren't you?" Mr. Molnar looked at Kira, surprised.

"Even though Dad was released from prison in Nineteen-sixty-three, he is still on probation for the next ten years, and a wrongly phrased sentence could send him back to jail for many years. If I were to claim refugee status here, the authorities would assume that Dad had given me information about the secret trial and details about the seven years he spent in prison, despite him signing an agreement of non-disclosure." Kira choked up, and then added in a whisper, "I'd rather die than put him in that situation."

An uncomfortable silence followed her outburst before Mrs. Molnar offered another solution. "What if you get married to a

Canadian citizen? I know quite a few women who stayed here that way and then applied for a Hungarian Consulate passport."

Kira admitted it was a tempting idea, but it had a few serious wrinkles. How easy would it be to find a willing suitor within the next three months to marry someone like her just to normalize her status in Canada?

Kira was unprepared for her first Canadian nightmare when she finally fell asleep on the Chesterfield in the Singers' living room that first night. She was so homesick in her dream that she went back to Hungary. *She was filled with the happy anticipation of reuniting with family and friends and hoped to find conditions that would allow her to follow her dreams and aspirations there. At the border, Thomas, her old boyfriend, wearing the uniform of a border guard, greeted her with a smirk. Instead of welcoming her back, he arrested Kira and hauled her to observe her dad's execution. She tried to scream, but no words came out of her mouth. After the execution, Thomas heaved Kira into a small, dark, dingy prison cell, warning her that she would be tried for spying. Stripped of all hope, Kira was left alone in the prison cell, where she could contemplate her stupidity for returning.*

She woke up crying, with tears streaming down her face and a monster of a headache, as if she had been banging her head against the cold stone walls in her nightmarish prison cell. Kira couldn't help thinking it was a warning sign to keep her homesickness at bay. As she sat up, the relief of finding herself in Montreal washed over her.

Chapter 10

Just two days later, Kira found herself aboard a train to Toronto, poised for a reunion nearly twelve years in the making with her cousin Cathy, who had departed from Hungary in late 1956.

Memories flooded back: of Cathy, a tiny figure swathed in Kira's cherished blue ski pants and matching jacket—a garment lovingly crafted from her father's old police uniform. Despite having nearly outgrown it, parting with it had been a struggle for Kira, marking perhaps the only piece of her wardrobe that ever passed between them. Their sartorial choices underscored their stark differences—Kira, the quintessential tomboy, favored comfort over style with her array of pants and sweat suits, while Cathy, ever the little princess, seemed perpetually dressed to the nines.

This created problems for the cousins when they were growing up together. Cathy was not free to play the fun games Kira enjoyed. She had to be careful not to dirty herself. While she preferred to play with dolls at home, Kira wanted to climb trees, build and defend sandcastles on the playground, or get into a satisfying mud fight. Kira often urged Cathy, against her wishes, to join her in rough games, relishing in seeing her cousin's pretty clothes get dirty.

Kira remembered that most of her visits with her cousin Cathy ended in tears. Cathy's mother, Aunt Paula usually spanked Cathy for dirtying her pretty dress, while Kira was locked in the bathroom as punishment for pushing Cathy in the mud.

Bored during the separation, Cathy tried to join Kira in the bathroom. However, by that time, due to the frequency, Kira had turned it into a place of tranquility, hiding a few books and a pillow under the bathroom sink. Kira, who hated tattletales even more than crybabies, refused to share her cozy hiding place, and after giving her cousin a few nasty pinches, she kicked her out of the sanctuary.

Kira's father laughed when he found her secret library and the hidden pillows under the sink. As Kira recalled, that was the end of using the bathroom as a place for punishment and marked the beginning of a new approach to her upbringing through friendly discussions about the reasons for misbehavior. But they were only little girls then, and she hoped that time and distance had transformed those childhood experiences into something to chuckle about.

On the long train ride, Kira contemplated how they would react to each other. It had been nearly twelve years since they'd last seen each other and they both had their share of troubles during those times. Cathy and her family stayed in Vienna for two years, where her father had an excellent job as an electrician. But Aunt Pauline found Vienna much too close to Hungary, besides being haunted by unpleasant memories of the concentration camp she spent in 1944 when she heard German spoken.

Shortly after they arrived in Canada, Cathy's father died of a sudden heart attack. Aunt Paula, at thirty-two, was left a widow, and Cathy, at twelve, fatherless. Kira could well sympathize with what a tragedy this must have been for them— after all, Kira had lived without her dad, in uncertainty for seven long years.

Cathy's mother, Aunt Paula, was the only cousin of Kira's mother, who survived the Holocaust, and for them, maintaining the relationship was necessary, even from the distance after they escaped from Hungary in 1956. Kira had to admit that she wanted a reunion where they could reacquaint themselves.

They knew about each other from the letters their mothers exchanged. Kira learned Cathy was engaged to be married a few weeks after her eighteenth birthday and that her fiancé, a successful businessman from a large family, was ten years older.

The train pulled into Toronto Union Station and Kira stood on the platform, looking around for a familiar face. The trouble was that she kept looking around at her eye level, until someone yanked the sleeve of her coat and yelled, "Hello! Are you blind, deaf, or both?"

Kira looked down and found Cathy looking up at her with a flushed face. Kira had no difficulty recognizing her since, even at first glance, it was evident that they came from the same mold, with slight variations. They shared the same oval face, high cheekbones, and large, dark, almond-shaped eyes.

Still annoyed, Cathy said, "Didn't you see me waving or hear me shouting at you for the last five minutes?"

Kira had to admit that in the big rush, she didn't notice her, and even if Cathy had been any taller, Kira would have had difficulty spotting her in the crowd.

Kira looked tenderly at Cathy and opened her arms to hug her.

Cathy frowned, stepping back. "Remember how you used to pull my hair and push me into the puddle? I won't tolerate that now." She stamped her foot to make her demand clear. "And remember that doll you got for Christmas in Nineteen Fifty-Six? You had no right to it! It was mine!"

Kira could only stare at her cousin, contemplating whether it mattered after all this time which one of them received that doll for Christmas. As Kira named her, *Angel* was a doll about the size of a seven-month-old baby with vibrant blue eyes. When dressed, she looked so real that people on the street often commented in shock when Kira took her out for a stroll. "I hope she's not her baby. She is too young to be a mother yet!"

Kira spent many happy hours dressing Angel in real baby clothes inherited from the children of friends and relatives. It was fun to tease the neighbors with the doll's authenticity.

Hearing her cousin Cathy complaining about the doll so many years later, Kira burst out laughing and pulled the elegant young lady close to hug her.

"Well, I'm glad you haven't changed, little Kitty. You still have the same sharp tongue and claws. I would have tried to bring Angel if I had known how important she was to you. Unfortunately, my papa presented her to a little girl of a family friend about three years ago. I was seventeen then, and he thought I was too old to play with dolls anymore. But if you insist, I will try to replace your coveted doll—maybe I can get one for you as a wedding gift?"

In one corner of her heart, she understood Cathy. It was hard to admit that it still hurt that her father gave away her precious doll without asking how important it was to her. But she also realized that the situation could not be rectified, as who would have the heart to take away such a gift from a four-year-old girl hugging her new doll closely to her heart?

Cathy looked up, hatred in her eyes, and in an icy voice, informed Kira, "Just a minute. From now on, I want you to call me Catharina, as in a few days, I'll be a proper woman, a wife of a respectable, rich man."

This outburst made Kira wonder why a proper woman married to a respectable rich man would still insist on lamenting the loss of a doll after all that time. And she couldn't see how changing her name to Catharina would turn a mean-spirited, wild tabby cat into a proper woman, either.

Cathy's wedding was to take place a week later. Kira was one of six bridesmaids, and a dress was tailor-made for everyone. Last-minute shopping and fittings filled their time, leaving hardly any moments for Kira to think about anything else.

The wedding was the most elegant, splendid occasion Kira had ever attended. Over three hundred guests filled the great hall at the Four Seasons hotel in Toronto and Kira was afraid that she would make herself a spectacle by tripping and falling on her face in her brand-new gown with a long train. The pink satin suited her white skin and black hair, and the princess style with the elongated waistline showed off her tall figure as she stood, a head taller than Cathy.

The Rabbi faced them, wearing a long, dark blue velvet robe and four-cornered ceremonial yarmulka. He was a charismatic, well-built man in his late fifties with thick black, slightly graying hair and a chiseled, handsome face. His voice resonated deeply, and he used it with mastery, leaving no eyes dry when he mentioned little Cathy's father, who couldn't witness this momentous and happy occasion.

Kira's tears rolled down her cheeks, and she had the terrible urge to blow her nose. Lacking pockets in her elegant evening dress where she could hide a handkerchief, she had no choice but to wipe her tears and nose in her long white gloves. The photographer's flash blinded her when he took a picture of her at that crucial moment.

Just before the wedding ceremony, Cathy introduced Kira to Ernest Gordon, a tall, handsome young man with large black eyes and black wavy hair. Throughout the ceremony, they exchanged glances. When the music started, he asked her to dance. But they were constantly interrupted by people who came to greet Kira, informing her they either grew up or used to work with her parents back in Hungary. They also shared stories about her beloved paternal grandfather and how fair and helpful he was before and during the war. Kira was beaming with happiness and pride. She hadn't felt surrounded by so much love for a long time.

Suddenly, her partner offered his arm and walked her outside, commenting, "Would you like to go somewhere else? Where we could talk alone?"

She closed her eyes briefly, then opened them in a rush. She suddenly felt lightheaded and dizzy, like floating in a bubble, and she nodded. She forgot her usual reaction to even the slightest amount of alcohol, and she had her share of champagne that evening. She saw him talking to Aunt Paula; he returned with her light coat, which he placed carefully on her shoulder, and walked her to his expensive-looking, brand-new car.

Seeing the car, Kira whistled in appreciation. The last time she saw cars like that was in front of the Royal Hotel in Budapest, where she used to stop with Thomas, her former high school boyfriend who was really into cars. Recalling the times when they walked past the hotel twice a day and admired the vast American luxury cars brought back a heartache that she pushed aside in a hurry to make a place for something new and altogether pleasant.

"Where to?" Ernest Gordon asked her after she was seated.

"How about Niagara Falls?" she inquired, thinking she was asking the impossible.

"Then Niagara Falls it is," he nodded, and started the car.

"What are you talking about?" She looked at him, alarmed.

"Hey, it's all right. Niagara Falls is only an hour and a half drive from Toronto. We can talk in the meantime."

Driving through the elevated bridge above Hamilton and approaching Niagara Falls, flooded by the many-colored lights in the early evening, was like a dream for Kira. When they approached the roaring water thundering over the fall, Kira raised her head and let the drops of water wash over her face.

Overwhelmed, she said, "I don't think I can take anymore! I have a colossal headache. Could we go back now?" Thoroughly exhausted, she fell asleep in the car. Ernest gently woke her when they arrived at the apartment, which she shared with her aunt Paula and her uncle Eugene. In Kira's overwrought imagination, for a time, Ernest Gordon, the tall, dark stranger with the sensitive mouth, became the same natural phenomenon as Niagara Falls.

Aunt Paula and Eugène exchanged glances and showered Kira with a new wardrobe. Night after night, Ernest took her to restaurants and nightclubs, and they danced until midnight. Kira couldn't remember what they talked about—somehow, it wasn't necessary.

Later, Kira couldn't recall the precise moment when she agreed to marry Ernest Gordon. She was still in the bubble, floating, letting the events carry her. She met Ernest's close friends and his mother, a visitor from Hungary. They were all smiling and happy to be acquainted with her. Somehow, it fit that she was engaged and married to Ernest Gordon within six weeks.

Friends and relatives gathered to celebrate again, and they considered it another major event of the year in the Hungarian Jewish community in Toronto. The same rabbi who married her cousin performed at Kira's wedding and kissed her in the end, wishing them all the best. Everyone congratulated Kira on her great fortune in finding such a fine man with a glorious future in such a short time. It also seemed to be the perfect solution for her immigration problem.

The night before Kira's wedding, Cathy invited her over to her apartment. The Diamonds had just returned from their honeymoon, which they spent in Europe and part of it was spent with Kira's parents in Budapest. It had been a total surprise for Cathy to have found out her cousin was engaged and ready to get married within such a short time.

Kira was bursting with curiosity. She had so many questions to ask Cathy about her honeymoon and their visit with Kira's parents and friends. Cathy was waiting for her at the door. She let her in and gave Kira a mandatory tour of her domain. It was a luxuriously furnished two-bedroom apartment, everything brand new and carefully coordinated.

Cathy introduced her to the decor. "French Provincial. I chose everything. It is directly from the factory. No store carried what I wanted. The sofa is so big that four people couldn't carry it here. It didn't fit in the elevator and the doorway wasn't wide enough either. So, they had to pull it up with a pulley to the sixth floor through the balcony." She sighed. "The rug was handmade in India. It took us many weeks to find the right colours—ivory and pale blue with gold trimmings."

Kira looked at her and then at the sofa. She couldn't imagine herself curling up in the corner and discussing anything personal with Cathy, who sat there like an unapproachable Ice Queen wearing a caftan matching the rug's colors.

Cathy jumped up. "Oh, I almost forgot. Look what I got from your mother as a wedding present." She ran to one of the bedrooms and came back with a brick-sized box wrapped in newspapers. Slowly peeling the many layers off revealed a beautifully engraved silver cigarette box. It was a gift presented to Kira's father by his colleagues many years ago, and she remembered how tenderly she cleaned and shined it so often while her father was in prison. She reached out to caress the box.

Cathy grabbed it. "Don't touch it. You will leave a fingerprint on it." The box fell on the carpet, spilling the photographs from its compartments. Bending down to pick them up, Kira recognized every one of them.

"But these are my high school class pictures…" Kira commented, ready to sit on the floor to look at them when Cathy intercepted her, pushing her roughly away.

"It isn't for you. Your mother gave them to me."

"Maybe the box, but surely not the photographs?" Kira wanted to protest. But all choked up, she realized her dream of finding a friend in Cathy was a futile one.

"Oh yes, about your wedding night," Cathy said in a cold, matter-of-fact manner. "I suggest you shower rather than bathe so you won't be too dry. And don't fight it, however painful it is. Let your husband do whatever he wants. Eventually, he will tire of it. I'll see you tomorrow at the wedding." Then she walked out to the kitchen, leaving Kira alone.

So, the audience is over, Kira thought as she gathered her purse and jacket to leave. She stopped momentarily, grabbed the silver box, opened it, placed all the pictures in her purse and left without saying goodbye. She felt a tinge of remorse leaving the box behind, but she didn't want to be accused of stealing. After all, it was a gift to Cathy from Kira's mother, and she must accept that. However, she was convinced that her high school pictures could only belong to her.

On her way home, she felt sorry for her cousin. *Desmond must be terrible in bed,* Kira thought when she recalled Cathy's weird advice. With a dreamy smile, she could still evoke the fresh smell of the green grass on the hill of Buda, Thomas's school jacket underneath them, and the sun spinning as they made love. How eager and inexperienced they were. Well, those stolen moments were over, and by tomorrow evening, she would be a legitimate wife of a good-looking gentleman, who, by the way he kissed her, had to be an experienced lover.

**

As the evening wound down, Cathy found herself alone on the balcony, the chill of the Toronto night biting as her thoughts turned inward. Below her, the city lights flickered like distant stars, starkly contrasting the darkness she felt inside.

"Why did I react like that to Kira?" she murmured, her breath forming small clouds in the air. She still held the empty silver box she found on the floor after Kira's abrupt departure, an anchor to a past she both cherished and resented. "She was just being herself, and I...I pushed her away again."

Cathy's mind drifted to the days following her father's death, the confusion and anger that had swelled in her young heart. Her mother's grief had been a silent storm, devastating in its quiet intensity. Left to navigate her pain alone, Cathy had built walls so high she no longer remembered how to lower them, not even for Kira.

"I wanted to be strong, like Papa always told me to be," she confessed to the night, her voice breaking. "But all I've become is cold."

A sudden image of Kira's laughing face, mud-splattered and bright, flashed through her mind. It contrasted her reflection in the glass door leading back inside—a composed, perfectly put-together facade. "Maybe that's why I envy her. She's everything I'm too afraid to be."

Cathy pulled the silver box close to her heart with a deep, shuddering breath. Tomorrow, she would give it back to Kira, not just as a peace offering but as a bridge—a way back to who she once was and might still become.

But deep in her heart, she knew it would never happen. The contrast between the two of them was too wide. Cathy's beloved father, her only buffer from her mother—the pretty woman with honey in her mouth but meanness in her heart—couldn't take the insatiable demands and died. He left Cathy at the mercy of her mother's greed and manipulation.

She would never forgive Kira for having her father survive while hers was dead. Did it matter to her the price Kira had to pay for it? Cathy didn't want to dwell on it. She was clinging to her hatred toward her cousin as if it were her sole protection against the cruel world. She never dared to admit that she diverted her inner rebellion against her mother to Kira, making it the sole object of her hatred. She never learned to dig deep into her soul, facing and disabling her devil.

Chapter 11

After the ceremony, Kira found solitude in the dressing room, the first in weeks. As the door shut behind the last guest, Kira stared into the mirror, alone with her reflections and a growing sense of unease. Her movement halted as memories of home—Budapest, her parents' laughter, the comfort of her childhood room—flooded back. She blinked away the nostalgia, only to be reminded by the silence that her new life was starting without them.

Earnest's mother broke the silence, her words a cold comfort: "He is a good boy; he will be kind to you. Come now; he is waiting for us. You will take me to the airport now."

As they drove, adorned with a *JUST MARRIED* sign and trailing cans that clanged on the highway, Kira's heart sank. The waves and jeers from strangers underscored her isolation. The farewell was mechanical at the airport, their touches devoid of warmth.

Back at the hotel, their clumsy attempt at crossing the threshold ended in laughter—not of joy, but of nerves strung too tight. Lying amidst the wreckage of their entry, Kira's laughter faded into the heavy silence that settled between them.

Earnest snapped, "It isn't a laughing matter. It could be a bad omen."

Attempting to lighten the mood, Kira raised her glass. "How about a toast to your fallen bride?"

Earnest uncorked the champagne and handed Kira a glass, which she downed in one long sip. Setting the empty glass aside, she reached out for another. This might help me get through...whatever comes next, she muttered.

She was about to stand when Earnest's voice stopped her, heavy with hesitation. "Kira, I—I'm sorry. This...this was a mistake."

Kira froze, her glass halfway to her lips. "A mistake? What are you saying? Are you...Is this about you being gay?"

"No, it's not that. It's just—" Earnest broke off, the words catching in his throat. "My mother, she's always making these decisions for me."

"And you just follow along?" Kira's voice rose, her frustration evident. "What about what you want? What about us trying?"

Earnest looked away, his voice low. "You don't get it, Kira. It's not that simple."

His reasons spilled out, unbidden and bitter. She listened, her heart sinking with each revelation until the room spun around her.

Earnest looked away as if ashamed, and lounged into his story. "I had a German girlfriend for many years, blonde and round. You are not even my type! I mean, you are a nice-looking girl and all, but I don't find you sexy. You are too tall, too slim, and a brunette."

As they sat in the dim light of the hotel room, Kira watched Ernest's face, marked by conflict. "If you loved her, why didn't you marry her?" she asked softly.

Ernest sighed, looking out the window. "You know, where I come from, there are old prejudices. Mother believed a Jewish boy should marry within the community. She feared mixing with Germans...after everything."

Kira's heart skipped a beat, her own complex identity momentarily forgotten. She remembered her father's whispered stories of wartime Europe, the deep-seated divisions that still lingered in the minds of those who had survived. "And she chose me?" she murmured, her voice tinged with irony.

"Yes," Ernest replied, his voice heavy. "She thought it was time I settled down and started a family with a *nice Jewish girl.*"

Kira swallowed—she was certain it wasn't the right time to enlighten Ernest about her real religious affiliation. Not that it mattered to her, as she grew up in an atheist household and until the age of eleven, nobody even bothered to ask if she had a religion. She knew that her mother converted shortly before they married in December 1944. She did it voluntarily, and to her surprise, Mother's father-in-law even chastised her. "We accepted you as you are; there was no need for you to change."

But Rozi Chopaky always followed her inner logic. She explained that she refused to be separated from her husband, even in death, by being buried in a different cemetery if registered to be of a different religion. She had Kira baptized as soon as she was born to make sure her only child would not be recognized as a Jew anymore. However, it was a topic her mother's relative in Canada was unwilling to discuss, so nobody questioned Kira's affiliations once she arrived in Toronto.

"And how does your German girlfriend feel about your sudden marriage to a so-called Jewish girl?"

Earnest swallowed; his face turned red. He mumbled, "I only called and told her about it while you were in the bathroom."

"Oh my God!" Kira's knees gave out, and she sat down. "What did the poor girl say?"

"She threatened to commit suicide."

As Earnest's words hung in the air, Kira felt the weight of reality pressing down; her next actions would define her future. This was becoming a nightmare, and Kira desperately wanted to wake up. And to make sure she wasn't dreaming, she pinched herself on her arm. It was no use. Earnest was still there, his white, tragic, handsome face silently begging her to be the one to decide about their future. Kira was getting angry. The sexiest girl in her neighborhood, men turning their heads when she passed them on the street and whistled in appreciation? Not sexy enough for her own husband?

Trusting her sexual power, she sat on Earnest's lap and faced him, unbuttoned his shirt, and reached in to touch his chest while she tickled his ears with her tongue. She felt his penis rising, and she reached into his pants, slowly circling it with her fingers. His breathing became rapid, and slipping out of his trousers, he dragged her to the bed. A huge penis entered her with no foreplay, without carefully lubricating her. The next moment, Kira felt like her inner part would tear into a thousand pieces, and felt something warm and liquid saturate the sheet under her. The pain in her abdomen was so sharp that she fainted.

**

Several hours later, she woke up in the hospital and saw two nurses and a young doctor bending over her, frowning. She asked for some water in Hungarian, but they shook their heads and replied in English. The room had four beds, two on each side. She tried to sit up, but the nurses and the young man in the white coat pushed her back, all of them shaking their heads, repeating, "The baby...you must not move."

"What baby? Why can't I move? Why am I here?" she shouted in Hungarian.

The nurses and the doctor looked at each other, and one left, returning with a visibly shaken Earnest. "You must not move. You bled and fainted. I had to bring you to the hospital. Did you know you were pregnant? Almost three months. If you stay in bed, you have a good chance to keep the baby."

Kira looked at him, gaping. She tried to understand what he was telling her when suddenly she realized. *My God, it's Rocky's baby... The cliff...*

Just as Kira tried to process the enormity of her situation, the door burst open, heralding yet another unforeseen challenge. She saw Aunt Paula and Eugene standing at her bedside while Cathy sat on a chair beside her bed. Kira looked at them, slowly searching their faces for sympathy. They all looked alike, as if a sculptor would have used the same mold repeatedly. Their mouths were a thin line; their eyes ice-cold and with the same frown on their face. What had gotten into them?

"How could you do this to us?" Cathy hissed. She counted on a finger. "Do you know how much trouble and money it cost us to bring you here? Desmond had to put a thousand dollars into my account so I could apply for your visitor's visa."

Then, a second finger. "It had to be under my name because only blood relatives could apply for a visitor's visa. And as you remember, you only got a special, non-renewable visitor's visa, allowing you to stay for three short months. And since your parents begged us to ensure you stay here for good, we arranged your marriage. You must have been quite a burden for them trying to get rid of you so desperately."

Cathy sneered and attacked. "Why didn't you tell us you were pregnant? Don't you realize that Earnest could ask for an annulment, and they would deport you within twenty-four hours?"

Cathy seemed on a roll and continued with the barrage without taking a breath. "Have you thought about how your pregnancy would affect our reputation? Desmond is a respected proprietor here in Toronto. You could ruin his business. You were always a stupid, selfish bitch."

Cathy's voice reached Kira in waves, some words louder than others. Kira looked at her uncle, Eugene, hoping he would stop the flood of insults. But he just stood there, glaring at Kira with the same disgusted expression as the others. Kira's heart sank when she saw his eyes. This wasn't the Eugene she used to know—this man wasn't her friend and protector.

She reached out with her left hand, trying to catch his attention, and pleaded, "Eugene, please don't let them judge me. I can explain it to you. You would understand me, I know."

She was hoping that Eugene, a known womanizer who left his wife while she was carrying his child—the only one surviving her close to twenty pregnancies—for the wife of her gynecologist would be more sympathetic.

But Eugene pulled back with a stern face. "What is there to explain? It is self-evident, isn't it? You got pregnant by Thomas again, and he didn't want to marry a slut."

Kira felt the blood drain out of her face. She reached to her throat with both hands and fell back onto her pillow. The pain in her heart was so sharp that she believed it would kill her. She closed her eyes again and muttered, "Leave me alone. Just leave me alone."

She turned away from her relatives, burying her face deep in her pillow. Maybe if she held her breath long enough, she could slip into a coma, blocking the pain forever. But at last, she covered her ears so she could no longer hear the barrage.

Then the woman lying on the bed beside her sat up and exclaimed firmly, "That's enough! Why don't you leave her alone? Can't you see she isn't in any shape to take your insults?"

They all turned around to see her, ready to reply, when the nurse, a large Black woman, rushed in and seeing the visitors swarming around the girl like flies on a dead body; she opened the door wide and stated firmly, "Out! All of you!"

Cathy raised her voice to protest. "You can't talk to me like that. My husband, Mr. Diamond, is an influential industrialist…"

Towering over Cathy, the nurse glared at her and snapped, "I don't care how influential or important your husband is. You're still not allowed in here without my permission." Then, to enforce her command, she shoved Cathy out, closing the door behind her.

With tears streaming down her cheeks, Kira smiled and chuckled when she heard her cousin explode in the hallway.

"Who the hell does that woman think she is? It is strictly a family matter, and I had the right to inform the stupid bitch what she did to us." Her voice echoed through the hall as they marched towards the elevator.

"Not in my hospital, and definitely not during my shift," the nurse replied sternly. "Don't bother coming back. I already alerted security to keep you out. You're endangering the patients."

Kira was drifting in and out of sleep. When she finally could sit up, the dark-haired woman in the other bed looked at her and smiled. "Would you like to read something? Here, I have some books you might like to look at," she said in Hungarian, pushing a few books toward her.

"You're Hungarian, too?" Kira asked, surprised that a fellow Hungarian could share a hospital room with her.

"Yes, I am. I'm Yvonne Frank." She reached out to shake Kira's hand.

"Hi! I'm Kira Chopaky. Can I really look at your books?" Kira said, her hands itching to feel them.

"Be my guest, here," Yvonne said, pushing the pile closer to Kira. The first book was *Winnie the Pooh*, translated into Hungarian by the well-known author Frederic Karinthy. She recalled how some people swore it was much better in Hungarian than in the original English. The other was *Colas Breugnon*, written by the French writer Romain Rolland, who won the Nobel Prize for Literature in 1915.

Kira recalled her last night back in Hungary. Before going to bed, the two of them, Dad and Kira, stood side by side in front of the large shelves in the living room, carefully selecting those books that one would wish to have as a companion, even in case of a shipwreck on a deserted island. Her suitcase was filled, so it was hard to choose.

While the two thick volumes of the Hungarian-English dictionary were essential, they picked the others for sentimental reasons, old favorites of Kira, some that had belonged to her dad as a child and had been rebound for Kira's eighth birthday. One, titled *Eclipse of the Crescent Moon*, written by Géza Gárdonyi, a Hungarian writer celebrated for his historical novels, was deemed essential. Set in the 16th century during the Ottoman Empire's expansion into Europe, the novel focuses on the legendary *Siege of Eger* in 1552. During this siege, a small Hungarian garrison led by Captain István Dobó famously held off a significantly larger Ottoman army. The story is not only about the siege itself but also about love, bravery, and the struggle for freedom and independence. It portrays the defenders of Eger as heroic figures, symbolizing the resilience and courage of the Hungarian people.

The other book, written by Romain Rolland, was a recent favorite. It is about *Colas Breugnon*, a cheerful, easygoing carpenter from the county of Burgundy during the Hundred Years War in France.

Kira remembered clearly when her dad pulled this last book from the bookshelf and handed it to her.

"Although I have no riches to give you for your trip, I think this book will help remind you that one can survive just about anything with the right spirit. Just remember the old Colas, how he managed to survive a siege, a rebellion, an epidemic, the death of his wife, and losing his house and carpentry workshop to a devastating fire— and still found the strength at the age of sixty to start all over again. So, keep your chin up..." her father concluded with a mischievous wink demonstrating his famous gallows humor; he slapped Kira's back so hard she had a coughing fit and he added, "While you can—said the executioner!"

**

During visiting hours in the late afternoon, Yvonne's husband, a middle-height man with light brown hair and big ears, arrived, wearing a light jacket despite the wet and cold early fall day.

"George, I want you to meet Kira Chopaky." Yvonne introduced Kira. "She had some unfortunate mishaps, but I think she will be fine soon."

Kira blurted out nervously, "Well, if a brand-new husband tells you that your marriage of a few hours was an error....then you end up in a hospital bleeding heavily after the consummation, where you are told that you are three months pregnant—I guess you can call it a rather unfortunate mishap. My problem at this moment is that I can look forward to being charged for misrepresenting myself and then being deported. Oh boy, what a mess!" Totally exasperated, she leaned back on her pillow.

George Frank whistled sympathetically and sat beside her. "How did this happen? Didn't you just get married a few days ago? I seem to recall I put the notice of your wedding in our Toronto gossip column. But you just arrived two months ago, didn't you?"

"How do you know so much about me?" Kira said.

"Oh, I own the Hungarian Jewish newspaper here, so it is my business to know about the Hungarian Jewish Community in Toronto. By the way, are you related to Alex Chopaky, the former chief of police who joined the Uprising of nineteen fifty-six?"

"I'm his daughter," she said, squeezing her eyes tight, wondering whether it was smart to admit. In Kira's experience, in the last ten years of her life, even at the best of times, it mostly caused disapproving frowns.

George Frank jumped up, pulled her close, and exclaimed with a smile. "Really? Oh, but that is wonderful! Welcome to Canada, girl. I admire your father; he is a great man. How is he now?" Then, seeing Kira's crumpled face, he stepped back and asked, "What's the matter now? Why are you crying?"

It took a while before Kira could speak again. It had been so long since she had heard anyone speak like this about her father, and she missed him so much! She was sure that he would never condemn her but would try to understand and find the most logical solution.

"Just that I'm so homesick, and I promised him I would stay...he tried so hard to get me out of there...no longer to remain there as a liability...and now they'll send me back..."

She stopped herself in time. Her training took over, and she was forbidden from talking about her father to strangers. And this man was a stranger—a friendly one, but still...Would he understand that the main reason for getting Kira out of Hungary was to remove the possibility of the Hungarian Secret Service using her as a hostage to coerce her father into doing things against his will? But who could she trust now with her plight?

The same Rabbi who married Cathy a month ago and Kira a few days before entered the room. His deep voice filled the room as he greeted Yvonne and George.

"May the Creator return your health as soon as possible, my friend? I hear you are leaving this place soon. Good, very good. I stopped by the editorial office this morning, and let me tell you, it looked empty without you, my dear Yvonne. They told me I can find you here, George."

"Aaron, see who else is here," George pointed at Kira.

"Why aren't you on your honeymoon? Now, that is funny. I just talked to Desmond Diamond half an hour ago in his factory. He mentioned nothing about you to me."

George said, "Aaron, you better sit down and listen. The girl is in real trouble. She needs all the help she can get. Kira, tell the Rabbi."

"Rabbi, can they really deport me?" Kira asked after she had told him about her troubles.

"Did you know you were pregnant when you left Hungary?"

She shook her head. "No, not a clue. I often skipped my period. According to the doctors, it was a nervous reaction to prolonged uncertainty. And ever since I arrived, I was so busy, I simply forgot about it."

Yvonne said, "Your uncle mentioned someone named Thomas. Was he your boyfriend? Is he the father of your baby?"

"He was my boyfriend for a long time but isn't the father."

"Who is the father, then?"

"Rabbi, it isn't important. It happened under rather unusual circumstances. Would you believe it if I told you he was saving my life while we conceived this baby? We were together only once. And ever since then, things have been happening to me at such a hectic pace...It came as a shock when I was just told I was pregnant."

"What are you going to do now? You know you can't have an abortion legally in Canada?" Yvonne said.

"Even if I could, I wouldn't have one. I had one already when I was sixteen, and I promised myself I would never have another abortion if I could help it."

"What about the father? Shouldn't you let him know about the situation?"

"No," shouted Kira, "it is my baby! Nobody will tell me again to get rid of it."

"Are you sure? That is what he would want you to do if he knew about it?"

"I don't know, but I will not tell him. I won't let him decide for me. This is going to be my baby."

"What about Earnest? How does he feel about this?" The rabbi said.

Kira raised her voice. "Who cares about him? He said he didn't really want to marry me; he only did it to please his mother. I guess he can ask for an annulment, can't he?"

The rabbi said, shaking his head, "Not if the marriage was consummated! And it was, or you wouldn't be here. Why don't you let me speak to him and your relatives and see what we can come up with? In the meantime, concentrate on getting better."

With a newfound resolve, Kira turned her gaze from the window back to the room, ready to face whatever came next.

Chapter 12

Rocky arrived in London in the first week of August 1967.

He had been busy all summer, as it took him a lot of time to sort out what he needed to pack and say his farewells to all his favorite people back home, not knowing when he would see them again. He had mixed feelings about his upcoming adventures—on the one hand, he was thrilled to leave Hungary behind and see his aunt and cousin in London, but the task that the Hungarian Secret Service thrust on him worried him a lot.

A few days before his departure, as he was sorting out his papers and books to take with him in his room, his father walked in and touched his shoulder lightly. Rocky turned around and looked at him., "You wanted to talk about something, Dad?"

André nodded and sat on the chair, waiting for Rocky to take the other one. "Something bothers you," he stated.

"Am I that obvious?" Rocky queried.

"Is it the task the Secret Service demands of you? With your cousin in the United States?"

"Yes, Dad. It is. I really don't want to get anybody in trouble, especially not a relative."

"Don't fret it, son. You can trust Lady Anne with the information. She has connections with the proper agencies and people to help you." André smiled and hugged Rocky.

They decided to spend Rocky's last day in Budapest at Mr. Varga's apartment. Recently released from prison, where he was sent for three years for illegal Bible teaching, Mr. Varga was happy to see them in his home, including cranky old Betty and Father Tibor.

It was a touching farewell party amongst close friends, raising their glasses filled with home-distilled spirits to wish happiness to their young charge, who was starting his life in a free country. And it was funny to observe the two old ladies, forever competing for Rocky's favor, secretly stuffing boxes of homemade pastry in Rocky's carry-on bag.

Only old Betty, Father Tibor, and André, accompanied Rocky to the airport the following morning. Hugging the last time before he stepped on the airplane, London brought enough tears to everyone's eyes to make their handkerchiefs thoroughly soggy.

The flight to London barely left room for Rocky to sift through the myriad thoughts and emotions swirling within him. Beyond the anticipation of reuniting with his mother's sister, Lady Anne, and her daughter, Clara, after so many years, there lay a tumult of concern and duty. The mission entrusted to him by the Hungarian Secret Service loomed in his mind, yet the prospect of embracing family offered a fleeting solace. For a short while, he felt guilty for not getting in touch with Speedy before he left, but he consoled himself with the promise that as soon as he settled, he would write to her.

At Heathrow airport, a large Black man, surrounded by several other people, held up a big sign with Rocky's name. Carrying his suitcases, Rocky made his way toward the welcoming committee. Arms enveloped him and everyone shouted, trying to introduce themselves, shoving and tugging at him simultaneously.

Rocky looked at them with wide eyes, trying to figure out the relationships these strangers had with him. Only a tall, slim woman in her late forties was familiar to him who, someone with tears flowing, opening her arms.

"Aunt Anne," Rocky whispered, hugging the woman resembling his dead mother.

"My sweet Peter," the woman said, but she couldn't continue as she choked up. Finally, she said after a few seconds, "You're here, with us, safe and sound. And with your future secured."

Rocky wasn't confident about his secure future, but it was not the time yet to discuss the nitty-gritty of his situation. First, he had to find out how he could get his university admission transferred from London to Toronto and figure out how much he could trust his aunt to help him with his other issues.

While they guided him towards a large limousine waiting outside the arrival terminal, his aunt introduced the small army of people who greeted him. The large Black man, holding the card with Rocky's name, towering over everyone, was Cyrus, a former refugee from Congo—he was Aunt Anne's bodyguard, driver, handyperson, friend, and confidant for the past twenty years. His wife, Iris, a plump, pleasant-looking Black woman, was the cook, housekeeper, and sergeant major, ordering and directing everyone around the household.

They shared a rather large mansion that belonged to Aunt Anne's deceased husband and family, with Cyrus' and Iris's grandchildren, the mischievous eight-year-old twin boys they helped to raise after their parents' accidental death a few years ago.

Much too excited about the new relative, the twin boys kept tugging at Rocky's sleeves, bombarding him with questions. "What's your name? Where do you come from? Did you bring anything for us? Where is Hungary? Are people living there always hungry? Are you staying with us for long?"

Iris finally put her foot down. "Get in the car, both of you. And keep quiet till we get home. You can have your chance to torture the dear boy only after he has dined and rested. And let Lady Anne have some time with her nephew. After all, they have a lot to catch up with."

**

Dinnertime was a zoo. In the large dining room, at least a dozen people walked around helping themselves, piling up their plates and carrying full glasses, circling around and chatting away. Lady Anne introduced Rocky to everyone as her nephew and the latest addition to her motley collection of friends and protégées, some of whom enjoyed Lady Anne's long-term hospitality.

To his utter delight, Rocky found Cyrus and Iris among the diners, treated more like guests than employees. The twins, the little rascals, were hiding under the table, with their plates and glasses filled, occasionally popping up from there and grabbing more food from the table. Everyone seemed to enjoy the party and no one objected to the rather unconventional setting and collage of people.

At one point, Clara, Lady Anne's daughter, a slim, tall girl with shoulder-length raspberry hair barely covered with a multicolored beret, arrived, wearing a checkered miniskirt, a plain white T-shirt and a pair of tall grey boots covering part of her thighs. Breathless from running, she headed towards Rocky, threw her arms around, hugged him tightly, and cried joyfully, "Dear Cousin! finally, we meet! I heard so much about you and the rest of the tribe back in Hungary. You must come to the pub with me, to meet my friends and tell me all about your life in that nasty Communist country of yours. And I promise to reciprocate and tell you about my rotting capitalist one."

Clara, who claimed she hated traditions, followed in her mother's footsteps, even in her choice of work and passion. An advocate for the plight of refugees, she was also a ballerina and according to rumors, quite a good one. Barely twenty years old, she was already a soloist at the London Ballet Company and had come directly from a performance. Nobody seemed to care about her late arrival to dinner, as people kept coming and going, all excited to greet Rocky.

It was close to midnight when Rocky finally collapsed in bed. With a smile on his face, he fell asleep.

**

The following morning, Rocky woke up to a gentle knock on his door. His aunt, wearing a lilac-colored floating housecoat and matching little slippers, carried a tray with two glasses of orange juice, two cups of steaming coffee, and two plates filled with pancakes saturated with Maple syrup.

"I thought we should have breakfast together," Aunt Anne said. "It will give us a chance to talk uninterrupted." After placing the tray on Rocky's lap, she sat down on the bed.

After the preliminary discussions about the well-being of Rocky's family back at home, his aunt said, "Peter, there's something you may not be aware of," Lady Anne began, her tone softening as she reached for a small parcel on the tray. "You're not just anyone; you're someone with a legacy waiting for him." She gently pushed the parcel towards Rocky. "This is yours. It represents more than just wealth; it connects to your mother, her love for you, and her dreams for your future."

Rocky stared at her, gaping. This was the last thing he expected. He was going to borrow money from her to cover his expenses and tuition, as he wasn't sure he would be eligible for the scholarship if he transferred to Toronto. As soon as he arrived, he would find a cheap place to live and a part-time job to cover all his expenses.

The small package was in his hand. It was a letter from the Bank of London advising him that the original 50,000 pounds invested in 1952 as his mother's life insurance had matured, and its current value was exactly 250,000 pounds.

Rocky gulped and then burst into tears. It was a fortune he never expected and he knew it would take some time to fully appreciate it before its relevance would sink in.

His aunt gathered him in her arms and rocked him like a baby until the tears dried. "Shush," she said gently, "I understand. You have thought little of your mother lately, and now, suddenly, you feel her arms reaching you. She was a splendid mother to you. And she was a lovely creature, capable of bringing joy with her singing for many people during a hard time. And yes, she would want you to have as much of a carefree life as you could manage, at least financially."

After Rocky recovered, his aunt suggested accompanying him to the bank to open an account.

But Rocky needed to tell his aunt about the change of plans. Rocky hesitated, realizing the gravity of the next topic. "Aunt Anne, there's a reason I must head to Toronto before anywhere else," he started, his voice carrying a weight of responsibility.

He unfolded the story of the Hungarian Secret Service's mission, emphasizing the delicate nature of his task and the urgency imposed upon him. The narrative was met with attentive silence from Lady Anne, who absorbed every detail with a mix of concern and contemplation.

She leaned back in her chair, eyes narrowing thoughtfully. "So, let me see if I've got this straight," she began, aiming to piece together the tangled web of espionage and family obligation Rocky had found himself ensnared in. "The Hungarian Secret Service, under the guise of assisting your family, has essentially enlisted you, an unwitting civilian, in a clandestine operation to reach out to Miklós Görgey, a relative of yours and, as it turns out, a notable figure in the CIA."

Rocky nodded, his expression a mix of concern and incredulity at hearing the situation laid out so plainly.

"They've spun a tale involving a humanitarian gesture," Lady Anne continued, "suggesting Miklós Görgey could return to Hungary to visit his dying mother without fear of reprisal, thanks to an amnesty. But the underlying motive is to lure him out of the safety of the United States, making him vulnerable to capture and exploitation for whatever intelligence he possesses?"

She paused, allowing the gravity of the situation to sink in. "And you, my dear nephew, were chosen for this task because of your family connection to Miklós Görgey and your planned move to Toronto, which they've manipulated to serve their ends. It's a plot thick with intrigue and danger, leveraging personal ties for political gain."

Rocky felt a chill at the succinct summary of his predicament. It laid bare the precariousness of his position—caught between familial loyalty and the machinations of international espionage.

Lady Anne's gaze softened. "But fear not," she said with a reassuring smile. "We're not without our own resources and wits. We'll navigate this minefield together, ensuring that your involvement ends without harm to you or Miklós Görgey. And who knows? We might just manage to turn the tables on those who would use you as a pawn in their game."

"Auntie, I'm sorry, but none of this makes sense. All I wanted was a passport so that I could come and join you and pursue my dream of going to university! I just hoped we can somehow entangle this web without harming anybody close to us!"

Lady Anne put her hand over Rocky's arm to calm him. "No need for you to worry. I promise we'll find a suitable solution to this problem. But right now, we have some planning to do. First, we must have some pictures to take for your British Passport. Here is your application. Fill it out, and I'll take care of the rest."

"Why do I need a British passport, Aunty?"

"Because as a British Subject, you deserve to have one. Your mother was British, and you were born in England. I have your birth certificate. The passport will make your life, wherever you go, so much simpler. Your mother was a so-called war bride, and you were born right here, in this very house, while your papa was busy fighting the Nazis, dropping bombs from his beloved airplane. We used to tease him that he had two wives, Lilly, your mother, and the Airplane, with a nickname of Lucy."

Before Rocky could interject again, she said, "How soon do you want to go to Toronto? I assume you want to start the new semester there."

"If we could arrange it."

"I'll take care of it. Today is August eleventh, and classes begin at the University of Toronto in the first week of September. So, we need to get cracking on this." Lady Anne stopped for a moment and looked at Rocky with suspicion. "Tell me, boy, is there another reason you want to go to Toronto?"

Rocky's face turned crimson, and he coughed.

Her Aunt slapped his back. "All right, no need to be embarrassed. So, there is a girl waiting for you there? Does she have a name?"

"Her name is Kira Chopaky, and we were classmates in high school," Rocky admitted.

"Oh, how sweet, a high school romance! Tell me more." Lady Anne, the eternal romantic, sat back in her chair, eager to listen to Rocky's tale.

"Not much to tell, Aunty. During High School, we were not involved romantically. But we had a very odd encounter a few months ago, back in May, in Eger, and the next time I wanted to see her, her parents told me she had already left for Canada. I sent her a letter to the address in Toronto, which her parents gave me to advise of my arrival, but it came back stamped, and the person at that address is unknown. And I'm worried about her, because...because when I last saw her, she was suicidal. And I have a strong feeling that she could use my help."

"And do you know where you could find her?"

"All I know is that she has close relations in Toronto. I'm hoping that the Hungarian community will help me locate her."

"But first, you need to find proper accommodation there. And in this, I can help you." She reached the little table beside her chair and, lifting a notepad and a silver pen, wrote someone's name and address.

"Baroness Dolly Lipnitsky. 568 Palmerston Street, Toronto. Dolly is one of my closest friends." Aunt Anne explained.

**

Lady Anne recalled the day she first met Dolly in early 1946 in Germany, in one of the Displacement camps where she worked with the UN to help resettle refugees.

Dolly was a strikingly beautiful petite young woman with long silver-blond hair, almond-shaped turquoise eyes, and a porcelain-coloured, heart-shaped face. But when she finally showed up at the camp requesting help, she was skin and bones and badly bruised all over.

Lady Anne later learned that Dolly was a seventeen-year-old beautiful girl from a wonderful family in Budapest, when a very charming, handsome, but thoroughly irresponsible aristocrat, Henry von Lipnitsky, seduced her and talked her into taking all the family jewels, eloping with him when he was forced to run from his creditors.

He kept gambling throughout Europe. When he was lucky, they lived big, in expensive hotels. Champagne, caviar, jewelry, and fur coats for Dolly. But when he ran out of luck, he sold Dolly to the highest bidder, mostly American soldiers, even for a bar of chocolate. She was barely twenty years old when she finally escaped from her worthless husband, who finally got what he deserved shortly after when the creditors finally caught up to him and killed him.

But as Lady Ann recalled, Dolly was not the type who would sit back, feeling sorry for herself. "Since she could speak perfect English, German, French, Hungarian, and Polish, I hired her to become an interpreter. In Nineteen-Forty-nine, after all the displacement camps closed in Western Europe, she went to Toronto, bought a large house, and rented rooms mostly to Hungarian refugees.

"We keep corresponding with each other. Her price is right, and she will also throw in a cooked meal when she sees fit. I understand she, too, fills her home with colorful characters, much like mine here. And, since her home is right in the center of the Hungarian community, it pretty much guarantees if Dolly doesn't know anybody there, the person is not worth knowing.

"I tell you what. If you're interested, I can call her immediately and ask her if she has a room for you to rent. By the way, you can tell her anything except the existence of your inheritance." She rolled her eyes and explained, "to avoid the temptation to talk you into investing in any of her dubious charities or business ideas."

She added, "The woman has a few hobbies I don't approve of, but that doesn't take away her charm or make me question my faith in her friendship any less."

**

By the end of that week, Rocky had a British passport, an airplane ticket to Toronto, and a letter proving his transfer from the City University of London to the University of Toronto, Electrical Engineering program. His room and board were secured at the baroness, Dolly Lipnitsky, and another letter from the Bank of Canada confirmed that he had access to close to 500,000 Canadian dollars.

Rocky spent his last night in London surrounded by his newly found relatives and friends, hopping from pub to pub to taste all the brews. The following morning, still in a daze, he was sent off to Toronto.

Chapter 13

Rocky's journey to his new Canadian home started smoothly, thanks to his British passport, which facilitated his entry through Toronto International Airport's immigration. He hailed a cab. Destination: the address his aunt had provided.

As Rocky settled into the backseat of a cab, the driver glanced at him through the rearview mirror. "Welcome to Toronto," he said, his accent tinged with a familiarity that piqued Rocky's interest.

"Thanks," Rocky replied, noting the driver's careful navigation through the city's bustling streets. The cab was immaculately kept, with personal trinkets that hinted at a story yet to be told—a small Hungarian flag dangling from the mirror and a well-worn history book beside the seat.

"Where from?" the driver asked, his curiosity apparent.

"Originally Hungary, but I've been in England recently." Rocky watched the driver's reaction closely.

"A fellow Hungarian, then!" the driver exclaimed, his face lighting up with a smile that reached his eyes. "I'm Joseph, by the way. Toronto's been my home for a while now."

Rocky reached out to shake the hand of his new driver and introduced himself. "Hi. My name is Peter Görgey. Nice to meet you, Joseph."

"Sorry, but I must ask. Is there any relation to *THAT* Görgey?"

Rocky, prepared for the unavoidable question, smiled and replied dismissively, "Only distant cousin."

As they navigated the streets of Toronto, Joseph shared his life story, mirroring the hardships and resilience that Rocky knew all too well. From a well-off family in Hungary that lost everything in the war to being branded as class enemies and exiled, Joseph's narrative was a familiar tale of loss and struggle. "…we had to suffer the added humiliation and privation, when the communists declared us to be *Class Enemies*, and forced us to pack up and go to the boonies. There to live in a dirty shack with leaking roofs and without adequate plumbing."

Rocky nodded, as if he was too familiar with the practice of being declared to be a class enemy, and deported somewhere in an isolated, unlivable part of the country.

"This also meant that I could not dream of attending even high school, never mind a university back at home. So, after completing grade eight in that little one room school in the Low Land, I made a living by helping the peasants to deliver their purchases to and from the neighbouring markets. Mind you," he added in a hurry, "the peasants were good to me; they always paid me with a little extra food that I could take home to my parents.

"I first heard about the uprising on October 23rd of Nineteen-fifty-six on the radio. I hopped on the first train heading to Budapest and joined the group at Sena Square. When the second wave of the Russian tanks re-entered Hungary in the first days of November, I headed straight for the Austrian border."

"And a good thing, too, as you could have been another of those young rebels hanged for the crime of fighting the invading Russian Army. What happened in Austria?"

"I stuck around in Austria for a while, although I moved away from the refugee camp as soon as I could. Too much fighting, drunkenness, and gambling. Who needs that? I went to the countryside and offered my help to the farmers again. They fed me well and helped me to decide where to go. I had a choice: to go to Canada, Australia or the United States. I decided beggars can't be choosers, so I applied to all of them, and whichever takes me first, that's where I'm heading. And guess what?"

"Was it Canada?" Rocky hazarded a guess.

"Wrong," Joseph exclaimed triumphantly, "it was Australia. And since I always wanted to see Australia, I went there first. Why not? They paid for my ticket. I put in a few years' service in one of the sheep stations in the outback. Saved my pennies, then travelled around and eventually ended up here in Toronto."

Arriving at their destination, Joseph's revelation that he was not just the cab driver but also a future housemate, piqued Rocky's interest.

"You're going to like it here. The Baroness, she's got a keen eye for students who are eager to work and study. As long as she can see that you're a hard-working person, eager and willing to study and work, she will go for an extra mile to help you. The other rules are: no boozing and definitely no gambling in her establishment. And she's very strict about it. She has what she calls a zero-tolerance rule. Once you break them, you're out, just like that." And he snapped his fingers to emphasize the point.

Rocky, who rarely drank alcohol and never touched cards, asked Joseph, with a serious face, "So, what are you allowed to do for fun? Go to church on Sundays and sing the hymns."

Joseph roared with laughter. "I didn't say you could never touch a drop of alcohol or stop having any fun. But until you experience any of our traditional Sunday brunches, you'll never know what you missed."

The taxi finally arrived. The house was in one of the narrow side streets, mostly filled with two storied homes. Joseph tried to point out the highlights of the neighbourhood with little success. To a newly arrived foreigner, after a long flight one street looked like all the others, side by side two-storied family homes and a few large, nondescript, multi-storied buildings scattered among them. Joseph stopped in front of a three-story building, which on one side had a large wooden outdoor staircase leading up to the third floor. A later addition to the original building made it somehow unbalanced, giving the impression of a drunken chimney sweeper wearing a top hat.

At the big, open, black double front-door with large brass knobs, and leaded windows embedded in its upper portion, a small, slim lady, wearing black, form fitting slacks and a multicoloured flowing blouse stood in high heel shoes. Her silver blond hair tied in a ponytail, with a long cigarette holder in her right hand, while resting the left on her narrow hip with the pose of a proud proprietor. With squinting eyes, she scrutinized the taxi stopping by her front door.

Joseph stopped in front of the building and turned the engine off, opened the door, ran around, and opened the passenger door to let Rocky out. Then he turned to the woman and exclaimed, "Dolly, look who I have brought you—a recent addition to your colorful collection, Mr. Görgey himself."

Rocky stepped out of the car and crossed the sidewalk without getting his suitcase. But before he could speak, Dolly pulled the long cigarette holder out of her mouth and looked at his face. Then she turned to Joseph and, after indicating to Rocky to follow her inside, said, "Joe, would you mind bringing Mr. Görgey's suitcases to the parlor?"

The double door opened into a spacious central foyer with a shiny wooden floor and panels on both sides of the walls. Immediately on the left was a coat tree, and right next to it were wide-open double French doors leading into a formal living room furnished by two antique settees and several armchairs, flanked by small ornately carved tables. A well-worn Persian rug covered the floor, and on the walls, Rocky spotted several, mostly modern paintings and a few large-sized mirrors. The other French door across the foyer opened to a stately dining room with a heavily carved dining table and upholstered dining room chairs. The foyer continued to a gracefully carved wooden staircase leading up to the second floor, where, holding on to the upper banister, several people looked down.

Dolly ignored them and, grabbing Rocky by his elbow guided him to the parlor. She closed the large double French door behind her and sat across from him. She scrutinized him for a while before she said, "So, you're Peter Görgey, my best friend's nephew."

Rocky nodded and tried hard not to stare at the woman's face. It was the most perfectly formed heart-shaped face, with a pointy chin, pale skin, and almond-shaped cornflower blue eyes. With her long silver blond hair, she should have looked like a small, ornate Chinese doll, except there was nothing fragile about her. Her eyes and mouth portrayed a powerful self-confident personality, which silently suggested a *Don't fuck with me* attitude. Those baby blue eyes penetrated deep and seemed capable of looking beyond the surface, like someone who knew how to make strong men stutter and reveal their most sacred secrets.

"I understand you switched your studies from London to Toronto. Why? I mean, why would you do that when you finally could have been with your aunt and her colorful gang after all those years and enjoy all the perks of her love and wealth? After all, the London University of Engineering already accepted you! Did you have a fight with your aunt? And don't lie to me about it, whatever your reasons were. I want you to know that as a professional lady of the night for nearly twenty years, little could escape or shock me nowadays."

Her directness impressed Rocky. And since his aunt already warned him not to reveal his newly found wealth to the Baroness, he was open about his other reason: the Hungarian Secret Agents forced on him in exchange for a passport. Namely, about enticing his uncle from Washington to Toronto,

"Ah," she said, with a mischievous smile on her face, "Very interesting. Well, we will deal with it when the time comes." Then she sobered up and asked, "Is there another reason you came to Toronto?"

Does this woman have a frightening talent for reading my mind? Rocky wondered. But since he was hoping to get Dolly's help to find Kira, he told her about his short involvement and his foreboding feelings about the girl.

"I don't insist on getting involved with her again," Rocky stuttered. "I mean, not if she doesn't want to see me again. I just want to make sure she is alright."

Dolly nodded, and out to him. "It's all right, my boy. We'll do our best to find her. In the meantime, come. I'll introduce you to my gang and show you to your room."

By then, the *Gang*, mostly people in their early twenties, were gathering in the foyer, waiting to meet the recent addition.

Joseph set about introducing everyone. He said, "You already know me. Here," and pointed to a tall, skinny youngster with flaming red hair, freckled face, and a wide smile, "is Smiley, otherwise known as George Ort. He is our future historian, hoping to become a professor of something. In the meantime, supporting himself, we take turns driving the same cab at different times of the day or the weekends."

Smiley stepped forward and shook Rocky's hand firmly.

Joseph turned to his other side and pulled forward a medium-height, black-haired girl trying to hide behind an enormous pair of glasses. "Now, don't let this little missy mislead you. She is a hugely talented artist. Wilma is her name, and most of the paintings on the walls in the parlor are hers. She is the only one of us, already supporting herself in her chosen profession."

The girl removed her glasses and, laughing, reached out to Rocky. "Welcome to our madhouse. I hope you'll love it here as much as we do."

Rocky smiled as he looked at her. She had short, unruly black hair falling over her forehead, hiding her unusual pair of mismatched eyes, one brown and the other grey, with an exaggerated pair of glasses. She wore a loose, black smock splattered with many colored paint spots and unlaced army boots without socks.

"She is renting the top floor with a skylight, using it as her own studio," Joseph said. Then he stepped away to reveal the person standing closely behind him. He was a short, stocky man wearing a chef hat and an apron, holding a large wooden spoon in one hand.

"Stephan is our delightful cook, who can create any dish your little heart desires. He hopes to become chef extraordinaire of the international cuisine scene. You'll taste some of his creations on our Sunday Brunch with invited guests when he can shine, and we can dine to our heart's content."

Stephan stepped forward, and bowed. Rocky, perplexed for a second, returned the greeting in the same fashion.

Just then, the front door opened, and a very tall youngster whirled in and, not waiting to be introduced, ran up to the new arrival and grabbed his right hand. "Servus," he said, "I'm Felix Dosa, a very modest and brilliant athlete and jazz musician. I love girls, booze, and parties, and I hope you can sing because I'm desperately looking for a singer for my new album. If you have some extra money, you can throw it in my direction because I'm planning to take the band on the road, and we need to buy a van."

Rocky could only stare at the boy and wonder how he could say all that in one breath. To show his talent, Felix inhaled, puffed out his cheeks into a pair of large balls, and said, "Oh, I have a huge lung…being an athlete and playing many instruments, including the trumpet."

Rocky's head throbbed from the impact of meeting all the residents. Dolly seemed to realize the situation and quickly stepped in, offering to guide her new tenant through the house and show him to his room. First, she led the way to the large kitchen, behind the dining room, and the equally large pantry. From the kitchen, a large, covered deck gave access to the backyard. A grassy garden divided the backyard, shadowed by a large tree, a large swimming pool, and a garage built for at least two cars.

From the open garage door, a loud banging followed by louder swearing made Dolly smile. "Don't mind him," she said when Rocky turned his head towards the garage. "It's only Danny, our handyman. Well, he's a supposed handyman, as he misses more than he hits with the hammer." And she added sympathetically, "I suspect he smashed his fingers again."

Sure enough, a minute later, a tall, solid man, wearing a grey, oily overall and a large handkerchief tied over his head, gingerly holding his left hand, emerged from the garage. Dolly walked to the first-aid box attached to the wall. She opened it and got out a roll of gauze and the small bottle of iodine, ready to administer the treatment. Danny, jumping on the deck without the use of the stairs, headed directly to Dolly and shoved his injured hand towards her.

"Fucking hammer attacked me again," he complained bitterly.

Dolly replied, "I'm glad your English is improving. By the way, meet your new roomy," and turned Danny to face Rocky.

Sucking on his injured finger, Danny apologized. "Please forgive my French." He shoved his non-injured hand towards Rocky. "I'm Danny, and despite nasty rumors, occasionally I can hit more than my fingers with the hammer." He chuckled. "I do not know why Dolly allows me to play with her tools in that garage. It shows you how great she is with her protégées, allowing them to learn from their own mistakes."

"Lucky for you," Dolly said. "Now wash up, my dear, and join us in the parlor later. I'm busy showing Rocky around."

"So you're the recent addition?" Danny asked. "We'll talk later after you settle down."

Dolly led Rocky to the other side of the deck, where another door led to her private apartment. It contained two small rooms and a bathroom. In one room, a large desk showed an office obviously used for business, and in the other, a combination of bedroom and sitting room, with a padded door opening directly to the main living room.

On the main floor, just underneath the enormous staircase, a two-piece washroom was obviously a fresh addition. Dolly explained, "We needed a washroom here more than a large coat closet."

Then she began climbing the stairs ahead of Rocky to the second floor leading to the bedrooms. Six of them, three on each side, with their own private bathrooms. The rooms were large and bright, each with a double bed, two armchairs, a desk, and a chest of drawers. Rocky spotted the radiators underneath the large windows as a source of heat, and he was relieved to know that he wouldn't need to carry coals up from the freezing shed to his room daily during the wintertime to heat it.

Dolly followed his gaze. "Central heating. The furnace is in the basement. We use oil for heat and hot water, as well." She walked to the end of the hallway and opened the door to the last bedroom. It looked just like all the others, except this one already had Rocky's suitcases on the floor beside his bed.

"This is your room. I expect you to keep it clean, including the bathroom. There is no room service here. You're responsible for your room and your own laundry. Right down the hall is the laundry room, with a washer and dryer." She pointed at the wallboard with a handwritten, pinned-up schedule. "You must coordinate its use with the rest of them. Breakfast is self-served. In the kitchen, you will always find fresh coffee and tea made, but in case we run out of them, whoever finds the pot empty makes it fresh for everyone. Bread is in the bread box, butter and jam are in the refrigerator, and milk is in the refrigerator. If you prefer cereal, you'll find them on the counter, beside the sugar container. There are always eggs and some cold cuts or cheese if you want to make a sandwich for yourself. And—" She raised her finger in warning, "you wash your own dishes. Are we clear about this? And if you see anything is running out, you write it down on the shopping list, stocked at the door of the fridge."

"Who does the food shopping?" Rocky asked.

"Once a week, I place the order through the phone, and the merchants deliver it to our door. Dinners are served at six. If you cannot make it on time, no problem, but you will have to heat the leftovers and clean up after yourself. Your monthly fee for room and board is exactly one hundred and fifty dollars, payable on the first day of every month. I hoped this would be agreeable with you." Dolly raised her eyebrows. "By the way, I'll let you know ahead of time. I'm not fond of lending money to any of my borders."

"And what happens if I can't pay the rent on time?"

"No such thing. I expect you to have the money on the first of each month. There are no loafers in this house. Now that you live in Canada, you have better learn to stand on your own feet. However, if you get into trouble through no fault of your own, get sick or treated unfairly, you come to me immediately, and I'll try my best to help you. My door is always open for my kids, but they know better than to abuse it. But, right now, I want you to pay me for the first and last month's rent, altogether three hundred dollars."

Rocky pulled out his wallet. He counted the money, six Canadian fifty-dollar bills and gently laid them in Dolly's open palm.

"Good," she said satisfied. Then, catching Rocky yawning, she said, "I guess jet lag is catching up with you. Might as well go to sleep, but for good luck' sake, don't forget to count the corners in your room and make a wish before you fall asleep—" She winked at Rocky, turned around and walked downstairs.

Chapter 14

The soft morning light gently filtered through the lace curtains of the spacious dining room, casting a soothing glow on the antique wooden table lovingly set for the communal brunch. The air was infused with the familiar scents of freshly brewed coffee and warm pancakes, intermingled with the delicate fragrance of flowers from the garden. It was a Sunday that promised leisure and camaraderie in the embrace of Dolly's expansive, inviting home.

Rocky paused at the threshold, taking in the sight of the bustling room. People chatted amiably around the table, plates clinking as they helped themselves to generous servings of food. His arrival was a subtle affair—he brushed off a hint of nervousness from his shoulders like lint and stepped forward with a tentative smile.

Dolly, spotting him from across the room, raised her hand in a warm gesture of welcome. "Ah, there you are! Come in, Rocky. You're just in time to join us," Dolly called out, her voice threading through the hum of conversations.

As Rocky moved closer, the details of the room became clearer—the fine china on the table, the vibrant paintings adorning the walls, and the diverse group of guests, each absorbed in conversation. The setting was a vivid tapestry of old and new, where antique decor met the laughter and lively debates of the brunch's attendees.

Rocky followed Joseph into the bustling dining room. A tall man with a commanding presence stood up from the table. He extended his hand with a warm, broad smile contrasting his deep, resonant voice.

"Welcome, young man," he greeted. "I'm Rabbi Aaron Salamon, and this is my wife, Rebecca." He gestured to the woman, who offered a graceful nod, her blond hair catching the light as she smiled.

"It's lovely to meet you, Rocky," Rebecca said, melodic and inviting. "We've heard much about your journey. I hope you find warmth and comfort here with us today."

- 97 -

Before Rocky could respond fully, another figure rose from his chair, thin and slightly stooped but with an unmistakable sparkle of humor in his eyes. "And I'm Father Tibor Ordog," he introduced himself with a firm handshake that belied his wiry frame. "Hungarian, as my name suggests, and yes, it does mean *Devil*. But fear not, I'm quite tame at the brunch table."

The priest's comment drew a light round of laughter from nearby guests, easing Rocky into the circle. His initial tension dissipated under their friendly welcome, replaced by a budding curiosity about the eclectic group he was about to join.

"Come, sit between us," Rabbi Salamon invited, pulling out a chair. "There's much to share and even more to enjoy, especially Stephan's culinary experiments."

Rocky settled into the chair between Rabbi Salamon and Father Ordog just as a large serving dish of steaming pancakes was passed down the table. He watched as Rabbi Salamon expertly navigated a serving onto his plate, adding a dollop of apple compote.

"Ah, you must try these," the Rabbi said, nudging the dish towards Rocky. "Stephan prides himself on his pancakes; I must say, they're worth the indulgence."

Rebecca, sitting across from them, chuckled as she sipped her coffee. "Aaron's right, though I tend to favor the salmon slices. I must admit it is nice of him to serve us kosher, even in this unorthodox setting."

Father Ordog, helping himself to the pancakes, leaned in with a conspiratorial grin. "And don't get me started on the coffee. It's a serious matter here. Given my name, I prefer mine black as midnight on a moonless night, which I find quite fitting." He gave Rocky a wink.

Rocky, amused and more relaxed, joined in the banter. "I'll have to take notes on who prefers what," he joked, accepting the pancakes and noticing how the simple act of sharing food seemed to weave him into the fabric of this community.

Joseph, who had been bustling around the room, ensuring everyone had what they needed, paused by their side with a fresh pot of coffee. "You'll find we're all quite passionate about our brunches here. It's more than just food; it's our little melting pot of traditions and stories. Make sure you try some of everything, Rocky."

As plates clinked and the guests continued to share and offer various dishes, Rocky felt the room's warmth grow. It wasn't just the food that made the brunch special—the company, the open hearts, and the laughter they shared.

As the laughter from the earlier jokes settled into a warm, comfortable hum of conversations around the table, Rabbi Salamon turned to Rocky with a thoughtful expression.

"What brings you to Canada?" the Rabbi asked, his voice mixing curiosity with a hint of empathy.

Rocky hesitated, the weight of his past experiences clouding his expression. "Well, Rabbi, I was looking for a place promising safety and new opportunities."

Rabbi Salamon nodded. "Ah, the search for safety. We, too, came here under similar pretenses. My wife and I escaped from Hungary during a particularly turbulent time. Canada offered us refuge and a chance to rebuild in peace."

Father Ordog interjected softly, "It's not just about finding a new home, but also about the peace of mind that comes with it. Knowing you're safe, you can finally sleep without fear—it changes you."

The Rabbi picked up on that, his eyes reflecting a mix of memories and present realities. "Indeed, it does. And yet, despite the safety, the shadows of old fears can linger. Rocky, have you ever experienced it?. How should I put it? Hauntings of the past that seem to follow you, even in a new land?"

Rocky looked at the Rabbi, surprised by the directness, but relieved to talk about it. "Yes, I've had my share of nightmares. Dreams where I'm still trapped back, unable to move forward."

"That's a common thread among us here," Rabbi Salamon said, glancing around the table where nods met his words. "Many of us have faced similar hauntings. It's one of the reasons this community is so tight-knit. We understand each other on a level that goes beyond simple friendship. It's about shared experiences, shared recoveries."

Father Ordog added, "We often discuss these topics—how to cope, how to truly start anew—not just in physical terms but emotionally and mentally."

Rocky felt a sense of belonging, a connection that had eluded him until now. "It's comforting to know I'm not alone in this," he admitted.

Rabbi Salamon placed a reassuring hand on Rocky's shoulder. "Here, you're not just understood, Rocky. You're supported. And in time, you'll find that these nightmares fade, replaced by new dreams— hopeful ones."

As Rocky and Rabbi Salamon's conversation about coping with past traumas and rebuilding new lives wound down, Rocky's gaze drifted across the array of technological gadgets lined up along the sideboard—a small testament to his passion for electronics.

"You seem interested in our little tech set up there," Rabbi Salamon observed, following Rocky's gaze.

Rocky smiled, a spark of enthusiasm lighting his features. "Yes, I've always been drawn to electronics. Back home, I spent much time tinkering with anything I could get my hands on. It's more than a hobby; it's a language I understand better than any spoken word."

At this, a hearty laugh erupted from the other end of the table, where a bald man with a jovial expression had been quietly enjoying the meal. He pushed his chair back and stood, walking over to join Rocky and the Rabbi.

"Speaking of languages," he said with a wide grin, "the language of electronics can sometimes cause quite the devilish mischief, isn't that right?" He extended his hand to Rocky. "I'm Reverend Mike Pokol, by the way. Hungarian for *Hell*, but don't let that scare you. I'm mostly harmless, except when it comes to my attempts at fixing my gadgets."

Rocky chuckled, shaking his hand. "Nice to meet you, Reverend. I've had a few mishaps myself with electronics."

Reverend Pokol's eyes twinkled with humor. "Oh, we'll have to swap stories then! I once tried to repair an old radio and ended up catching the attention of the local fire department. Smoke signals are not the best way to tune into your favorite station!"

Their laughter drew a few curious looks from others, but it also broke any remnants of formality that might have lingered around the table. Rocky felt an immediate kinship with Reverend Pokol, whose lighthearted approach to life—and electronics—felt both comforting and familiar.

"Perhaps you can help me later with setting up some new equipment we got for the community center," Reverend Pokol suggested. "It's sitting in boxes because everyone's afraid they'll end up sending more smoke signals."

"I'd love to," Rocky replied, pleased to be able to contribute something meaningful to the community.

As the laughter from Rocky's and Reverend Pokol's shared stories began to ebb, the room was suddenly filled with the comical sight of Isabella Seraph wrestling her way through the doorway with a stubbornly open umbrella. Despite the sunny day outside, Isabella, ever the eccentric, and prepared for all eventualities, had brought her large, floral-patterned umbrella which now seemed to have a life of its own.

"Every time with this umbrella!" she exclaimed, her voice filled with frustration and amusement. The guests turned, some chuckling, as she battled the unyielding spokes.

Joseph, quick to come to her aid, approached with a smile. "Isabella, let me help you with that. It seems you've brought some of the storm inside."

With a deft flick and a twist, he closed the umbrella, eliciting a round of applause from around the table. Isabella bowed theatrically, her bright eyes scanning the room until they settled on Rocky.

"Ah, you must be the famous Rocky," she said, striding over with the umbrella now neatly tucked under her arm. "I'm Isabella Seraph, professor of philosophy and resident skeptic. And before anyone else labels me—yes, I am often called Dr. Lunatic, but only affectionately, I assure you."

Her introduction sparked laughter and a few nods of recognition from those who knew her well.

Rocky, intrigued by her vibrant personality and unorthodox entrance, smiled warmly. "Nice to meet you, Dr. Seraph. I've never seen someone make such an entrance with an umbrella indoors."

Isabella waved off the compliment with a laugh. "One must always be prepared, Rocky. But tell me, have you settled in well? Are there any existential crises I should know, or have we staved them off with pancakes and sausages?"

After a chuckle, the group's attention turned towards Rocky, asking him where he came from and his plans. Which university and what faculty accepted him? Did he have enough money to pay his tuition and support himself? Rocky explained that the City University of London had initially accepted him but switched to Toronto for family reasons and that he was planning to get a part-time job.

"What kind of part-time job did you have in mind?" Reverend Mike Pokol said.

"I don't know. But something involving electronics would be nice since that is one of my passions and chosen field."

Rabbi Salamon put his small espresso cup down. "I could call the Diamond Industry owner and see if he will hire you."

"That would be wonderful, Rabbi. Thank you. What do they manufacture?"

"Diamond Industry is one of the up-and-coming leading manufacturers of fine Hi-Fi systems in and around Toronto. And you can use public transportation, which is a definite plus if you go to the U of T without access to a car." The rabbi stopped and slapped his forehead, "That reminds me. Dolly, I need to talk to you in private. Do you mind?"

Dolly walked ahead to her office. The others didn't mind it either, as they were used to these private talks between Dolly and any of her other guests who were all closely involved in their communities and performed not only the role of a spiritual leader but often acted as social workers trying to solve their problems. So, they turned to Dolly for advice, as they knew her to be level-headed and practical, capable of cutting through unnecessary and unproductive emotions.

She sat down in one of her armchairs and pointed at the one beside her. Rabbi Salamon sat down and wiped his forehead with a starched handkerchief that he pulled out of his pocket.

"Dolly, I need your advice in a very delicate situation. One of my newly arrived people found herself in a real mess, and I'm apprehensive about her well-being."

Dolly pulled her feet under her skirt, ready to listen and think about a suitable solution.

The rabbi described Kira's situation, including how the husband claimed his visiting mother, who was unhappy about his long-time German girlfriend, coerced him into marrying Kira. "The mother is a holocaust survivor who took it as a personal insult that her only surviving son is cohabiting with the murderer."

Dolly grimaced.

"I couldn't agree with you more," the rabbi replied with a sad face. "Intolerance, no matter where it comes from, is repulsive, especially when it punishes the innocents. And in this case, the poor girl, I mean the so-called German girlfriend—if I understand correctly—is from a third-generation Canadian family."

"How long were the two of them together?" Dolly said.

"At least four years. Earnest only told her about his marriage on the day of the wedding. The poor girl collapsed and is currently in the hospital with a total nervous breakdown. She is under heavy sedation, as she is suicidal."

"What a mess!" Dolly said, reaching towards the little table beside her chair, where she kept her cigarettes and the long silver holder. "So, there are two girls in trouble. The first is suicidal and in the hospital under heavy sedation. The second one, who is also in the hospital, is pregnant and with a child, not by her husband. Did I sum it up correctly so far?"

"Yes, but there is more. The pregnant girl came with a unique three-month visitor's visa, which was not renewable. She could have stayed here permanently if her marriage had succeeded. The girl can't return to Hungary, as her father, a former politician, had been found guilty in a secret trial, where he nearly landed on death row. She faced serious discrimination. But she is hesitant to ask for refugee status here, as she is afraid of the consequences her parents back in Hungary might face because of that.

"But now, because of her pregnancy, the Canadian authorities could accuse her of duping the poor boy to marry her so she could stay in Canada. Her relatives consider themselves upstanding citizens in their community and are more than ready to eliminate this so-called shameful problem that could damage their precious reputation. Bad for business, they claim."

"Holy fuck!" Dolly waved her cigarette holder in agitation, "So, Aaron, my friend, what are you proposing to do?"

"I had a long conversation with the Diamonds—they're the second girl's relatives, and the husband last night and twisted their arms to forget about calling the authorities and having the girl deported. I told them that since I was the one who officiated their wedding, I would testify on the girl's behalf, and I certainly have seen no evidence of coercion on her part. The bleeding happened as the result of the consummation of the marriage; therefore, annulment should not be an option. I also spoke to the girl in the hospital, and she swore she wasn't aware of her pregnancy. There were so many things happening to her recently that she completely lost track of her menstruation period or lack of it."

"Did you believe her?" Dolly said.

"Yes, it was hard not to believe her."

"Where is she now?"

"Still in the hospital for the next few days. I also talked the new husband into staying with the girl until the baby was due and taking at least financial responsibility for her. The Diamonds seemed to be pleased with that arrangement."

"But you're not sure about it, is that it?" Dolly said.

"I didn't tell you yet that the way I found out about the girl in the hospital was when I went to visit Yvonne Frank, who was in the same room with her. And she told me about the dreadfully unpleasant and horrible scene she witnessed between the girl and her beloved family when she was finally coming around. Yvonne thinks it would be an awful injustice to let the girl return to the bosom of that ever-loving family of hers. And frankly, I'm worried about it, too. Nothing good can come out of it."

"What is the girl's name?" Dolly asked.

"Kira Chopaky."

"You're kidding!" Dolly replied.

"Why would I kid you about it?"

"Oh, but it is a peachy business, Aaron. And no, I did not lose my mind." She sobered up. "However, now it is your turn to listen and see if we can devise a suitable solution for all concerned. Rocky Görgey just arrived from London, where he was originally going. Although accepted at the University in London, he suddenly changed his mind and switched to the University of Toronto. His reason was that he was looking for Kira Chopaky, a former high school classmate. He told me about their recent and brief involvement and that she had already left Hungary when he looked for her. He said he had a foreboding feeling about the girl, as when they met in the summer, she was seriously suicidal."

"Wait! So Rocky Görgey had a brief relationship with Kira? When?"

"In early May."

"Then Rocky must be the father of Kira's baby! The timing is right!"

The two stared at each other and then clasped hands in great delight.

"The girl can't possibly go back to the husband or near that monster of her family," Dolly declared. "Bring her here. She could share the upper floor with Wilma."

"Well, that might be a problem as the girl refused to tell me who the father was, as she was afraid he might force her to give the baby up. And she said she'd rather die than do that. How would she react to finding Rocky here?"

"We'll cross that bridge when we have to. In the meantime, you don't have to tell her yet that you know who the father is. And I don't have to know who she is until she arrives here and introduces them to each other. The whole thing is strictly a coincidence. Then, let the chips fall where they may. With God's help, of course."

"Of course. It couldn't be any other way. But I promised Rocky I would try getting him a job in the Diamond Industry. How would that seem under the circumstances?"

"Simple. You don't need to reveal to the Diamonds that you know the relationship between Rocky and Kira. I promise not to tell Rocky about the relationship between Kira and his future boss. Just introduce the boy to Desmond and see what happens. Knowing the cheap and snobbish bastard, he will be happy to get reliable and cheap labor from the son of an aristocrat, a university student. Just think of the irony: without knowing, the Diamonds will support the girl, anyway."

The Rabbi stood up. "In that case, I might as well go directly to the hospital and present the options to her. I'll let you know which one she prefers, and take it from there."

Chapter 15

As Rabbi Salamon entered the hospital room, Kira looked up from the book she was trying to read, her eyes betraying the turmoil beneath her calm exterior. Her forced smile was a thin veil over the despair that had taken root in her heart.

Rabbi Salamon outlined the arrangement he'd secured for her—a chance to start anew, away from the judgment and constraints of her past—Kira's initial shock gave way to a flood of relief and disbelief. For the first time in what felt like an eternity, the glimmer of hope began to pierce the shadows of her despair. But with hope came fear—fear of the unknown, fear of another disappointment, and fear of trusting again, only to be let down.

Kira contemplated the offer to become a housekeeper in exchange for room and board, her mind raced with questions and possibilities. Could this be the sanctuary she longed for, a place to rebuild her shattered life and provide for her unborn child? The thought was both exhilarating and terrifying. Accepting the Rabbi's help meant stepping into the unknown and trusting strangers with her well-being and that of her child.

**

The following morning, Rabbi Salamon parked his new car, a giant black Cadillac with an automatic transmission, by the back entrance of Mount Sinai Hospital. After placing the sign *CLERGY* on the windshield, he left it confidently in the NO PARKING zone. He then went to the administration to advise them to send all Kira's bills to Mr. Gordon. As he explained to Earnest the previous night, since it was his brutal action that put the girl there, the least he could do was pay for her medical expenses.

Kira, already dressed in her room, was waiting for him.

"I see you're up and ready to go," the Rabbi said. "I took care of everything—all we have to do is wait for the wheelchair to roll you out of here."

"I don't need a wheelchair," Kira protested. "I can walk out of here on my very own feet."

The large Black nurse with the empty wheelchair arrived quickly and said, "You can walk from the back door to the car, but I'm wheeling you out of there in a wheelchair. It's hospital policy, and it's no use arguing about it. So, sit, honey, and enjoy the ride."

Before she could rise, the Black nurse stooped, hugged her, and said gently, "Good luck to you. I'll see you soon before the baby comes."

The Rabbi opened the passenger door for Kira, took her bag, and placed it on the back seat.

It was less than five blocks from the rooming house. Dolly was waiting at the door and ushered them into her study.

After introducing them to each other, the Rabbi reassured Kira, "I leave you in Dolly's tender care. From now on, you have no more worries. I'll see you around." He waved goodbye to Dolly and left.

"Have a seat there," said Dolly.

Kira gingerly sat on one of the armchairs, ready to bolt. Dolly took the other armchair and waited. They both sat and stared at each other, Kira with quiet defiance and Dolly with open curiosity. Dolly liked what she saw. A tall girl with short black hair and honest hazel eyes, pale and worn at the edges, but with a straight back, ready to face whatever came her way. A fighter, Dolly decided. Dolly liked fighters. And she would not begrudge helping them when the need arose.

"So, You are Kira Chopaky."

Kira nodded, waiting for Dolly's judgment of her situation.

"And you're in trouble." Before Kira could react, she added, "I know, I know, it is not your making. But you are here and in trouble. I understand that you're planning to keep the baby."

"Yes, I do, and nobody can force me to abort it."

"Now, that's a given since, in Canada, abortions are illegal. However, you can give the baby up for adoption. It happens all the time."

"Not to my baby, it won't. I'll keep it, and I'll raise it."

"And how do you plan to do that? Do you know how difficult it is to be a single mother?"

"No, I don't, but I guess I'll find out, won't I?" Kira said with quiet defiance.

"All right, my girl, I just wanted to know how strong you feel about this. Now, let's see what we can do. To begin with, let's keep quiet about your condition. I'll introduce you to the rest of the gang as Mrs. Gordon, a woman abused by her husband and in need of refuge here. You will stay upstairs with Wilma on the top floor. It is a self-contained two-bedroom unit, so it is up to you whether you want to socialize with anybody down here. The doctor suggested a few weeks of complete rest, which means off your feet. So," Dolly raised her voice, "up you go to bed with you. Joseph will help you with your luggage, and Wilma will set your room up and cater to you for a while. These two are the soul of discretion, so you won't have to worry about what they think or say about you to anyone."

Kira, instead of getting up, looked at Dolly.

"Is there anything wrong?" Dolly asked.

"I should say so," Kira sputtered in anger. "If I go upstairs and play the invalid, how can I earn my keep? I refuse to be a charity case. The rabbi told me that you needed a housekeeper in exchange for room and board. So, that is what I plan to do, starting right now. Tell me what to do," she insisted.

Dolly stepped back with a mixture of annoyance and respect. "And I say the best thing you can do right now is to go upstairs to bed. Nothing is going to be gained if you faint from loss of blood or lose the baby. Right now, you're responsible for another human being inside you. If you want to keep the baby, you must be strong enough to care for it. And I promise you won't be a charity case. Those responsible for your present condition will pay for your room and board, plus your medical bills. But right now, get up, go with Joseph and Wilma before I lose my temper." Dolly stormed out of her study.

**

As soon as Kira was settled comfortably in the apartment, Dolly changed into a pair of tight black slacks, a black silk shirt, and a light, form-fitting black jacket, completing it with a black pair of spiky high-heeled shoes. Snapping her small purse on the left side of her silver belt around her slim waist, she looked into the mirror to inspect the result. She decided it was good enough to intimidate her foes. But she still looked around and, spotting the large black umbrella with a sharp end in the stately ceramic stand in the hallway, she clenched it in her right hand like a sword. Now, she was ready for combat.

Joseph, waiting for her with the taxi in front of the house, gave her a curious look, as there was not a single cloud in the sky, but Dolly just shrugged her shoulders and, firmly clutching the umbrella's handle, sat in the back of the car.

When they arrived at the factory, Dolly said, "Joseph, wait for me. I'll be back shortly," and marched up to the front door. Once inside, she said to the man in the booth, "Let Mr. Diamond know that Baroness Lipnitzky is here to see him. And don't bother telling me he is not here because I know better."

Diamond showed up quickly, still wearing his suit, as he had just arrived at the factory. His face was red, and he was visibly nervous. "Baroness," he said, pulling at his tie, "what do I owe this pleasure?"

"We have some business to discuss in private. So, lead the way," Dolly commanded.

"Baroness, I have little time. I'm expecting some people soon."

"So, they will wait until I'm finished with you. I promise to be short and to the point."

Desmond led her to the side office he used to greet other clients. It was a small but comfortable place, with a large antique desk and two armchairs. There was a large canape by the wall, the kind one can expect to see in a movie director's place, where they supposedly try out the future stars for their other talents. Knowing Desmond, Dolly suspected the canape was also used to hire new secretaries.

Eying Dolly's umbrella, Desmond rushed behind his desk for protection.

"So, baroness, what do you want to discuss with me?" he asked nervously.

Dolly took her time to settle down in an armchair, hanging the umbrella on its left arm within reach. "I have Kira Chopaky at my place. She is pregnant, and she is not well. Since your wife is her closest relation, I expect you to pay for her room and board besides her medical expenses. That would come to about three hundred dollars per month."

Diamond jumped up as if a wasp stung him and shouted, "You're out of your mind if you expect me to pay you a penny for the upkeep of that slut. She is finally out of my house, and I have no more responsibility for her. So, get lost, woman!"

"Tut, tut, my dear. I would not be too hasty if I were you. Just a little reminder about that business a few years back when I helped you out with that very delicate situation about your young girlfriend. You remember the fourteen-year-old that you raped and then asked me to arrange the abortion for?"

"I paid dearly for that, didn't I?" Desmond asked nervously.

"Well, my dear, if I remember correctly, you paid me to refer you to a doctor willing to perform an illegal abortion, and for my discretion, I will not report you to the authorities. Raping a fourteen-year-old could have landed you in prison for a long time, and as far as I know, it is one of those crimes that has no time limitations. Even if, in the meantime, she became your wife." She rose and reached for the telephone. "But of course, if you want clarification, I could call my lawyer from here."

Desmond unbuttoned his shirt at his neck—sweat glistened on his chest. His hands shook as he pulled out the top drawer of his desk and grabbed his checkbook. "You realize this is blackmail?"

"No, it is not." Dolly snapped confidently. "It is simply a donation to the Lipnitsky Foundation, set up to aid young people freshly arriving in Canada after they escaped Communism. So, be kind and write in the check that it is for charity. I'll even give you a tax receipt at the end of the year."

Desmond squeaked, "Fine, Baroness, how much did you want?"

"About four hundred dollars each month would just about cover her expenses. I'll be back for next month's installment by the first of October."

Desmond tried to argue. "But Baroness, you mentioned three hundred dollars before."

"Well," Dolly shrugged, "I changed my mind. Since the beginning of our conversation, the price has just jumped another hundred dollars. Who are you going to complain about it?" She reached out to take the check from him and then, after placing it firmly in her purse, strolled out with her last words, "DD, it is always nice doing business with you."

**

Her next destination was a Bay Street office building, housing several high-profile companies dealing with investments. She took the elevator to the seventh floor and approached the young woman receptionist operating the switchboard.

"I'm here to talk to Mr. Ernest Gordon. Please announce me."

"Is he expecting you?" the receptionist asked.

"He will see me," Dolly said confidently. "Just mention that Baroness Lipnitsky is here to see him.

The young woman stood up to inspect the baroness and, shaking her head, muttered, *'Earnest sure has some weird taste in his women.'* But she picked up the phone and called Earnest to the front office.

Earnest arrived, fixing his tie and smoothing his hair, ready to meet the Baroness. He did not know who she was, but he was used to meeting all kinds of people in his line of business. Investing was a game for only rich people, and they came in all sizes and shapes. This time, he saw a modish, slim, middle-aged woman with baby blue eyes, long silver blond hair in a ponytail, and a firm but well-shaped mouth—supposedly with money to throw his way. It was probably a referral from some of his moneyed, middle-aged ladies with solid libidos. With a broad smile, he said, "How may I help you, Baroness?"

Dolly was happy to play the game if it suited her purpose. "Well, Earnest, an old friend of mine, has referred you to me after I mentioned that I need a very discreet and superb financial advisor. You came highly recommended. Is there a place where we can chat in private?"

Earnest could feel the needles in his palm that usually came with gleeful anticipation of both financial gain and fulfilled sexual fantasies. He pointed to the door leading to a small conference room and stepped ahead of Dolly.

Dolly was not impressed. In her world, the men opened the door for a lady. She also observed the cocky expressions when Earnest took his chair behind the large desk and graciously offered a seat to her across from him. She recognized the type: a swaggering stud, very sure of his power of masculinity, who believed his sole existence was to pleasure ladies of all ages for their fortunes. And Dolly took a perverse pleasure in anticipating the crush on his ego and turning him into a trembling jelly. She leaned towards Earnest and lunged into her business. "Well, Earnest. It is about your wife."

Earnest's eyes opened wide from the shock. "What about her?" he stammered.

"She is pregnant, sick, and in my care. What are you planning to do about it?"

"Nothing," he hissed. "I offered to take her back after that fiasco that followed our so-called wedding night. She refused my help, so I washed my hands off her. I'm convinced that she tricked me into this marriage so she could stay here legally and legitimize her bastard. She should be grateful I don't go to the authorities and demand to have her deported for providing false information upon her arrival at immigration."

His handsome face turned into an ugly snarl as he rose from his chair, ready to leave the room.

"Not so fast, bastard," Dolly said, her voice dripping with malice. "Sit back and listen." she ordered. "I know about the circumstances of your marriage. It was not Kira who coerced you into it. You're just a spineless, weak Momma's boy who didn't even have the guts to stand up for your long-standing German girlfriend. So, now you have not one but two victims in doctors' care. What you intend to do about your former girlfriend doesn't concern me. But Kira's fate does. You attacked and brutally raped her. As a result, she nearly bled to death. She was lucky enough to survive and even luckier that the doctors saved the child. She is in my house, and I intend to take good care of her. It will be several months before she can get up and do anything. However, I refuse to pay for her upkeep and medical expenses out of my pocket. So, until she is on her feet and ready to take care of herself and the baby, you'll get the bills, approximately four hundred dollars a month."

Earnest's eyes popped like he was a sick beagle. He was both shocked and furious. He jumped up from his chair and shouted, "You have a bloody nerve coming here and making demands like that of me! Not a penny! You understand? Not one penny!"

Dolly looked at him, as if watching a nasty bug landing in her soup. "Ernie boy," she said softly, "I somehow doubt that you want me to inform your superiors about your gambling addiction. Some of your clients might take a strong opposition when they find out their portfolios are diminishing, not necessarily because of market fluctuation. Can you risk it?"

Earnest turned red as a beet, gasped for air, and sunk back in his chair.

Dolly nodded. "I didn't think so. So, be a darling and cough up the first and last month's installment. That will be eight hundred dollars. Please fill out the check for the Lipnitsky Foundation, a charitable organization established to help young people escape from Communist countries to help establish themselves in Canada. And, of course, I'll send you a tax receipt at the end of the year."

Earnest pulled out a check book and a silver pen. He filled it out and ripped the check, demonstrating how he itched to rip Dolly apart with his hands. Dolly smiled, grabbed the check from his hand and, without looking back, left the conference room. She only looked back from the elevator door and blew a mocking kiss to the dumbfounded man still standing in the doorway.

Dolly went to the nearest bank and opened an account under the Lipnitsky Foundation. As soon as she got home, she planned on calling her religious friends to inform them they had just become the directors of this brand-new charity organization and to come by as soon as possible to sign the papers.

Chapter 16

In the quiet of the early morning, with the city still stirring outside his window, Rocky sat at a small, worn desk. The task before him was simple, yet urgent—his hands trembling slightly as he held the pen. He was about to bridge worlds with a few lines on a piece of paper, to reach out to a relative he had never met on behalf of friends left behind in Hungary. The gravity of the situation pressed down on him, a reminder of the promises made and the stakes involved.

"Dear Miklós," he began, his handwriting steady despite the turmoil. *"I am a relative of yours, requested by your friends in Hungary to inform you about an urgent, sensitive family matter. This is something I can only relate to you in person. Please contact me as soon as possible at 526 Palmerston Street, Toronto. Regards, Peter Görgey."*

With the letter sealed and safely tucked into his jacket, Rocky prepared to start the bustling day. Today, he would meet Desmond Diamond, the enigmatic owner of Diamond Industries, a man known as much for his rapid ascent in the manufacturing world as for his unorthodox methods. As Rocky navigated the bustling streets of Toronto, he couldn't help but reflect on the path that had led him here—a journey fuelled by ambition but shadowed by caution. The promise of a job was tantalizing, yet the whispers of Desmond's unconventional practices echoed in his mind, urging him to tread carefully.

As Rocky approached Diamond Industries' formidable red brick facade, he paused, allowing himself a moment to take in the sight. The building, with its half-open narrow windows and steam whispering secrets into the morning air, was a testament to the industrial era's enduring legacy. It was here, in the heart of this mechanical labyrinth, that Rocky hoped to carve out a new chapter of his life.

He took a deep breath, the cool air mingling with the faint scent of wood and metal, a reminder of creation's tangible, raw essence. With determination and apprehension, Rocky stepped forward, ready to confront whatever lay beyond those large double doors with the large sign advertising **Diamond Industries** above it.

With sweaty palms, Rocky approached the door and pushed it open. He stepped into a large foyer with a small office without a door.

A white-haired pensioner sitting in the little office looked at Rocky, his face contorted with curiosity. "Can I help you?"

Rocky cleared his throat. "I'm looking for Mr. Diamond. I have an appointment to see him at ten o'clock."

"And your name?"

"Ro...I mean, Peter Görgey. Rabbi Salamon—" Rocky stuttered.

"Oh, yes, certainly. Mr. Diamond is expecting you. I'll let him know you arrived. Just wait here." He pointed at the door before he pushed a button on the phone and said, "Mr. Diamond, your guest has arrived. Shall I send him up? All right, you'll be down in a second."

A few seconds later, a small-framed, red-haired man came through another door. He was wearing an oily overall and cleaning his hands with a red flannel cloth.

"Excuse my dirty hands," he said as he greeted Rocky. "I had to take one of our machines apart for maintenance. Rather than an outsider, I prefer to do it myself. Oh, I shouldn't forget my manners. I'm Desmond Diamond, or as everyone refers to me, DD, the owner of this company. And you're Mr. Görgey from Hungary, looking for a job."

Rocky wasn't sure what to expect. A factory owner who wasn't shamed to put on overalls and get his hands oily was a different image from the fat, cigar-smoking, and well-dressed manufacturers with manicured hands portrayed by the fervent anti-imperialist pamphlets back in Hungary.

Desmond, indeed, was notable in his own right. A self-taught and self-made man, starting with nothing and building up his empire, was pleased to boast about his success. Growing up in rural Hungary, as a boy, he was lucky to be befriended by a former Wehrmacht communications officer, who, after completing a few years prison sentence after the war, set up his shop in Desmond's stepfather's tool shed. The man was an expert at building and repairing radios. As the village had no electricity, most of the radios were battery-operated. Desmond remembered the tool shed, filled with old batteries and big light tubes, and recalled the old brochures from German factories about radios, turntables, and other wonders.

"Bodo Schnell was his name, and being childless, took to me and patiently explained what was," Desmond said. "When I finished grade eight, I attended a prestigious technical high school in Budapest. One of my uncles lived in Budapest with his wife, and being childless, they offered to put me up for the duration. I graduated in the spring of nineteen-fifty-six and got a job at the Telephone Company. It was an exciting place to work, but by the end of October, the revolution came, and in the middle of November, my whole family left Hungary.

"We ended up first in Vancouver and then moved to Toronto. By then, I knew I would not be working for anyone but myself. So, I started in the basement of our rented house, repairing radios and televisions, and then moved into a slightly bigger place, buying used tools and machinery. And," he said, with evident pride, "I found this old factory dirt cheap, bought it, and even had some of the machinery included in the deal. They work, most of the time, with a bit of coaxing.

"I no longer make house calls and repair old broken radios and tubes. Diamond Industry is rising to become one of the leading manufacturers of high-quality sound systems. And we offer it in a cabinet of your own choice."

As Rocky followed Desmond through the din of machinery and bustling workers, the air was thick with the scent of sawdust and oil. The factory floor was a labyrinth of activity, each turn revealing a new facet of Diamond Industries' heart. With a proud step, Desmond guided Rocky through the divided sections: the electronics area, pristine as a laboratory, and the woodworking shop, where the air buzzed with creative enthusiasm.

"Here, at Diamond Industries, we're not just making sound systems; we're crafting the future," Desmond proclaimed, gesturing towards the glass-encased design booth. Despite the grime on his overalls, his eyes sparkled with a zeal that bordered on fanaticism. "We operate on the edge of innovation, and I built this empire from the ground up. My team—my family—is the backbone of this success."

Rocky observed the workers, noting the intensity of their focus and the efficiency of their movements. They were a mosaic of backgrounds united under Desmond's vision. Yet, as Desmond spoke of equality and opportunity, Rocky couldn't help but notice the shadow of hierarchy beneath the surface. The promise of equal pay for all sounded generous, but the reality of minimum wages and under-the-table dealings hinted at exploitation masked as benevolence.

"What about when the work slows down?" Rocky ventured, his curiosity piqued by the implications of Desmond's business model.

Desmond's response was swift—a rehearsed assurance. "We manage, and my people understand the business. They're loyal because they know I have their best interests at heart."

Rocky wasn't entirely convinced. The disparity between Desmond's self-portrayal as a benefactor and the potential vulnerability of his workers left a lingering question about the actual cost of success in the Diamond Empire.

They reached the glassed-in booth and stepped inside. The engineer and the designer rose from their seats, and Desmond introduced them. "Eugene, my brother-in-law, a relatively recent arrival from Hungary, is the engineer. And Ivan, from Romania, is our designer."

Eugene, a tall, skinny fellow with a worried expression, stood up and shook Rocky's hand. Ivan, a stocky black-haired man with a blank face, just nodded his greeting and pointed at the package of cigarettes on his desk. After offering one to Eugene, he picked it up and left the room.

"Most of my workers are relatively recent arrivals from behind the Iron Curtain. They are good workers and grateful to get a job from me," Desmond boasted.

"What about when you have to fire them because of slow work? Are they still grateful to you then?" Rocky said.

"Why? Of course, they are." Desmond looked at Rocky with wide eyes. "In my factory, I pay everyone the same basic fee, regardless of their skills, with cash, which is more money in their pocket than if we would pay tax. But I spell it out to them. I expect them to put the difference in their bank so they can live on it on those rainy days. It's brilliant if I say so myself." Desmond rubbed his hands with glee.

Rocky wasn't sure how that was supposed to help the unemployed, but he made a note to investigate it at the first opportunity. He wouldn't be at all surprised if his workers had called DD a Double Dealer, or Devious Devil, Dirty Dog, or even Doggie Doo behind his back after he laid them off at his whim without too much notice.

Impressed with Rocky, Desmond planned to boast to his friends and relatives about a genuine aristocrat working for him. However, he still offered Rocky the same deal as the others: a dollar fifty an hour for as many hours he could squeeze in during the week or on the weekend after his classes.

As the tour concluded, Desmond extended an invitation to dinner, a gesture that felt like a test as much as a courtesy. Rocky left the factory with the job offer in hand and a mind swirling with doubts and decisions. The tour had peeled back the layers of Desmond Diamond's world, revealing a complex interplay of ambition, innovation, and the delicate balance of power.

**

It was time for Rocky to return to his new home, get organized, and catch up with sleep.

As the shadows lengthened and the hustle of the city settled into the quiet of the evening, Rocky found himself alone with his thoughts, the letter burning a hole in his pocket. The decision to send it was no longer just a matter of fulfilling a duty; it had morphed into a crucible, testing his values, loyalty, and the fabric of his identity.

Rocky replayed the words of the letter in his mind, each syllable a heavy step in the dark labyrinth of his conscience. "Am I doing the right thing?" he wondered, the question echoing in the silence of his room. The potential consequences of his actions loomed large, casting long shadows over his resolve. To send the letter could mean dragging Miklós into a quagmire of political intrigue and personal risk. To withhold it was to betray the trust of those who relied on him, who saw him as a bridge between worlds.

The weight of history pressed down on him, the stories of his family's struggles and triumphs, their brushes with danger, and their acts of courage. "What would they have done?" he asked the empty room, seeking guidance from ancestors he had never met but whose blood coursed through his veins.

The stakes were clear: on one hand, the safety and well-being of a relative stranger; on the other, the expectation of those who considered him a lifeline. The choice he faced was a microcosm of the immigrant experience, straddling two worlds, belonging fully to neither, constantly balancing on the edge of divided loyalties.

As Rocky sat in the dimming light, the letter in his hands felt like a talisman, a key to doors he wasn't sure he wanted to open. The temptation to let it go, to release himself from this burden, was a siren call. Yet, a deeper part of him resisted, urged on by a sense of duty and the faint whisper of hope that his actions might make a difference.

In the end, he stood, the letter still clutched in his hand, his decision teetering on the brink of action and inaction. Night had fallen now, a blanket of darkness punctuated by the distant glow of city lights. Rocky moved towards the door, then paused, a silhouette framed against the backdrop of his uncertainty.

"Talk to Dolly first," he whispered, the words a lifeline in the tumult of his thoughts. It was a delay, a momentary retreat from the precipice, but it was also a decision to seek wisdom before plunging ahead.

With that, he tucked the letter away, its fate still undecided, its message unspoken. The chapter closed with Rocky standing at the crossroads of his conscience, the path ahead shrouded in mystery and the echo of his aunt's advice ringing in his ears. What would tomorrow bring? Only time will tell.

**

Before he went to bed, Rocky went downstairs to speak with Dolly. He found her in the kitchen with a small plate of cookies and a glass of milk.

"A bit of a night snack?" Rocky teased.

Dolly looked at him with a big smile. "Just the person I was hoping to call to join me. I believe we have some important matters to discuss."

Rocky looked at her, wondering whether Dolly was a mind reader. Since his strange episode at the mailbox earlier at the University, when his inner voice stopped him from mailing the letter to his uncle, he had been eager to talk to her.

"I'll be happy to join you in a minute, Dolly. I'll just run upstairs to get some advice about something. I'll be down in an instant," he said, sprinting up the stairs.

He returned in a minute with the letter he'd written but not yet mailed to his uncle and put it in Dolly's hand. "Something is not quite right with this picture, and I would not be happy to cause any trouble to anyone, but especially not to a relative. Do you have any suggestions, Dolly?"

Dolly sat down in the armchair in her room, gesturing for Rocky to take the other, then pointed at the telephone between them. "We will have a three-way international conference call in about five minutes. This phone has a secure line, and the calls are from your Aunt Anna in London and your uncle Miklós Görgey from Washington, DC."

Seeing Rocky's confusion, she quickly added, "Just for your information, the three of us, your aunt, Miklós, and I, have been longtime friends and co-workers. When you told your aunt in London about your dilemma with the Hungarian Agents, she contacted Miklós. She informed him about the devious plan the Hungarian Agents are trying to involve you. And it was she who sent you in my direction and also called to let me know she had gotten in touch with Miklós. So, in a few minutes, the phone will ring, and we'll devise a plan between the four of us. Is that agreeable to you, Rocky?"

Rocky could only nod and express his heartfelt thanks. When the phone indeed rang, it was Dolly who picked it up, "Well, hello Anna, and hello Miklós! Rocky sits beside me, so let me put him on the extension. That way, we can all communicate."

"Hello, Rocky and Dolly!" Lady Anne said, "Greetings from Clara and the gang! And hello, Miklós, once again. So, what's the plan?"

A warm baritone replied, "Hello to you all! And greetings to you, Rocky! I'll be happy to make your acquaintance in your beautiful city of Toronto in person! I heard about your new city hall! Would you mind sending me a black and white postcard with your new address?"

Holding the phone to his ear with a sweaty hand, Rocky replied, "Of course I will. Is it alright if I mail it tomorrow?"

"Not just yet," Miklós said. "Hang on to it until the person insisting that you get in touch with me shows up and demands to know if you already sent the note to me. Make a big show out of it. Invite him to join you at the mailbox. If possible, let him handle the postcard. Dolly will let me know the mailing time, and I'll take it from there. And Rocky, thanks a lot. We'll talk in person soon—and Anne, hugs and kisses to all of you in London. Keep me posted. Except for Dolly, I say good night to you all."

After a brief conversation, Dolly hung up and turned to Rocky. "I hope this puts your mind at ease. Don't worry, Miklós is brilliant; he knows not only how to avoid the traps set for him but also how to let them dig their trap to fall into."

Dolly opened one of the drawers of her desk, pulled out a postcard with the black-and-white photo of the new Toronto City Hall with the outdoor skating rink and handed it to Rocky.

"This is the postcard Miklós referred to, ready for you to sign and mail at the right time."

Chapter 17

The following morning, people lined up on the ground floor of the University of Toronto's Galbraith building to register. Pushing and shoving, people shouted greetings to each other. Rocky's registration as a foreign student took longer. When he completed all the forms and was told when and where to attend his lectures, he was ready for a well-deserved break.

He walked over to the International Student Centre. The old Victorian mansion had seen better days, mostly furnished by cast-off tables and chairs, and even the chesterfields scattered around. People stood around the enormous fireplace on the main floor, chatting away, and some sat on chairs around the square tables, eating from paper plates with plastic utensils. The atmosphere was festive and loud with the multilingual gibberish.

Rocky climbed the wooden stairs to the third floor, hoping to find the new friend he had met the day before. Sure enough, he was there, sitting by the table with a chess set in front of him, facing a Japanese student who was staring at the board as if he could mesmerize the pieces into making the winning move by themselves.

Rocky had just settled into the comfort of an aged, overstuffed armchair when the ambient chatter of the International Student Centre seemed to hush as if the air grew tense. He glanced up, sensing a shadow looming over him. A middle-aged man stood there, his presence cutting through the room's warmth like a chilled breeze. The man's suit, a three-piece ensemble that seemed out of place amidst the casual university setting, was impeccably tailored, hinting at an almost unnerving meticulousness. His tie was knotted perfectly, not a thread out of place, contrasting sharply with the relaxed attire around them.

The man's sharp and assessing eyes fixed on Rocky with an intensity that seemed to bore into him. He held a photograph in one hand, his grip on it betraying a hint of underlying tension as if clutching onto a piece of evidence. As he stood there for a moment, surveying Rocky, the silence around them became palpable.

"I beg your pardon, are you, by any chance, Mr. Görgey?" the man asked, his voice smooth yet carrying an edge that made Rocky straighten in his chair. Though politely phrased, the question felt like the beginning of an interrogation rather than a casual inquiry.

Rocky was taken aback by the sudden focus of attention, and he felt a mix of curiosity and wariness. "Yes, I am. And you are?" he responded, his voice steady but his mind racing.

"Mr. Kovács," the man said, and pulled up a chair with deliberate slowness, the scrape of its legs against the floor cutting through the hum of conversations around them. He sat, leaning forward slightly, invading Rocky's personal space in a calculated and intimidating way. "We need to talk," he said, his tone suggesting it wasn't a request but a foregone conclusion.

Around them, the festive atmosphere of the International Student Centre continued unabated, yet within their small bubble of interaction, the air was charged with an unspoken tension. Mr. Kovács discreetly wiped the sweat from his brow with a large handkerchief, a humanizing gesture that belied his otherwise composed exterior.

"Phew!" Kovács exhaled softly, "Who would have thought that the weather in early September could be this warm in Toronto?" It was a mundane comment, yet it hung in the air, a momentary diversion from the weight of their encounter.

Rocky pondered the man's true intentions, the undercurrents of danger, or perhaps desperation, that seemed to underlie his polished demeanor. Was this man a diplomat, a spy, or something else entirely? Rocky waited, his body tensing for the revelations that would follow.

"Mr. Görgey," Kovács began in a low, measured tone, "I trust you haven't forgotten your promise to reach out to your relative in the States?"

"Of course, I have not forgotten my promise! I'm just about ready to mail him a nice postcard with the black-and-white picture of the new Toronto City Hall instead. Why don't you come with me, sir?

The nearest mailbox is right at that corner, by the Central Library. This way, you can witness the event in person."

The man seemed satisfied with the proposal. He reached out. "You mind if I look at it, my boy? Just to make sure you included everything your relative needs to know?"

DEAR MIKLÓS, I HAVE AN URGENT MESSAGE FOR YOU ABOUT A CLOSE FAMILY MEMBER. MEET ME IN TORONTO AS SOON AS YOU CAN.

The man looked up and shook his head. "You forgot to write your address, and you still need to sign it, boy."

With a sigh, Rocky hastily scribbled his Toronto address on the bottom with small letters and signed the card, *With love, Rocky.*

Rocky made a big show of opening the mailbox flap, showing the card through the slot, bending down, and shouting: "It is urgent!"

Mr. Kovács could hardly contain himself. Things went much better than he ever expected. He pulled out his business card and passed it to Rocky with a wide smile, "Good job! All we need now is to wait for the man, and as soon as he shows up, we'll take it from there. Call me anytime, day or night, if you hear from him." And added with a concerned face, "I hope he won't dilly-dally too long for his mother's sake."

**

Dolly made the expected call to Miklós that evening. The call went through a secure line directly to the CIA in Washington, DC.

"Thanks a lot, Dolly. I'll take it from here and let you know about the timing of my arrival. In the meantime, business as usual; keep an eye out for unexpected friends. Bye for now!"

Dolly smiled, hung up, and turned to Rocky. "There, my boy, it is done! At least this part of it. So, I suggest taking it easy and living your life because the next act will not take place for a while. But," she added seriously, "it won't hurt to keep your eyes and ears open for strangers lurking about. So, if you notice any suspicious activities, you'll let me know immediately, OK?"

Rocky nodded. He was ready for bed. Lectures at the university and, most likely, broken machines were waiting for him the next day at his new job.

**

The following morning, Miklós Görgey stood at the head of a sleek, sunlit conference room, facing a unique assembly: seasoned agents from the CIA, FBI, and RCMP, all casually dressed but unmistakably professional. Their attention was riveted on him, a sense of anticipation in the air.

"Good morning," Miklós began, his voice filling with gravitas and excitement. "Today marks a first in our collective careers—a joint task force spanning agencies and borders. Cecilia Gaston," he gestured to the woman beside him, her sharp intellect matched by her striking appearance, "is the architect of this collaboration. Her insights will be invaluable."

Cecilia nodded, her gaze sweeping the room. "Our mission is straightforward but challenging. We're to outmaneuver a plot as cunning as it is dangerous. Each of you brings a critical skill set to this table. Let's use them to turn the tables on our adversaries."

The agents leaned in, the air crackling with renewed focus. Miklós outlined the operation, briefly drawing on the flip chart to sketch their strategy. The plan was clear: leverage their collective experience, anticipate the enemy's moves, and act decisively.

"As we proceed," Cecilia added, "communication and adaptability will be our greatest assets. We're not just aiming to thwart their plans but setting a trap."

The meeting transitioned into a dynamic exchange of ideas, each contribution sharpening the strategy. As they wrapped up, the sense of camaraderie and purpose was palpable. They were ready to face whatever came next, together.

**

Days after Miklós's prediction, two newcomers from Hungary joined the scene in Washington, posing as trade delegates but with the true intent of surveilling the post office. During a strategy session, RCMP agent Zameck asked, "Why send additional agents?"

FBI agent Kozich, eyes on the surveillance footage, responded, "They're fresh faces, unknown to our network. It's a smart move, but we're one step ahead."

Their focus shifted to the surveillance feed where a seemingly homeless man, Jimmy Bingo identified by Kozich as their own operative, positioned strategically outside the post office, caught their attention. "He's ours," Kozich assured, "Watch this."

As Miklós emerged from the post office, he engaged with Jimmy, their planted agent, in a brief but animated conversation. His joy was palpable, even from the grainy footage. "There," Kozich pointed out, "Miklós is playing his part perfectly, signaling that the operation is proceeding as planned."

"What if they try to grab Miklos at the Post Office?" Andrew Zameck asked.

"I don't think they would risk it," Kozich replied. "They do nothing risky during the day in a busy and public place like that Post office."

"So, from now on, we let them follow Miklos?" Andrew said. "How far are we willing to let them play their game?"

"Since we'll be right behind them observing their every move, we'll just wait until we can actually catch them doing something illegal. Miklos already has a plan to lay a trap for them."

"Like what?" Andrew said.

"Just watch the screen–and listen! Can you hear him describing how he plans to move into a new apartment building within a week? We're pretty certain that they will try to use this time to plant some bugs in it, using a few of their agents as telephone or electrical workers. We let them plant one in the crevices of the wall outside the post office, directly above Jimmy Bingo's head."

"So, in your estimation, when and where do they plan to grab Miklos?"

"We don't think it would happen in Washington. The few agents they have here will strictly follow him and find out when and how he's planning to leave for Toronto. When Miklos received the card from Toronto, they expect him to rush to Toronto to find out about the urgent family matter. "

"But it won't happen that way, right?"

"Not exactly. Just watch the surveillance tape."

On the tape, they saw Jimmy Bingo, seeing his friend, smiling widely, asking, "You must be excited beyond words and curious about the news your new relative wants to share with you! So, when are you planning to see him?"

Miklós, leaning close to the man sitting on the ground at the post office entrance, softly but clearly said directly to the bug in the wall just above the head of the blind veteran. "Just between you and me, I planned to leave within a few days but was called in to complete a few urgent assignments. And as you know, my friend, duty comes first. So, I will have to postpone my trip."

"That's too bad, my friend! I know how eager you must be finally to meet with your young relative! For how long?" Jimmy replied, with all the sympathy he could muster.

Miklos sighed. "In our line of business, that is never certain. I'll leave as soon as I can, though."

The agents watching the surveillance tape burst into laughter. "Now, this will screw up the planned schedule of the Hungarian agents arriving in Toronto."

**

Within two days, the RCMP from Toronto reported. "A group of eight Hungarian Agents, pretending to be part of a Trade Mission, landed in Toronto. They are hoping to complete their mission within a maximum of ten days. We are on their tail, following their movements."

"Thanks, guys," Miklos said. "They must have arrived with a chartered MALEV airplane, but more than likely, they also have a get-away plane standing by, ready to fly at the moment of notice, preferably with me all rolled up in a carpet. So, try your best to find the plane and remove it from service."

Miklos saw the RCMP officer put that down in writing as well.

"Also, find out how long their visas are valid, which hotel in Toronto they booked, and for how long."

"We already did," came the reassuring reply. "Their short-term visas expire in less than ten days, and they're booked in the Hotel Danube for that time."

"So, if I miss my flight to Toronto because some other important jobs need to be completed right here in Washington, the unexpected delay of my arrival will thoroughly mess up their schedule! It will force them to get their temporary visas extended and scramble to find cheap accommodations for the unforeseen duration." Miklos chuckled.

Mr. Markovitz nodded. "Aye, that would do it! To keep them on their toes!"

In the dimly lit room, the atmosphere was electric, charged with the anticipation of Miklós's next words. He stood, a strategist among warriors, outlining the final phase of their operation.

"Our actions in Toronto will not just catch our adversaries off guard but unravel their entire scheme, exposing vulnerabilities within their ranks," Miklós declared, his voice steady and commanding. "Our surveillance has already laid the groundwork within the Hungarian consulate. We'll see and counteract every move they make before they even realize they're playing into our hands."

Laughter briefly lightened the room's tension as an officer joked about Miklós's cunning. But the moment passed quickly as Cecilia, ever the professional, redirected the focus. "The logistics, Miklós. How will you enter Toronto undetected?"

Miklós smiled like a chess master seeing the endgame. "We'll deploy diversions across three locations, ensuring our enemies watch shadows while I move in the light. But specifics are on a need-to-know basis for now."

Zackary Simon, finally voiced the question in everyone's eyes..."And the timing? When does this all come to a head?"

Miklós's answer was as dramatic as their plan. "Halloween. That's when I'll enter, not as a spy, but as a spectacle. Imagine, amid the masquerade, a figure descends, not just any figure, but Mary Poppins herself. There, amidst the festivities, is where our trap springs."

The room fell silent, absorbing the plan. It was bold, theatrical, and carried the weight of their collective hope. At that moment, the team was unified by a mission and the sheer audacity of their endeavor. Toronto wouldn't know what hit it.

Chapter 18

Within six weeks, Mr. Kovacs's once orderly office transformed into a chaotic hub, teeming with newcomers draped in coats, clutching suitcases, and bulging briefcases. Their voices rose in a cacophony of shouts, arguments and demands for immediate service, creating a palpable tension that threatened to burst the seams of the small space.

Mr. Kovacs, the consulate's unassuming deputy, was overwhelmed by the sudden invasion of his workspace. Seeking refuge, he retreated to the sanctuary of his modest back office, a room cluttered with papers and personal memorabilia that told the story of his lengthy service. With a build more suited to a scholarly life than the clandestine world his job occasionally brushed against, his average height and gentle demeanor belied a keen intellect and a steadfast commitment to his duties. His hair, though thinning, was meticulously combed, and his glasses perpetually slid down the bridge of his nose, a testament to the countless hours spent poring over documents and reports.

He found Mary, his fifty-year-old overweight secretary, hiding in his room.

"Who are they, and what are they doing here, Mary?" Mr. Kovacs demanded an explanation, his voice laced with urgency.

"They claim to be part of a Trade Mission, setting up an export business for Hungarian wines and jams in Ontario," Mary responded, her voice betraying a hint of unease. As Mr. Kovacs's gaze met hers, he saw a shadow of fear flicker across her face, uncharacteristic of the usually unflappable secretary.

Mr. Kovacs was puzzled over this mystery. "Do you recall any request from the Embassy to make them a hotel reservation? Or to set up appointments with the liquor board and food distributors?"

"Well, apparently, someone from the Hungarian Embassy in Ottawa took care of that for them."

Mr. Kovacs shook his head. "Without informing us about them? That's what I call poor communication! But do you know what they are doing in our office now? And why they didn't go to the hotel directly from the airport?"

"There was a major fuck-up with their reservation! I don't know the details! They either mixed up the dates or the number of people arriving! So, they want to wait until the hotel sorts out their problems. But apparently, the hotel administration was friendly and patient. Even offered to upgrade their rooms to make up for this inconvenience as soon as they sort it out to their satisfaction!"

"Oh! That's all right then," Mr. Kovacs replied sarcastically, "and what do I do with them in the meantime?"

"Feeding them would be a good idea!"

"Right, Mary, and who will pay for it?"

Mary looked at him with a twisted smile. "As usual, charge it back to the office. You always do, anyway."

"All right, big mouth," Mr. Kovacs responded with resignation, as if the money would have come out of his own pocket, "get ready to either call for pizza delivery or a reservation for about eight people at a Swiss chalet downstairs."

"Why eight people, boss? There are six people, plus one of you,"

"Because I assumed you wanted to be included, don't you?"

"It's awfully generous of you, boss, but someone must stay behind and wait for the call from the hotel, don't you think?"

"Good thinking, Mary! Do we know who is heading this delegation?"

Mary paused, her hand trembling slightly as she adjusted the frames on her nose. "Go and meet him yourself," she said, her voice a whisper of its former self. "Just don't expect me to stay around while he is here with his bullies." She took a deep breath, steadying herself before she continued, "You know what, boss? As of now, consider me off sick till further notice." With that, she grabbed her coat and purse, her actions swift and decisive. As she marched out the door, leaving a bewildered Mr. Kovacs behind, it was clear this was more than a simple aversion.

Mr. Kovacs stood in stunned silence, realizing that Mary's reaction was out of the ordinary. Mary, who had been with the consulate through thick and thin, who had seen her share of difficult situations and demanding visitors, had never exhibited such a visceral reaction. It dawned on him that her fear might stem from a deeper place, perhaps whispers in the community or rumors of Colonel Salma's reputation that had reached even her ears. With her extensive network within the Hungarian expatriate community, Mary likely knew more about the dark tales surrounding Colonel Salma and his methods than she let on. Her decision to distance herself at the first sign of trouble spoke volumes of the fear Salma instilled in those who knew of his past.

Mr. Kovacs opened the door and stepped into the reception area. He looked around and raised his voice so everyone could hear him.

"Your attention, please! Let me first welcome you to the small Hungarian soil our Consulate represents in this big country of Canada." People quietened and paid attention to him. He continued, "Forgive us for the confusion, but your arrival in this office was unexpected. You must be hungry, so I am pleased to invite you downstairs for a full dinner at the Swiss Chalet while they sort out your misunderstanding at the hotel! Just give me a few minutes to chat with the head of your delegation, and we'll be all heading down to eat."

Comrade Salma, clad in the attire reminiscent of his days in the Secret Service—an organization marked by its complex role in Hungary's recent history—entered the room. His long brown leather coat, cinched with a belt and paired with light brown shoes, was not just a uniform but a symbol of a fraught era in Hungarian history. Like many of his generation, Salma was a man shaped by the tumultuous events of his country's past, wrestling with the legacies of choices made in times of crisis.

His hair, peppered with grey, betrayed his years in the field. Yet, his sharp, eagle-like eyes missed nothing, radiating an intensity born of decades navigating the shadowy corridors of espionage. Despite his short stature, he carried himself with an air of undisputed dominance, a living testament to the old guard of intelligence, still as dangerous and relevant as ever.

He removed his coat and dropped it over an unoccupied chair, then without being invited; he sat on the chair belonging to Mr. Kovacs. Arrogantly planting his feet on the top of the desk, he turned toward Mr. Kovacs and came to the point immediately.

"I'm Colonel Salma, and I'm here to conduct a mission deemed to be top secret. And we demand your full cooperation."

"So, you're not here to promote our wine and jams?" Mr. Kovacs stammered, clearly confused.

Colonel Salma glared at Mr. Kovacs and replied in a tone of voice that implied he was not really obliged to give the man an explanation, but as a great favor, he would share information, even with such an idiot as Mr. Kovacs. "My primary task here is to get rid of one of the thorns on the Soviet Union's side. I know we must keep up with the cover of the trade mission, but since I know nothing about the wine and jam business, I will delegate the negotiations to you."

Mr. Kovacs did not expect to do the job of the newly arrived Trade Mission alone. He could help with some negotiations, try to set up an import business and sell Hungarian wines and fruit jams, but he had assumed that there were several meetings already set up. Of course, there was still the handling of the samples to deal with.

But when he voiced his misgivings about the logistics problem, Comrade Salma impatiently waved his hands as if he would chase away an annoying insect. "You'll find a solution. I got your samples; someone will deliver the boxes here tomorrow. What more do you want?"

"If I could trouble you for some of your men to help me with the samples...To deliver it to our future customers..." Mr. Kovacs stammered.

"I think I can accommodate you by loaning you one, maximum two muscles for the duration." Comrade Salma smirked. "It will be good for them to mingle with the natives and pick up some manners. Don't let them smile too often, as we had no time to fix their teeth yet. And don't let them practice their English just yet, either! I did not choose them for their intelligence but purely for their muscles. Would that be satisfactory?

"My sole reason for being here is that I'm the right, no…" he stopped and specified, "Let's be honest about it: the only man to deal with this guy, Görgey. He is obviously a pro, who, among others, had been instrumental in the exposure of Kim Philby as a KGB agent!

"He is a very talented man, and I would admire him if he were not my worst enemy and nightmare. He is like a slimy eel, constantly escaping us. Not this time! By God, not this time! I will close every escape route he ever invented! He is mine, and I'll finally take him back!" Comrade Salma almost salivated just thinking of his expected triumph.

Mr. Kovacs, shocked to the core, could only stare at the seriously obsessed man in front of him. Just then, the telephone rang, and the hotel let them know their trouble was over and that they could return at their convenience.

**

The following morning, Mr. Kovacs, outranked, had no choice but to take over the legitimate side of the delegation. He had to prepare to attend his first meeting of the day, discussing the details of setting up a separate section by the Ontario Liquor Board for the proposed Hungarian wine and spirits business. He didn't really mind the unexpected role they had forced him into, as it guaranteed a large percentage of the profit ending up in his own pocket, soon to be placed somewhere in a small tropical Island in a nameless, numbered bank account. One had to be smart in cases like this to grab the opportunity and plan ahead.

So, he didn't complain when Comrade Salma ordered him to rent a car for ten days for two of his agents to conduct surveillance around the house, where Mr. Görgey expected to show up in person. What he minded was the extra-long hours that were added to his working days, as Comrade Salma, not wanting to show his face in public, insisted that Mr. Kovacs stay with him late into the night at the consulate office, forcing him to absorb, and of course applaud his very detailed, and brilliantly laid out plans ready to be implemented in a moment's notice. Often, Mr. Kovacs saw him bending over the maps of North America, drawing lines on them, and muttering.

Then, one morning, Mr. Kovacs caught Comrade Salma in his office at the Consulate, sitting in his chair, covered by his own coat, in deep sleep. It was obvious he never left the building during the night. He woke up and stupidly looked at Mr. Kovacs, trying to figure out why he was so familiar. Then, it slowly dawned on him where he was, and omitting an enormous yawn, he rubbed his eyes with both fists before trying to get up from the chair.

Holding his sore back with both hands, he gingerly tried to walk up and down, then swallowing a couple of painkillers, he turned toward the map of Washington pinned on the board in front of him. He pointed at the big red circle on it. "Here is the Post office where Mr. Görgey rents a box. Thanks to you, we know the exact time the boy posted his card, asking his uncle to meet him in Toronto ASAP and providing the correct address."

Comrade Salma went on with detailing the plans for action, "...so, it worked out just fine to have waited for him to go there to pick up his mail. We know it had arrived approximately two days ago, and he picked it up the same day, just before lunch. From that point, our surveillance team is sticking to him like glue, hoping to find out what kind of transportation he plans to use to come to Toronto."

Mr. Kovacs said, "If he is, as you claim, such a pro, won't he notice your surveillance team hanging around the Post Office?"

"We don't need to be too obvious about the surveillance team. Fate provided us with a blind and dirty homeless person sitting by the door with a lame dog. He's been there for ages. I understand Mr. Görgey, a bleeding heart, is regularly feeding him a sandwich and a cup of coffee for lunch. By this time, they're best buddies, chatting away!" Comrade Salma rolled his eyes.

"So, what has the beggar have to do with anything?" Mr. Kovacs asked, a bit mystified.

"We put a little device on the wall above his head on the outside wall of the Post Office, and all conversations between him and our guy come through like a charm. So, we know that he recently rented a new apartment in Washington, DC, and is ready to move in within a few days. It will give us enough time to plant some bugs in his new place. We don't know the exact date he plans to visit Toronto, although he mentioned a splashy costume party he hopes to catch. Or maybe he said crash? However, neither the time nor the location have been mentioned yet. I hope it will happen sooner because our hotel reservation and visa permits expire in the middle of October."

Mr. Kovacs couldn't help himself. "You sound a bit worried. Is there any problem with your plan?"

Comrade Salma waved his hands, trying to minimize the problem, but admitted, with a sigh, "For the time being, we had lost sight of him. But we don't panic yet. We assume that they just called him away in a vague, work-related, urgent business. In our line of business, we can always expect the unexceptional, don't we? So, we sit and wait for a while."

Mr. Kovacs couldn't help himself; he had to find out. "Comrade Salma, if you know where he lives and the location of the Post Office he regularly visits in Washington, why don't you try to catch him right there? Instead of making such a complicated plan involving so many people?"

Comrade Salma looked at Mr. Kovacs as if he were an ignorant six-year-old boy. "Obviously, you're not familiar with Washington. It is the center of the FBI and the CIA, keeping very close eyes on our embassies and the comings and goings of our agents, so we have very limited freedom of movement there. "

"What about the Canadians?"

"The Canadian borders are more porous, and their RCMP agents more relaxed than their American counterparts. But you're right; we should still cover all our bases." He looked at his watch. "Just about now, the house surveillance should be ready to go. Kovacs, you rented the car as directed, didn't you?"

"Of course, Comrade Salma. Here are the papers. Would you be kind enough to sign them?" Mr. Kovacs pointed at the line, as he wasn't prepared to cover the expenses of this dubious operation by Comrade Salma's association. When the man put his signature on the paper, Mr. Kovacs asked for further instructions. "Anything else, Comrade Salma?"

The man, obviously used to giving orders, spelled them out.

"Call Sam and Bernard at the hotel and tell them where they can pick up the car and the correct address for their surveillance. They need to find out how many people live there. And warn them not to be too obvious. Once you're done, report back to me. I need a soundboard."

Mr. Kovacs had no choice but to pick up the phone to follow through with the order.

After meticulous preparation, Colonel Salma laid out his plan with cold precision, his voice steady, betraying no hint of the tension.

"The operation hinges on intercepting Görgey before he realizes he's walked into a trap," he began, locking eyes with Mr. Kovacs to ensure the gravity of the situation was understood. "As soon as our intelligence confirms Görgey's imminent arrival in Toronto, we have three scenarios to consider, although each leads to the same conclusion: Görgey will be in our custody before he can meet with his contacts."

Comrade Salma launched into his speculation:

"Scenario One: The Direct Approach. If Görgey flies directly to Toronto, we'll have agents posing as taxi drivers at the airport. His expectation of a taxi awaiting him plays into our hands. Once he's isolated, our agent will divert him to a secure location instead of his intended destination.

"Scenario Two: The Ground Intercept. Should he opt for the bus, the same principle applies. One of us, disguised as a cab driver, will approach him under the guise of transportation. It's straightforward—pick him up, and instead of driving him home, take him to our extraction point.

"Scenario Three: The Longshot. The least likely but still possible scenario involves him driving. It's a long shot, considering the distance and the surveillance complications, but we'll monitor the major routes just in case. Our focus, however, remains on the airport and bus terminal—these are our primary battlegrounds."

Salma paused, allowing the details to sink in. "In all cases, the element of surprise is our greatest ally. Görgey is skilled, but he's not infallible. Our preparation, adaptability, and the element of surprise will ensure our success."

He concluded, "This operation is the culmination of months of planning. Failure is not an option. We adapt, we anticipate, and we execute with precision. Kovacs, everything has been arranged to ensure minimal risk and maximum efficiency. It's now just a matter of execution."

Salma looked at Mr. Kovacs with great satisfaction, expecting loud approval for his wisdom.

Upon learning the true nature of the mission and Colonel Salma's intentions, Mr. Kovacs was caught between his duties as a consulate official and the ethical implications of assisting in what appeared to be a dangerous and possibly illegal operation.

Mr. Kovacs sat back in the dimly lit confines of his office, the weight of Colonel Salma's revelations pressing heavily upon him. The quiet hum of the night's activity outside his door did little to drown out the turmoil in his mind. For years, he had served the consulate steadfastly committed to his nation's interests, always navigating the delicate balance between diplomacy and personal integrity. But Salma's plan thrust him into uncharted waters with its dark undertones and moral ambiguities.

He gazed at the worn photo of his family on the desk, a stark reminder of the personal stakes involved. How could he reconcile the role he was being forced to play in Salma's scheme with the values he held dear? The thought of aiding in the kidnapping of a CIA agent—a man who, in his own way, was fighting for his country's safety—left him feeling hollow. Yet, defiance against Salma's directive carried risks to his career and potentially to his and his family's safety.

Although he was only a trained diplomat and not a spymaster, he could still see a few big holes in the man's logic. But he didn't want to be too closely involved in what he now believed to be a very fishy operation, so he decided not to mention his forebodings.

Chapter 19

Between university and his part-time job at Diamond Industries, Rocky had no time to spare. Days and weeks passed, marked only by the cooling weather and the leaves turning yellow to red. Whoever claimed engineering was easy was surely mistaken, he muttered every evening, attempting to solve the next day's lecture problems.

The work at Diamond Industries proved more frustrating than challenging. Initially assigned to the cabinet-making section, Rocky spent more time dismantling than using the equipment. Most machinery was outdated, some having been in use since the beginning of World War Two. Rocky soon learned that D.D. avoided investing in new technology and safety equipment, leading to numerous accidents. However, the workers never voiced their complaints, a silence Rocky attributed to their illegal status in Canada. He decided to keep quiet about his own workpermit situation while remaining alert about any other illegal activities.

One evening, as October waned, Dolly's unexpected invitation to her parlor caught him off guard. "Hello, my boy," she greeted him, her voice a mix of warmth and mystery.

Rocky followed, curiosity piqued, yet cautious. Sitting across from Dolly, he felt a strange sense of anticipation.

"How's school?" she inquired.

"Challenging," he admitted, but his mind raced beyond academic woes.

The conversation shifted to his work at Diamond Industries, and Rocky found himself opening about his concerns. "It's not just the machinery. There's a shadow over this place, something unspoken but palpable."

Dolly's advice to document everything resonated with him deeply. *She's seen more of the world's dark corners than I ever have*, Rocky realized, a newfound respect for the woman before him taking root.

"Don't be alarmed," she added in a more serious tone, "but last week, the boys spotted a strange car parked by the house with the same two people sitting in it. We believe we are being observed. My assumption is that whoever is so interested in your relative means to capture him once he contacts you here."

Rocky admitted that while waiting for his relative from Washington, he received only a couple of letters from home; one was from Speedy, inquiring if he had advised his relative about his mother's condition. And since there was nothing to report, he never called the number Mr. Kovács gave him.

"But before I jump to conclusions," Dolly explained further, "I needed to rule out the likelihood of the mafia monitoring us, courtesy of DD, as he has been annoyed with me lately. But my associates reassured me that everything is quiet on that front, so I must assume that now the Hungarian Secret Service keeps us under scrutiny. That's fine. It is easy to rattle them. Just watch."

She got up, put a warm shawl around her shoulders, and grabbed a camera before she marched out front of the house to the parked car. Rocky stepped out front and watched as Dolly leisurely circled the vehicle, took several pictures of it and the occupants, and finally knocked on the driver's side, indicating to the guy to roll down his window.

The guy, first hesitating, rolled down his window a crack. Rocky couldn't hear what Dolly said to him—he just saw her motioning towards the house and imitating her to drink from an imaginary cup in her hand. The man rolled his window up in a hurry, started the engine, and stepped on the gas as if the devil was after him. Dolly took an elegant bow to show her appreciation to Joseph and Danny, standing beside Rocky and clapping their hands.

"What was that?" Rocky, still puzzled by the performance, asked the boys.

"Dolly did it again," they said in unison, still sputtering.

"What did Dolly do?" Rocky repeated.

Joseph replied, "First, she took pictures of the car, its license plate, and all. Then she graciously offered them the use of our bathroom or a hot cup of tea during what must be a boring surveying."

Rocky looked at them with wide eyes, clearly not comprehending. The dangers he'd considered abstract were suddenly at his doorstep, threatening not just him but those he'd come to care about in this foreign land. The sight of Dolly confronting their watchers was both surreal and empowering.

"So, what was their hurry? All they need now is to be stopped by the cops for speeding. They must have been pushing one hundred kilometers an hour on the street, posted to be thirty!"

**

The phone call from the Metro Police about the two busted agents had come as a very nasty surprise. Mr. Kovacs took the call, requesting him to appear at the local station to identify the two men claiming to be part of a Trade Mission from Hungary. They had been accused of keeping a house in Toronto under illegal surveillance for several days and speeding three times the legal limit when accosted. The discovery of Hungarian passports and short-term visas confirmed suspicions. But with their swift expulsion from the country, the threat momentarily seemed to diminish.

Mr. Kovacs hated being put on the spot but had no choice over the matter. Even if the police believed the agents' explanation that being new to the country, they just got lost and kept looking at the map, what suitable explanation did they have for repeatedly returning to the same spot day after day and then speeding three times over the limit when Dolly accosted them?

Declared to be first offenders, they were discharged into Mr. Kovacs's hands with the condition that they board the next flight back to Hungary.

Driven directly from the Police station to the Hungarian Consulate, the two busted agents faced the irate Comrade Salma, ready to charge them with treason.

"Idiots," he roared. "I told you to be discreet!" He stopped in his tracks as he realized, "Thanks to you two idiots, we are down to three agents! Hardly enough to cover all the terrain!" Obviously, the void left by the expelled agents must be quickly filled. He began his nervous marching up and down in the office, thinking. Then he grabbed the phone and dialed a number.

"Zdvastute Tovarish!" he greeted someone in Russian on the line. By the sound of it, he relayed his trouble and received a satisfying solution as he hung up with a grin. "Comrades! You're bloody fortunate! I have two Bulgarian special agents seasoned in covert operations on loan, just freshly off the airplane. And," he raised his arms to emphasize his luck, "in addition, I'm also being offered four heavily armed local boys as a backup. It looks like we'll be able to provide the City of Toronto with a spectacular fire works display for All Saint's Day!"

He returned his attention to his two recently busted agents and in a benevolent mood and a wildly sweeping gesture, requested Mr. Kovacs before he left the office, "Kindly remove these two wilted stems of weeds from my sight before I'm tempted to shoot them!"

Mr. Kovács, with his mouth open and in shock, stared at the man. Did he hear it correctly? Was Comrade Salma promised the help of two highly trained foreign agents, and in addition, four heavily armed local muscles, to deploy in an armed kidnapping in the middle of Toronto? Living in Toronto for the last several years had been the best in his life, and he wasn't planning to give that up soon. Not for anyone, including, or maybe especially not for, Comrade Salma! He decided to keep a close eye on them and try to stop them if possible.

**

October 31st unveiled a brisk, cold morning. The first hints of frost glistened on the abandoned swimming pool, creating a crystal sheen over the water's surface. The house, usually quiet and reserved, buzzed with unusual energy as the day progressed. Doors creaked and slammed with the rhythm of excited preparations, footsteps thudded on the wooden staircase, and voices echoed, blending joy and anticipation in a cacophony of human warmth against the autumn chill.

In the dining room, several giant pumpkins sat regally on the table—their innards scooped out to make room for flickering candles. The sharp, earthy scent of freshly cut pumpkin mixed with the sweet smell of wax and the lingering aroma of spiced apple cider simmering in the kitchen. Laughter and chatter spilled from the heart of the house, where pots and pans clanged in a symphony of culinary chaos. The air was thick with the smell of baking treats, cinnamon, and nutmeg weaving through the atmosphere, promising delights yet to come.

Rocky, caught in the whirlwind of activity, paused at the staircase, momentarily overwhelmed by the transformation of his usually subdued residence. Joseph donned an elaborate costume that obscured his identity and bumped into him, the rustle of fabric and the faint jingle of accessories adding to the day's enchantment.

"Halloween, my man!" Joseph's voice, muffled through his mask, carried a contagious vibrancy. "Tonight is Halloween, and we have a huge costume party tonight. Don't be late and make sure you're dressed. If we recognize you, we won't let you in. So, get cracking. You must find something to wear before the evening. We start promptly at sunset."

Rocky, who did not know what this party was about and why he was expected to wear a costume, went to work confused. D.D. wasn't around, and the workers, most recent arrivals from various refugee camps in Western Europe, were equally in the dark about Halloween. Only the older man at the factory gate could give Rocky some answers.

As Rocky navigated his new life in Toronto, the cultural tapestry of North America was a constant source of wonder and, sometimes, confusion. Halloween, with its roots stretching back to ancient Celtic festivals like Samhain, had evolved from a night of superstition and warding off evil spirits into a festive celebration full of costumes, candies, and jack-o'-lanterns. This tradition, unfamiliar to Rocky, symbolized blending various cultural heritages into a unique event celebrating the macabre with a sense of community and joy.

The contrast with All Saints' Day, a solemn day observed on November 1st by many cultures worldwide, including Hungary, to honor the deceased, was stark. This day, marked by visiting graves and lighting candles, reflected a contemplative respect for the past and the departed, a sentiment Rocky understood but had seldom observed with such ceremony.

"Oh, but of course!" the old man nodded his understanding. "Coming from Europe only recently, you would celebrate All Saints' Day on November 1st, visiting your loved dead ones in the cemetery and somberly lighting the candles on their tombstones. You wouldn't be familiar with Halloween, celebrated on October 31st, the Eve Before All Saints' Day. Over the centuries, Halloween transitioned from a pagan ritual to a day of parties."

The Old man shrugged and rolled his eyes. "I only know that tonight people, young and old, will dress up in weird costumes, go door to door, mutter something under their nose, and then people will give them candies. It is rather a bizarre and morbid way to celebrate your dead relatives!"

Rocky, who never celebrated All Saints' Day in Hungary and was not in the mood for partying, forgot about the whole thing, as he needed all his concentration to take apart the lathe he was working on. The darn thing broke again, and luckily, D.D. wasn't around to scream at him, as usual, and blame him for holding up production. It was as if it were Rocky's fault that D.D. refused to invest in better-quality equipment and parts.

It was close to five o'clock in the afternoon when Rocky finally got away from work. He arrived home dirty, tired, and starving. The transition from day to evening draped the neighborhood in a twilight glow, the setting sun casting long shadows and painting the sky in hues of orange and purple. Children's laughter and the sound of distant doorbells began to fill the air, the anticipation of trick-or-treating palpable. The smell of autumn leaves, damp earth, and the occasional whiff of a distant bonfire completed the tapestry of Halloween night.

The crisp air nipped at his cheeks, a stark contrast to the warmth of the house. The front yard was a spectacle of Halloween spirit, with carved pumpkins guarding the entrance, their faces a grotesque parade of smiles and grimaces, illuminated from within to cast dancing shadows. A mock tombstone peeked from behind a bush, a skeleton seemingly emerging from the earth, its bones clicking softly as a gentle breeze passed.

Standing amidst this orchestrated chaos, Rocky felt an unexpected surge of excitement. The sights, sounds, and smells enveloped him, drawing him deeper into the celebration of a tradition he had never known but was beginning to understand—the celebration of the eerie, the spooky, and the communal joy found in shared fright and delight.

Rocky entered through the backyard, but the two masked monsters guarding the gate grabbed him and propelled him toward the swimming pool.

"Hey!" He screamed from the top of his lungs, "What's the idea? Let go of me at once!"

Hearing the commotion, Dolly opened her backyard door to the deck and pool. Laughing, she said, "Leave him be, boys!" Then she motioned for Rocky to enter her sanctuary.

Rocky, annoyed by the unexpected rough handling, looked at her with angry, wide eyes. "What was that for?" he demanded.

"Relax, it was just innocent fun," she smiled and pointed at an armchair.

Rocky, shaken by the day's revelations and the unexpected rough handling by the masked monsters, found solace in Dolly's calm presence. Her words, "Tonight, we are expecting some guests. Some are invited, some are not," lingered in the air, heavy with unspoken implications. As he settled into the armchair, a blend of annoyance and curiosity clouding his thoughts, the festive chaos outside seemed to fade into the background, replaced by a growing sense of unease.

"The ones not invited," Dolly continued, her voice dropping to a conspiratorial whisper, "are likely unaware of our traditions. But their ignorance of Halloween will be their downfall. We know what they want, and we're ready for them."

Rocky's mind raced. The idea that their quaint celebration could be a battleground for more sinister forces was absurd and terrifying. Yet, Dolly's confidence in tone offered a sliver of reassurance. As he mulled over her words, a sudden chill swept through the room, not from the autumn cold but from the realization that tonight's events could set the stage for a confrontation far beyond the scope of trick-or-treaters and costume parties.

In the distance, the sound of a slow and deliberate car engine broke the evening's silence. Rocky glanced towards the window, but the night's shadows obscured the view. The vague yet undeniable sense of an impending encounter hung in the air like a promise.

As the clock ticked closer to the witching hour, the line between friend and foe, between the living and the spectral, seemed to blur. Rocky knew that this Halloween would be unlike any other, a night when the masks worn by friends and strangers could conceal the faces of a far more dangerous game. The question of who would unmask whom loomed large, a puzzle whose pieces would begin to fall into place under the cover of darkness.

Dolly's final words, a mixture of warning and wisdom, echoed in Rocky's ears as he prepared to face the night. "Remember, my boy, the most frightening masks are often worn by those who wish to hide in plain sight. Keep your wits about you, and trust that not all spirits tonight are here for the festivities."

With that, Rocky stepped into the Halloween night, armed with his newfound knowledge and a determination to uncover the truth behind the masks. The stage was set, the players ready, and as the first of the uninvited guests approached, the story of Rocky, Dolly, and a Halloween of hidden agendas was about to unfold.

Chapter 20

By seven o'clock in the evening, it was dark. The streetlights threw dim light patches on the sidewalks and revealed many children and adults wearing weird, scary masks, carrying paper bags, going door to door, screaming and screeching. Most houses on the street were decorated, some with gigantic spiders on their doors, some, like Dolly's, with tombstones and skeletons scattered around the front yard. Without exception, they all had carved pumpkins illuminated by lit candles.

A black-capped witch manned Dolly's front door, wearing a long black wig, sporting a huge warty nose and the broom between her legs. She had a large wooden bowl beside her on the stairs, and every time children walked up to her and said, "Trick or Treat," she reached into the bowl and followed by a sinister cackling, dumped a handful of sweets in their bags. Far from being frightened, the children giggled, then turned around and happily skipped away to the next house, which showed that they would welcome the little ones by having their lights on.

Many people were on the street, all coming and going, mostly on foot, except for the cars circling around, looking for a parking spot. Out of the cars came people dressed as pirates, skeletons, black widows, bride, and groom joined at the hip, a Popeye, and a group of four very tall, blonde-wigged nurses carrying huge syringes. And they all headed toward Dolly's home.

The witch manning the door at Dolly's house had a clear view of the car parked too close to the curb, observing two men sitting on the front seat, wearing identical ill-fitted grey suits and raincoats. They were munching potato chips from a bag and sipping from a can of pop.

They kept looking at a piece of paper, then at Dolly's house, making sure they had the correct address and taking pictures of all the guests arriving and gaining admittance.

They were the two Bulgarian agents who had been transported and loaned by the KGB at the last minute to Comrade Salma's operation. It was to be their last mission before retirement and a last opportunity to reclaim their standing. Paired in their last mission, they seriously fucked up a few months before, when they were supposed to shadow a known dissident in Prague and lure him into one of the dark alleys in the worker's district, stab him with the poisoned sharp end of an umbrella.

They had many assignments together before and learned to rely on each other's strengths. Misha had the talent to blend in, becoming totally invisible, an excellent trait when following a suspect, while Yasin was an expert in quick decision-making.

But hard as they tried to analyze their last and only failed mission, they were still unable to pinpoint what and where it went wrong. Not only did they lose sight of their target, but they ran into a group of heavy bikers in the dark alley, and who, surrounding the two of them, beat them up before the cops arrived. Thus, bringing public attention to themselves, they had to be rescued and have their presence and supposed actions in a friendly nation explained. Both felt rather fortunate that instead of being sent to the Gulag, they were offered a second, albeit a last, chance to redeem themselves in the eyes of the Agency. Not that they were given too much choice. They both realized their special training as KBG undercover agents, interrogation, and assassination could never be traded for a peaceful civilian existence.

With resignation, they braced themselves for their next and, hopefully, their last assignment. It looked like a relatively easy job since all they had to do was identify the CIA agent, who was supposedly attending a private custom party at that address.

But they also knew the stakes were high. The person they were supposed to shadow and identify was a highly trained CIA agent with a long list of successful missions catching high-profile KGB agents deeply infiltrating the West. It was an assignment where failure was not accepted. It would end their careers, most likely their personal freedom, if not their lives, and the future of their own families as well.

They knew it would be difficult to blend in tonight since neither of them was given enough time to purchase adequate customs.

"Don't sweat it, Misha!" Yasin reassured his partner. "Just pretend that we're dressed as undercover KGB agents. See," he pointed at the two tall men, dressed as RCMP officers in full regalia, emerging from the car just arriving. "Just like them. If they can dress like that, we certainly could fit in. So come on, my friend, let's get the show on the road."

They took a deep breath, opened the doors and stepped out of the car. Misha headed toward Dolly's front door, while Yasin headed toward the garden gate, intending to sneak into the backyard unnoticed.

Keeping his fingers twisted behind his back for good luck, Misha stepped right behind the two tall guys wearing the RCMP uniform and complimented them.

"Great costume, guys! Do you mind if I join you?" Not waiting for a response, he stepped close behind them, pretending to be part of the group. A head shorter than the two ahead of him, he was hoping to use them as covers to sneak in behind them.

The witch, accompanied by a tall skeleton, stopped each of them at the door and whispered something to the guys dressed as RCMP officers. They nodded in response and whispered something back. The door opened, and they were let in. That left Misha, the Bulgarian undercover agent, alone at the doorway, facing the Witch and the Skeleton. The Skeleton grabbed his collar and asked him, "What were the two things Dolly inherited from her late husband?"

"What is this?" Misha, confused, asked in a huff. "Twenty questions? I thought it was an open party."

"You guessed wrong, Buddy," the Skeleton informed him. "Just answer the question, and you'll be free to enter."

"I have no clue," Misha admitted, speculatively adding, "I hope she got lots of money and jewelry."

The Witch and the Skeleton looked at each other, nodded, opened the door, and let him enter. They stepped in right behind him.

Before he could utter a word or warning to Yasin, his partner, the Witch and the Skeleton wrestled Misha to the floor. Stripped of his gun, they tightly bound and rolled him into a carpet in the hallway.

Someone screamed as he was pushed into the swimming pool. It took some time before they dragged him out, fully clothed and dripping, and presented him to the masked, laughing people. And although the two of them had no clue what was in store for them, they couldn't help but foolishly grin back.

Two Metro police officers at the front door interrupted them, requesting a quick word with the guys dressed as RCMP officers attending the party.

"We just arrested four rowdy, fully armed individuals idling in two rented cars a few houses down the street in a no parking zone. These yahoos kept harassing the children and threatening the adults going from door to door. They were drunk, and it turned out to be fully armed. And they had enough explosion in their trunks to blow the city block! They were also on the Wanted List for several armed robberies in the neighborhood for at least two years! Whoever called the police forestalled a hideous and possibly bloody incident, endangering many innocent lives," the officer blurted out in a hushed voice.

Still not quite comprehending the immediate dangers they've escaped from, most of the party attendees removed their masks and, still laughing, dragged the two Bulgarian agents into the living room. Except for the four detectives, dressed as tall nurses with giant syringes, and the two men dressed as RCMP officers, along with the immediate members of Dolly's household, the rest of the guests were still convinced that they were just a part of an innocent, funny charade.

Dolly emerged from her office, bringing a large towel, and ordered the soaked agent to undress. He looked around, seeking a way to escape or at least cover himself, but observing the unmasked crowd around him, he decided there was really no need for false modesty under the circumstances. So, he dropped his trousers, peeled his wet shirt off, and sat down on a chair to remove his shoes and socks. He stood up in his wet boxer and white t-shirt and covered his eyes with his hands.

He knew what was coming, and he was right. Since their trip was a last-minute deal, they had no time to pack anything for themselves, so he picked up some boxers at the airport. He didn't picture himself ever standing before a crowd and being laughed at wearing the boxers with pink hearts printed all over it. The whole situation was beyond embarrassing. It was downright humiliating. For a minute, he couldn't decide which was a better fate for him, being humiliated in public or staring at the guns at the execution yard.

The person dressed as the Black Widow, stepped forward and, removing the black veil covering his face, faced the two agents. "I believe, gentleman, you were hoping to find me here. And you were right for a change. However, the joke is on you because you're caught in the act."

As the laughter and chatter of the party enveloped them, Misha and Yasin shared a glance that communicated more than words ever could. For the first time since their arrival, the jovial facade of the Halloween party seemed to peel away, revealing the grim reality of their predicament. The playful shrieks of guests in costume, once amusing, now echoed like alarms in their ears.

His hands bound behind him, Misha felt a cold sweat on his forehead. He leaned slightly towards Yasin, his voice barely a whisper against the cacophony of party noises. "Yasin, do you think they know? About us, about who we really are? We could always claim to be just two strangers accidentally wandering into a private Halloween party!"

Yasin, usually the more composed of the two, couldn't mask the tremor in his voice. "I...I don't know, Misha. This was supposed to be a simple mission: identify the target and report back. But now..." His gaze darted around the room, taking in the faces of their captors and the other guests, trying to discern any sign of recognition, any hint that their true identities as KGB agents were known.

Realizing they were not merely intruders at a party but potentially exposed as spies on foreign soil hit them with a sobering clarity. The playful nature of their mission—the disguises, the sneaking around—all seemed foolish now, child's play in the face of real danger.

Misha's thoughts raced to the worst-case scenario. "If they hand us over, if they know who we are...Yasin, our families, our..." He couldn't finish the sentence, the weight of what their failure might mean for their loved ones back home, crushing him.

For a moment, the festive atmosphere around them faded into the background, replaced by a stark tension that seemed to stretch taut and unyielding between them. It was a moment of silent acknowledgment between the two men, an understanding that they were in a deeper situation than they had ever anticipated, with far more at stake than their own lives.

The two RCMP officers stepped forward and, reading the interlopers their rights, handcuffed the two agents and escorted them to the police cruiser. As they were dragged away, the raucous laughter and music of the party resumed their dominance, a stark contrast to the turmoil unfolding between Misha and Yasin. At that moment, the Halloween celebration felt like a macabre dance, with them as the unwitting jesters at the court of fate.

"Poor buggers," Dolly commented as the police cruiser swallowed the two Bulgarians.

"Don't feel too bad about them," Miklós said. "They don't know yet, but they are the luckiest devils. Being caught as a spy in North America practically saved their lives. Now, they have the option to ask asylum after being briefed or exchanged at a later date with some American Spies. Let me tell you, the consequences for them returning to the bosom of their Agency, with a failed mission, would not have been pretty."

The remaining guests, still dressed in costumes but without masks, gathered around the dining room table laden with food. Rocky, wearing a large apron and the big chef's hat, holding a big spatula in his hands, ready to strike, stood at the kitchen door, still stunned by the unexpected event. He kept staring at his relative with wide eyes and an open mouth. And the relative stared back at him, although with a twinkle in his eyes.

But before he could approach, a tall girl with short black hair and a little Red Riding Hood costume came in from the back door. Spotting Rocky at the kitchen door, she uttered a toe-curling scream and flew out to the deck, accidentally falling into the swimming pool.

"Damn it," Dolly swore, "they were not supposed to meet just yet." She promptly turned around and said to the skeleton beside her, "Joseph, fish her out."

But before Joseph could move, Rocky spurred into action, jumped into the pool after her. He blindly reached out into the dark and grabbed the first things he could reach. It was Kira's red coat that pulled her down to the bottom of the pool. Instinctively, he gathered her in his arms and emerged from the pool, with the help of many hands reaching out for them.

Quickly bundled into warm blankets, they were both ushered inside. Having gulped many mouthfuls of water, they were both coughing. Dolly grabbed a bottle of brandy off the table and handed it to Kira and Rocky. They each swallowed a large swig with no argument, just staring at each other.

"All right," said Dolly firmly, "the show is over. It is time for everyone to retire." Recognizing the voice of authority, most of them obeyed.

Wilma steered the hysterical Kira back to the third-floor apartment while Joseph escorted Rocky to his bedroom—he was still sputtering, trying to take in the sudden reappearance of Kira at the same time his uncle surfaced,.

"Kira! Wait!" Rocky screamed, and when she didn't stop, he stood there blabbering incoherently, "But, but, when did she ...? And how ...? I didn't dream it, did I? It is Kira! I must talk to her!" Rocky insisted feverishly.

Ignoring Rocky's demands, Joseph dragged him upstairs, tucked him into his bed, and stood over him till he fell into a deep sleep.

**

Comrade Salma kept vigil by the phone in the Hungarian Consulate that night. He was sitting in Mr. Kovács' chair, staring at the phones and enticing them to ring with good news. The first call informed him that both Bulgarians got caught red-handed and were on the way to being indicted. The next call came to report that in the same neighborhood, the local police force caught two sets of yahoos harassing the kids and their parents on the street. They couldn't have done a better job arousing suspicion than idling in a no-parking zone, being drunk and disorderly while armed to the teeth, with enough explosives stored in the trunk of their rented cars to blow up the whole neighborhood! And now it looked like the police were looking for a connection between both events!

Comrade Salma was not impressed. His fingers were twitching, and he had to restrain himself not to reach for his revolver, ready to shoot the imbecilic, useless idiot.

But he still waited for calls from the airports and the bus station.

"Colonel," the agent responsible for observing and assisting in the kidnapping operation called solemnly.

"Cut the crap!" Comrade Salma snapped, "Give me your report! Did our guy, Görgey, arrive? Did you catch him? That's all I want to hear! Otherwise, heads will fall—understand, Comrade!"

"There was a man looking very much like Mr. Görgey arriving on the plane and spotting his name written on a card held up high by one cab driver, headed straight toward him. But just before the man reached the driver, two police officers intervened and escorted him to another section. Sadly, though, they spotted my partner and duly arrested him. I barely escaped for now by mingling with the crowd. And since I have no intention of experiencing another stint in a foreign prison for trying to kidnap a foreign national, forgive me for flying directly to a warmer climate. So long, my dear Commissar! Better luck next time!" he sang as he he dropped the phone and ran.

In less than ten minutes, another call came through, this time from the Greyhound bus depot, with practically the same story. As in the description, a man showed up and headed toward a cab driver. Two police officers intersected him, shoved him into an unmarked cruiser, and drove away in a hurry. And they arrested all Comrade Salma's agents present at the bus station.

Comrade Salma could only stare at the phone in his hand. He had no words left to express his feelings. It was a major fuck-up, no matter how he looked at it. All the time, careful planning and hand-picking of his agents! And nothing to show for it! All his agents were caught practically red-handed, and he could only hope that the Bulgarians were better trained to tolerate torture and wouldn't spill the connection between comrade Salma and the Russian Generals.

The only thing left for him to do now was to disappear. He gathered his suitcase and bulging briefcase, picked up the phone and dialed a number.

He barked his order, "Come and pick me up. Let the plane, fully filled, ready to leave, wait for me at the Cargo entrance." Leaving the doors wide open behind him, he called the elevators but didn't wait for them—he rushed down the stairs to the side entrance, stepped out on the dark street and slid through the back door of a large black limousine pulling up beside him. He knew that he had to catch the standby flight on time or got arrested by the Canadians for breaking International Law and for trying to kidnap a foreign agent. He wasn't sure what worried him more: to be caught by the Canadians or to face his bosses, waiting for him back in Moscow, trying to explain how a perfectly planned operation had failed.

Chapter 21

Dolly woke up with a smile on her face. It had been a long time since she had a man in her bed, especially the man she had loved for a long time.

Miklos yawned as he stretched and sat up. "Good morning, gorgeous. Nice to see you again," he said, his smile warming her heart.

Dolly stood, her attention caught by the silence. "It's too quiet."

Miklos listened and nodded; his gesture understated but clear.

Dolly said, "It is Saturday morning, and the house is unusually quiet. I wonder what the kids are up to." She sniffed the air as the aroma of freshly brewed coffee, bacon, and eggs hit her.

Always the early riser, Joseph had taken it upon himself to organize the morning's gathering. His meticulous nature was evident in ensuring every place setting was perfectly aligned—his glasses pushed up on the bridge of his nose as he double-checked each detail.

With her ever-present notebook and pen, Wilma scribbled notes. Her role as the group's unofficial chronicler had made her the keeper of their adventures, and her keen observations often captured the nuances that others missed.

They stood around the table formally set for ten people. It was as if a commando group was waiting for their commanding officers to evaluate a mission. Only two people in the group were not yet aware of last night's events. The others, grinning, were waiting to be praised for successfully carrying out their assigned roles.

Dolly stepped out of her apartment, followed by Miklos, and a loud cheering greeted them. Summing up the situation, Dolly took her place at the end of the large table, suggested Miklós take a chair on her right, then lifted her glass filled with orange juice and said, "To our good health and successful operation!"

Seven people lifted their glasses in unison and repeated, "To our good health and successful mission."

Rocky, the youngest at the table, seemed almost swallowed by the grandeur of the morning's assembly. His wide eyes flitted from face to face, absorbing every word and gesture with the eagerness of a sponge. His admiration for Miklós was palpable, a shy smile creeping onto his face whenever their eyes met. It was clear he was wrestling with the weight of his gratitude, the words he sought teetering on the edge of his tongue but never quite making the leap. Seated across from his relative, he kept looking at him shyly. Dolly reached over and patted his hand.

"You didn't think we would just let them grab your uncle without fighting back, did you?"

Rocky shook his head, trying hard to find the words to thank her and to satisfy his curiosity about last night's event.

Dolly looked around. "Shall we tell him what happened?"

Joseph, Danny, Wilma, Smiley, Stephan, and Felix nodded.

Dolly looked around and spotted one empty chair. She turned to Wilma, "Where is Kira? She should be here, down with us. There is no reason for her to hide her face up there anymore. So, please tell her to join us down here now."

Wilma rose, walked out the back door, and returned shortly with Kira.

Kira entered the room as if she were stepping into a stream, cautiously, almost reluctantly. Dolly pointed to the empty seat beside Rocky, and Rocky stood up, politely pulling the chair out and offering it to Kira. Her gaze lingered on the empty chair beside Rocky before she took it, her movements deliberate, starkly contrasting the chaotic warmth that filled the room. The others might not have noticed the subtle tension she carried in her shoulders or the way her fingers nervously twisted a strand of hair, but it spoke volumes of her feeling, like an outsider being suddenly thrust into the heart of a family's intricate dance.

"Thank you," she mumbled, as she busied herself with buttering a slice of bread.

"Welcome to Dolly's assembly." Miklós lifted his juice glass again to extend the greetings to the new arrival. "And since I'm the one who caused all this excitement last night, I might as well introduce myself. I'm Miklós Görgey."—he pointed at Rocky—"this young man's cousin. We know that this young man, who desperately wanted to leave Hungary to attend a university of his own choosing in the Western world, was given a task by the Hungarian Secret Service. The price of his freedom was to entice me, his distant relative, to come and visit him in person at the earliest opportunity so he could give me sensitive information regarding a close family member of mine."

Miklos looked around, smirking, "Although I was happy to learn of the existence of a distant cousin, I couldn't help being suspicious. As far as I knew, I had no close relations living in Hungary anymore. I made sure of that back in early December Nineteen-fifty-six,"

**

Miklos could still remember the cold and wet day in the first days of December 1956, when he drove the ambulance with an Austrian plate across the border to Hungary. He and two of his buddies, all dressed in white coats with the Red Cross armband on their sleeves, delivered first aid supplies to the hospitals in Budapest.

The Hungarian guards were suspicious and ordered them to unpack everything from the van. However, finding only medical supplies instead of the expected arms from the fascists in the West, they begrudgingly let the van pass across the border. Miklos drove on to the first crossroads, where he pulled in, looking at the mess the border guards made in the car while searching for the illegal arms.

"Why did we stop here?" Jeff, one of his buddies, said.

"Other than cleaning up this mess?" Miklos pointed at the disarrayed boxes thrown all around the floor. "I also want to ensure we would not arrive at our destination during daylight. I want to get to the hospital just about sunset, unpack our cargo without uninvited observers, swiftly exchange it for our passenger, and be on our way back to Vienna."

"You said nothing about a passenger before!" Jeff said, in a panic.

"Relax! I arranged everything."

It was already dark when they pulled into one of the side entrances of a hospital. A man, wearing a bloodstained smock, stood by the door, casually leaning against it, smoking a cigarette. He stepped forward and shook Miklos's hand. "Nice to see you, my friend. You do not know how badly we need your supplies! Did you, by any chance, bring some blood as well? We're down to our last bag, and many injured people are still lining up for it."

"We brought as many as we could quickly grab. But what about my cargo?"

"She is fine and deeply asleep. She won't wake up for at least another four hours. We tucked her into many layers of warm blankets. Here are her papers. Everything is in order. The doctors in Vienna will take care of her."

When the first-aid kits and other medical supplies were unloaded, another man appeared with a gurney. They placed the gurney on one side of the ambulance and pulled a mobile screen around it, blocking the view from outside. The people from the hospital stood guard, making sure no one had witnessed the exchange. Then, they locked the back door of the ambulance and gave it a reassuring bang with their fist.

It was late at night, and many trucks on the road were heading toward Austria. Hungarian army trucks and the occasional private cars passed them. A lone Russian officer looking for opium stopped them once, but after convincing him they didn't have any, he let them go. They arrived back at Vienna without incident. Just in time for Miklos's mother to gain consciousness and enjoy the happy reunion.

**

"And currently, she is in a posh retirement home in Arizona," Miklos added proudly.

"You mean, you snuck in during that time and brought her out?" Dolly looked at him with wide eyes. "You never told me that!"

"Sorry, my girl, but it was strictly on the need-to-know basis. I'm sure you understand the game by now. I couldn't risk leaving her behind and being a source of blackmail." Miklós looked at Rocky with a forgiving smile.

"So, if your mother was no longer in Hungary, why would they assume they could use her to manipulate you?" Rocky said.

"But the authorities didn't know she was no longer in Hungary. It so happened that around that time, many people disappeared, either by escaping the country or by meeting with accidents. The morgues were packed with unidentified victims, and the authorities were not eager to identify them, nor the reasons for their demise."

"So, they figured if they didn't know her whereabouts, you wouldn't know it either? And created a mystical mother for you, hoping you would fall for their trick?" Horrified, Rocky exclaimed. "But that's monstrous!"

Miklos nodded. "This wasn't the first time the Hungarians tried to entice one of their former agents back to Hungary. I knew a junior captain in the Hungarian Secret Service, who, after the revolution, ended up in the United States and was employed by the CIA. He had an old, widowed father at home, a good-standing member of the Communist party. One of those from the old guards, who considered the communist Party his closest family, blindly trusting them, ready to follow their rules, without a question. The Hungarian Secret Service persuaded the poor man to go to the United States and entice his son with the promise of amnesty and promotion. As soon as they arrived back, instead of the promised promotion, they arrested the son, accused of espionage, and promptly court-martialled and executed him. And the father, learning about his son's fate and his role in it, committed suicide. This was a lesson for all of us to learn.

"So, when I received Rocky's letter, I smelled a rat, and since it gave me Dolly's address, I got in touch with her. I assume you all realize by now that we are old acquaintances." And he sent a wicked wink and a smile in Dolly's direction.

Dolly playfully slapped Miklos with a backhand and took over the narration. "About ten days ago, Danny and Joseph noticed a few strangers leisurely strolling on our street, taking lots of pictures, mostly of our house. Now, granted, that alone would not be suspicious, as the house indeed has a few architecturally interesting features. It is also within walking distance of the corner of Bloor Street and Spadina, which are filled with European-style coffee houses and Hungarian restaurants favored by all Hungarian tourists. So, it is almost inevitable that some would stumble on our street.

"I figured it could be a fluke if they came by once. Come by twice, it could be because they want to take a picture of our unique, picturesque home to show others at home. But when the same bunch, wearing identical brown leather coats and matching sets of leather hats, kept coming back as regular as a clockwork over the week, taking pictures upon pictures from every direction. I have to admit, that triggered my suspicion.

"One of them actually had the nerve to take a leak on one of my bushes on the front lawn during bright daylight!" Dolly fumed, thinking of the event. "I marched right out and informed him we don't use our gardens for that purpose. If they need to go to the toilet, there are plenty of restaurants on Bloor Street, a walking distance from here, where, for the price of a cup of coffee and a sandwich, they could use their facilities."

"What did they say?" Miklós said. He laughed.

"They were just smirking. One of them replied in a heavy Hungarian accent, "Sorry, Madam. We meant no harm! Only this bush here looked a bit parched, needing some watering!"

"The cheeky bugger!"–Dolly fumed. "You would think this incident would have chased them away for good. However, the next day, we spotted a car parking across the house, with two people sitting in it and staring at us for a long time. They were so obvious that I couldn't help but play a game with them."

Rocky laughed. "Ah, I wondered…that explains that evening when you walked up to that parked car and offered the occupants to come in and use the facilities. Instead of graciously accepting it, they took off in a hurry."

"Of course. But the timing was also important. The Hungarian agents in the car were clearly busted, and they had only two short days to be replaced. Judging by our frantic activity to prepare for a Halloween costume party on the night of Miklós' expected arrival, they needed to be ready. But we screened all the attendees at the door just in case the new agents would try to sneak in by wearing masks and full costumes."

"How?" both Kira and Rocky queried,

"By asking a question at the door that only those in the know could answer correctly."

"So, what was the question?"

"What were the two things Dolly inherited from her late husband?"

The room immediately was filled with screaming, hooting, and clapping.

"And? What were they, Dolly?" the group asked in unison.

"Other than an empty title and a large amount of gambling debt? Nothing good or valuable!" Dolly replied, with a mischievous smile.

"Poor bugger!" Danny sighed, referring to the duped foreign agent trying to enter the front door. "No wonder he was speechless. Nobody, unless they knew you closely, would know that!"

When the laughter subsided, Rocky asked, "What about the other guy, the one trying his luck, coming in from the backyard?"

Dolly replied, "We took the light bulb out above the garden door. I instructed Joseph, standing guard in the shadows, that anyone trying to enter there should be shoved in the pool. We suspected he would more likely prefer to get air in his lung and get out of the pool than to reach for his gun."

"And the RCMP guys, how did they get involved in this?" Wilma said.

Miklós cleared his throat, trying to get their attention. "Actually, they had been very much involved from the beginning. As soon as I realized the Hungarian agent's intent, I started the ball rolling and formed a three-way coalition with the FBI, the CIA, and the RCMP to catch the Hungarians in action.

"The RCMP was happy to get involved as they had come across reports about KGB agents actively trying to recruit informants, mostly at the university campuses all over the country. However, the KGB also knows that the Russian consulates and their agents are constantly observed. For this reason, they use the services of their friendly satellites. So, it was not a complete surprise for the RCMP to learn about the recent arrival of a few more Hungarian agents in Toronto."

"Admit that the RCMP guys dressed as legitimate officers gave our party a certain piquancy," Joseph leaned back in his chair, patting his aching stomach from too much laughter. "Who knew those guys had a sense of humor?"

Rocky's expression was a worried one. "Shouldn't we worry about the Hungarians' reaction to this fiasco? I mean, all of their agents, including the two Bulgarians, got caught red-handed and arrested! It is an internationally embarrassing situation! They might blame me for it and try to retaliate by hurting my father!"

Miklos stepped forward and hugged the young man reassuringly.

"I disagree, my friend. It will force both the Hungarian and Russian agents to lie low for a while. They need time to lick their wounds, reassess, and re-group. And it will give us some time to arrange for your father to get out of harm's way."

An urgent telephone call to Miklós led him away, and resumed when he reappeared with a wide smile on his face twenty minutes later.

"That call just came from the RCMP's headquarters. Early this morning, they paid a visit to the Hungarian Consulate on Bloor Street in Toronto, intending to ask a few questions of Mr. Kovács about his involvement in this matter. They found the door to the office open, but the premises were empty. No employees, no documents, nothing. They called the Hungarian Embassy in Ottawa, trying to find an answer, but only a low-level secretary could take their call because, as of last night, the ambassador and all the staff, including their families, had packed up and flown out. And, of course, nobody seemed to know the reason for it. I asked the guys at the RCMP whether they had a chance yet to figure out the reason and the level of the Bulgarian agents' involvement in this case. Not surprisingly, the Bulgarian Embassy denied knowing anything about their existence. But we know the Russians get them involved on special occasions. It would be good to find out who exactly had been their direct target. I wonder whether there was a relatively recent arrival of an important person from behind the Iron Curtain, requesting refugee status?"

"You think the Canadian government will follow up with an inquiry?" Dani said.

"It will grant at least one visit from the Canadian Minister of Foreign Affairs with the Russian Ambassador, demanding an explanation," Miklós replied sarcastically. "Knowing from experience, the ambassador most likely will walk out of the meeting, huffing and puffing, accusing the Canadian Government of trying to steer up some shit just to give them a bad reputation internationally. Same old, same old," he waved impatiently.

"By now, we all know that the coordinated actions at the Toronto airport and the Greyhound bus were a charade, and you needed to have at least three people impersonating you. So, how did you arrive safely with no one noticing it?" Stefan asked.

Miklós smirked and said, "While I had three doubles, one for the airport, one for the bus station, and another at the Niagara Falls border crossing, the real me drove directly to Buffalo in a military truck. From there, I flew in on a privately owned small four-passenger plane to the Toronto Island airport, to be picked up by Joseph early yesterday morning. But it was such a hectic day for everyone preparing for the party that it was easy to sneak into the house unnoticed."

Chapter 22

Rocky, overwhelmed yet still seated at the table, turned to Kira. "I didn't know you were living here. I've been trying to find you—"

Kira jumped up and dashed through the back door, her steps echoing as she ascended the stairs to the third-floor apartment.

"So much for peacemaking," Dolly muttered under her breath before addressing Rocky louder, "Let her be, Rocky. She's clearly not ready to talk to you."

"But I don't understand! When did she...? Why is she here? And why didn't you tell me? You knew I was looking for her..." Rocky protested..

Dolly raised her hand, signaling him to stop. "Rocky, this is a private matter. Let's discuss it without an audience, shall we?" She led him to her office, where he sat, his expression a mix of stubbornness and anticipation for an explanation.

Dolly settled into her armchair. "You may feel I owe you an explanation, but I don't. It's not my place to disclose why she's here. If she chooses to share her reasons with you, that's her decision. For now, I suggest you give her space."

"But why? I'm not her enemy," Rocky insisted.

"She's not in a place to trust anyone right now, and I understand her reasons. If you care about her, you'll respect her need for space. Unless you want to push her further away, I suggest you leave her be. If you'll excuse me, I must ensure she knows she's safe here." With that, Dolly left the room, leaving Rocky alone with his thoughts.

**

Rocky was determined to discover why Kira needed to stay concealed in Dolly's place. He recalled the conversation at D. D.'s home when Eugene mentioned his niece went to the same high school with Rocky, but he never revealed her name, as both D. D.'s wife and mother-in-law rudely interrupted. And even though there were opportunities to chat at work, Eugene avoided talking to Rocky about personal matters.

Well, Rocky thought with renewed determination, *it was time to change that.* As he glanced at his watch, he considered Eugene a colleague from_work always kept his private life a guarded secret. Despite their daily interactions at the office, Eugene rarely spoke of personal matters. Today, Rocky decided he would bridge that gap. He picked up his phone to invite Eugene for coffee at one of the new Hungarian cafes along Bloor Street, hoping to delve into more personal territory in a casual setting.

After his phone call, Rocky got dressed, put his coat on, and strolled from Dolly's towards Bloor Street and from there to Brunswick Avenue. He stopped at his favorite store selling candies, tobaccos, newspapers, and books, to chat with the owner, Mr. Thorn. It was one of those cases when the name didn't match the person, as the man couldn't have been a nicer, more easy-going person, even if he tried. Rocky bought a few Hungarian newspapers, including a locally printed one, the *Masada*, which Mr. Thorn pointed out as one of the most liberal in the free world.

"You should meet the editor," Mr. Thorn suggested, "George Frank. He lives in Toronto and is a close friend of your landlady. Which is not really a surprise, is it?" He grinned, "as she keeps superb company."

Rocky watched Eugene disappear into the *Continental Cuisine Diner.* He paused, leaning against the cool exterior of the candy shop. He remembered the first time he met Eugene in the bustling office where they both worked. With his quiet demeanor and reserved smile, Eugene seemed like an enigma. Rocky had always sensed there was more to Eugene's story, especially after overhearing a brief phone conversation about the family left behind in Hungary.

Rocky crossed the street, reflecting on their sporadic, guarded exchanges over coffee breaks, wondering if today might finally offer a glimpse into the man behind the façade.

As Rocky suspected, Eugene was unusually talkative and happy to be away from his cousin and boss. They talked about Hungary and family. Eugene missed his wife and daughter, whom he left behind about a year ago. The fact that they left Hungary spoke volumes of their disillusionment with the regime, and their belief that they could fare better in the West.

After finishing their second cup of espresso and their third crepe Suzette—one filled with cream cheese, the other with crushed walnut, and the third with strawberry jam—Rocky brought up his original subject.

"Eugene, you mentioned that you have a niece who attended the same high school as mine. Is she in Toronto, by any chance? It would be so nice to meet a familiar face so far from home. I'm sure you understand the feeling...." Rocky looked at Eugene with the hungry look of a newly arrived person aching to bump into someone he knew from home.

"Well, to tell you the truth," Eugene said, squirming in his chair, "my niece became an embarrassment to us."

Rocky nodded sympathetically, waiting for the explanation.

"I won't bore you with the details, Rocky. The gist of the story is that it was DD who paid for my niece's trip to Canada, and it was Cathy who arranged for her to get married to a friend of theirs. Now, I don't really know what happened on their wedding night, other than my niece ended up in the hospital, heavily hemorrhaging, and..." Eugene suddenly stopped. It seemed as if he suddenly got fed up with being controlled by Paula and blurted out the rest.

"It turned out that my niece was three months pregnant when she arrived in Canada! No wonder my sister begged DD last summer to get her off their hands!

"Mind you, her new husband, even after this fiasco, offered to take her back and to take care of her until the bastard is born. But no! She had to have her own way and refused the offer. So, with Rabbi Salamon's help, she moved somewhere, and I tell you, good riddance to Kira Chopaky!"

Rocky felt the blood rushing to his head. Horrified, with an ashen face, he looked at Eugene, and all choked up, he asked, "Your niece is Kira Chopaky?"

Surprised, Eugene looked at Rocky. "Why, of course? But what is it to you? Do you know her?" Then he slapped his forehead and exclaimed, "Of course, you probably know her from High School."

If Rocky had the strength, he would have been happy to dunk Eugene personally in the Devil's boiling cauldron. But he could only stare and try to breathe, grasping the news about Kira's pregnancy.

"How far ahead was she when you found out?" Rocky finally sputtered.

"I already told you, three months. Why?"

Rocky finally rose and walked out of the restaurant, leaving Eugene with his mouth open and an unpaid bill.

**

Rocky ran all the way home and stumbled into the backyard. Still shaken, he collapsed on the bench by the swimming pool. He welcomed the icy wind as he needed to calm down and gather his wits to face the situation. He noticed Miklos' presence when the man sat down on the bench beside him.

Miklos said, "You look troubled. What's up?"

Rocky mumbled, "I got somebody in trouble when I literally saved her life. Now, she is all alone, and her family thinks the worst of her. And I do not know how to fix this mess."

Miklós replied, "It would help if I knew what you're talking about."

Rocky took a deep breath, then told Miklós about the circumstances of their meeting with Kira last May. "But by the time I called her, she had already left Hungary. Her grandmother mentioned Toronto, so I figured I could find her here. And Dolly promised to help me locate her. Can you imagine how I felt when I saw her last night, right in the same house where I live? And how terribly confusing it was when she fell into the swimming pool, ready to escape me?"

"So, why do you think she wants to avoid you?"

"My best guess is that she wants to avoid being the subject of another rejection in her life. Because I'm pretty sure that she is pregnant with my child. I just learned from her no-good uncle that she arrived pregnant. She only found out about it on the very night of her wedding, which her cousin had arranged for her. Apparently, she ended up in the hospital heavily hemorrhaging, and that's when the doctors told her she was pregnant and that they barely saved the child."

"Now, that's a mess," Miklos said, "but it still doesn't explain why she wouldn't want to see you. unless she wants to keep the child and is afraid, you might want her to get rid of it. Or she believes that you totally want to deny your involvement with her, to begin with."

Rocky shook his head. "Hell, I don't know what I think! I know it is the worst muddle I have ever encountered, and I don't know how to fix it."

Miklós stroked his hair back with one hand, huffed, and said, "Maybe Dolly will help you sort things out with Kira. Women are better suited for such a task than men. But in the meantime, come inside. I'm sure you could also use a little brandy to regain warmth in your veins."

Rocky was happy to follow Miklós back to the house and hoped he was right.

**

Still shaken by Rocky's presence in her new home, which she believed to be a safe place, Kira sat on her bed. *What could I do now? Run? Where? Back to Hungary? No way! How could I face my parents, who believed me to be in a safe place, far away from the constant humiliation and persecution since my father's imprisonment in the late fall of 1956? Being out of the country must be one big load off my parents' minds.*

But her pregnancy had come as an enormous shock to her. It wasn't that she was unaware of the consequences of being sexually involved with anyone, but lately, due to ongoing stress in her life, her periods became unpredictable. In the last six months, before she left Hungary, she had stopped bleeding altogether. The doctors reassured her that it was normal in her continuously stressful situation. And since Thomas broke up with her at least two years ago, she didn't have any sexual relations with anyone, so it was safe to rule out Thomas as her child's father.

Since she tried to block out her extreme experience with Rocky on the cliff last May, it was a wake-up call to find herself pregnant with his child.

She was stroking her slightly bulging belly when she suddenly felt a little motion inside her, as if a little butterfly flipped its wings and, a little later, again. What was it? She wondered. Was it the baby's first movement inside her? Was it sending her a message?

She heard a knock on her door, and, believing it to be Rocky, she said harshly, "Rocky, I don't want to see you. Go away!"

"Kira! It is Dolly. May I come in, please?"

Kira jumped off her bed, opened the door, and hugged Dolly.

They sat in the two armchairs facing her bed. With a conflicting motion, she turned to Dolly and, still caressing her stomach, exclaimed, "The baby just moved! The first time!" Then she said accusingly, "Why didn't you tell me that Rocky lived here too?"

Dolly looked at her sternly. "And what would you have done if I had told you? Run away? Where to? As far as I'm concerned, you're safe here, regardless of who else lives in this house. You live on the third floor, and he lives on the floor below. If you choose to associate with him, that's fine. If not, that's fine, too. So, what's the problem?"

Kira was confused and angry. "What do you mean, what's the problem? And what if he demands I get rid of the baby?"

"He couldn't do that," Dolly replied calmly. "First, I told you already, there is no legal abortion in Canada, and second, he would have to establish paternity before he could dictate anything to you about the baby. Only the mother may decide whether she wants to keep the baby after birth or put it up for adoption. So, relax!"

"But what if he wants to be involved with the baby after its birth, or even worse, taking it away from me, declaring me unsuitable as a mother?"

"That is at least another four or five months away! Many things can happen in those times, so why worry about it?" Dolly said,

"However, it would be only fair for you to talk to Rocky and try to come to a somewhat fair balance since the two of you, in all likelihood, will live in proximity. And let me tell you, I won't let anyone turn my home into a bitter battleground. Do we understand each other?"

Kira nodded. Before she could find her voice, Dolly added, "But I must add to Rocky's defense that when he first arrived, he told me he wanted to find you. He also told me that your last encounter still back in Hungary left him deeply concerned about your well-being, but by the time he could look you up, you already left. The only thing he could learn about you was that you had moved somewhere in Toronto. So, please don't jump to the wrong conclusion about him. At least hear him out. He is downstairs, barely holding up. Can I call him up, or what?"

**

Rocky was standing outside the door. He took a deep breath and knocked. "Kira," he called out, "It's Rocky. May I come in?"

"The door is open," she replied nervously.

Rocky stepped in and stopped. This was the first time he had ever been upstairs, even though he knew there was a two-bedroom unit on the top floor that Wilma had occupied alone, until now. The living room had a skylight, which made it a perfect studio for Wilma's paintings. It still had her canvases leaning against the wall and one on the stand covered up, implying it was a work in progress. But the homey, brightly painted vintage furniture showed a woman's touch. The living room combined the living and dining space and the kitchen. Behind the large living space, the two bedrooms flanking the bathroom, were at the back.

Kira stood in the middle of the living room, looking frightened like a lonely deer caught and paralyzed by a car's headlights on a dark night. She placed her hands on her abdomen as if protecting her unborn.

Rocky walked up and pulled her silently into his arms.

Kira shyly returned the hug and sobbed.

Chapter 23

When Kira and Rocky came downstairs, they joined the lively circle in the formal living room on the main floor. People moved over to make room for them on the large sofa in front of the fireplace.

"So, Miklos, now that we can finally greet you amongst us in person, tell us why the Hungarian Security Service is so adamant about capturing you?" Danny addressed their guest of honor.

"You mean, why do they consider me a great thorn in their side?" Miklos replied with a wicked twinkle in his eyes. "It is simple. I exposed some of the agents they thought were secured in the West. Including Kim Philby."

"I heard about Philby," Rocky pitched in, "since they made a big deal about him in 1963 when he finally surfaced in Moscow. Were there others as well?"

Miklos paused, ensuring he had everyone's attention before he continued. "The Portland Spy Ring incident, perhaps not as widely recognized outside intelligence circles, was a seminal event in the Cold War's shadowy espionage game. In the early sixties, this spy ring, operating from the heart of Britain, passed crucial naval secrets to the Soviet Union.

"Their unmasking resulted from an unprecedented Anglo-American cooperation between MI5, Britain's security service, and the CIA, America's Central Intelligence Agency. This came after *Sniper*, a code-named Soviet defector, revealed that the Admiralty's Underwater Weapons Establishment on Portland Island was compromised. The spy ring's exposure averted potential catastrophic security breaches and exemplified the fragile balance of power during the Cold War. It underscored the era's paranoia, where allies and enemies alike were caught in a perpetual dance of deceit, intelligence, and counterintelligence. I was just one guy in the know. That's all." He ended with modesty.

"Miklos, the modest one! Now that's a switch." George Frank hooted and then turned to Rocky with his right hand extended. "Hello Rocky, I'm George Frank, an old friend of your relative. And," he turned toward the plump, middle-aged woman with raven hair sitting beside her, "this is Yvonne, my wife and right hand." He smiled. "Welcome to our crazy world."

He walked up to Kira and hugged her. "I see that the two of you reconnected already. I'm glad. So, sit down and enjoy the show. We are about to hear the tale of Miklos Görgey and the Hungarian Secret Service."

"Well," Miklos began, "all you need to know is that during the German invasion in nineteen forty-four, I participated in many illegal anti-German activities as an army cadet in the Ludovika Military Academy. It involved shielding army deserters, hiding some American pilots shot down behind the lines and giving a helping hand to Wallenberg, feeding and protecting Jews in Budapest.

"After the war, I became a police officer in Budapest because I believed I could help create a safe, crime-free environment in the capital. Although I wasn't a Communist, during the war, I worked closely with László Sólyom and learned to respect him. He became my immediate superior officer in the police force. Eventually, I became heavily involved with counterespionage and worked out of the newly established Ministry of the Interior, closely with the chief of security, Gabor Peter.

"Then, in the fall of nineteen-forty-nine, overnight, with no explanation, the atmosphere in the Ministry became oppressive and people in high positions, like Laszlo Rajk, who by then became the Minister of Foreign Affair, then Szőnyi, chief of cadres; Szalay, and my boss, Sólyom, one after the other, disappeared. It was rather mysterious until we were called into the ministry one morning for an ultra-secret meeting.

"They bolted the doors of the room before they informed us about the *treason of Laszlo Rajk and his band of vulgar agents* and cited the long list of their crimes, like being the spies of Tito and the imperialists, police informers since their adolescence, and currently organizers of a plot to assassinate Comrade Rákosi and topple the government.

"By then, I'd learned to distinguish the regime's mindset, its need to point the finger at the people in the security business for not finding the traitors in time. And since I had close relatives who fought in the Spanish Civil War with Rajk, I knew that, given the reasons for their close associations, I, too, would be under suspicion.

"That same day, I left the office earlier than usual. But before I left, I put my uniform jacket on the tailor's mannequin that stood in my office and pinned all my medals on its breast with a note: *ALL THIS WASN'T ENOUGH FOR YOU?*

"I went home, waited until it turned dark, grabbed my service revolver and put a handful of extra bullets in my pocket, escaped from the sixth floor. Jumping from one balcony to the floor below, I made my way down carefully. I knew the city better than any members of the AVO commando, and I was also familiar with all the back roads through the mountains to the boggy Fertö Lake bordering Austria.

"Two days later, I was in Austria and soon in Paris. Then I went across the channel to England, where MI5 debriefed me. It was then that I first mentioned an incident when Gabor Peter, as the head of the State Protection Authority— ÁVH, Hungary's secret police, boasted in a rare, reckless drunken moment, how he recruited a British guy in a high-power position, during the thirties in Vienna. And I hoped that his report would have helped raise some suspicion about Philby then."

Rocky interjected into Miklos' musings, "But the Philby case came to light in nineteen-sixty-three. So why would the Hungarian Secret Service and the KGB want to lure you back four years later?"

Miklos leaned forward; his fingers tented in contemplation, a shadow of concern briefly crossing his weathered face. "Good question, my friend," he began, his voice low and measured, betraying a lifetime of navigating treacherous political landscapes. "They must believe I possess knowledge worth the peril of capture. The winds of change are sweeping through Praha, and I suspect they play no small part in this intrigue."

**

The same evening, Rocky walked up to the third-floor apartment, carrying his toothbrush and a book, ready to make himself at home.

Already in a nightgown, Kira stood speechless at the door, with wide eyes. When she found her voice, she demanded. "And what do you think you're doing here, Rocky? I don't remember ever inviting you up here for an overnight party!"

Rocky, looking embarrassed, stuttered, "But, I thought...this afternoon, when—"

"What about this afternoon? We haven't said a word. And we certainly didn't come to any agreement about anything. Or did I miss something?"

"No, but I thought that when you came to me and cried, there was some sort of agreement or at least an acknowledgment between us. I assumed—"

"You assumed what? That crying on your shoulder was a clear sign I would hand the reins over to you for my life? Nobody, you understand; nobody will ever dictate how I should live. That means I will be the only one to decide about my child's future. You understand me?"

Rocky nodded and, for a moment, was tempted to turn around and march downstairs. It didn't look like Kira was in the right frame of mind to discuss anything clearly and logically. He got as far as the door when he turned back and, grabbing Kira by her hands, steered her towards the sofa. He sat beside her and calmly said, "Before you decide to sentence me to oblivion in our child's life, let me tell you how I see things."

Kira raised her hand, ready to interject. Rocky ignored it and continued. "I know what some of your relatives think. I spoke to your uncle Eugene this afternoon, and the dear soul generously gave me his version of the truth. He suspects the child belongs to Lajos. I know better. You broke up with him at least two years ago. I can count. The child is mine. And," he raised his voice, "I'm glad. I always wanted to have children."

"Even under these circumstances?" Kira whispered.

"We don't always choose the circumstances, but when it happens, we have choices. And let me tell you, Kira Chopaky, I'm glad you're carrying my child. Whether you believe me, but that's the truth. I couldn't have chosen a more upstanding, decent person to be my child's mother than you."

"What about Speedy?"

"What about her? It's true that we have become friends lately, but I would never choose her to be my soul mate if that's what you're wondering about. Speedy is like a racehorse. She needs constant excitement in her life and must win at all costs. Could you trust her with a child? She wouldn't have the time and the patience for one. And I want to make sure that the mother of my child is a person of dignity and love."

"I'm not sure I can love you, Rocky."

"But you can love our child, and that, for the time being, is enough for me. And I'll be happy if we can become friends. I promise not to put any demand on you, and in exchange, all I want is a place in my child's life. You know where to find me. If you need me for anything, Kira. Good night."

And he walked out of the room.

**

The following week, Rocky was too busy to go to work after school. He showed up early Saturday morning, and just as he expected, D.D. was waiting for him at the door.

"Come to my office," D.D. said.

Rocky followed him. D.D. pointed to the chair across from his desk, and Rocky sat down, waiting for the storm. He didn't have to wait long.

"I understand you spoke with Eugene about Kira," D.D. said.

"If you mean Eugene admitted his niece is none other than Kira Chopaky, my former classmate from High School, then yes, we had a conversation about her. Is that a problem?"

"Well, that depends on what you know about her. She is trash who came to Canada knowing she was pregnant by heaven only knows whom, and she tricked us into finding her a husband here so she could stay. No matter how you cut it, she is here on false pretenses. Now I understand why her mother begged me to move heaven and earth to get her out of there."

Rocky looked at him with great disdain and steady determination.

D.D. averted his eyes and said, "Why are you looking at me like that?"

"Like what?"

"Like you could murder me?"

"Do I? Let's see. You called me into your office to inform me about your opinion of Kira Chopaky, whom you have known for only a few short months. I've known her since nineteen sixty. By the way, why is my opinion of her any of your business? And why is that relevant to my working here?"

"Of course, it matters to whom I hire to work for me. It is a matter of trust."

"Since when is my performance related to who I know and what my personal relationship with or opinion of them is?"

"All right," D.D. snapped, "let's cut to the nitty-gritty. Judging by your attitude, you don't agree with my opinion of my wife's slutty cousin."

"Damn right, I don't." Rocky stood up and stepped closer to the desk. "You know nothing about her and her circumstances."

"But you do? Pray tell me all!"

Rocky shook his head. "Why? So, you could twist my words and turn it against her? If you knew half of what Kira and her family had endured in the last many years, you would be ashamed to talk about her like this."

"You know I could easily fire you for insubordination, right?"

Rocky laughed. "Insubordination? What of your orders did I refuse to carry out that would make you fire me?"

"I'm sure I can find something," D.D. muttered. "For instance, I could report you to Immigration, saying you tried to get employment without a legal work permit. Somehow, I doubt a person arriving with a student visa from Hungary would be given a working permit in Canada!"

Rocky smiled. "And the joke would be on you, DD, since the law clearly states that it is the employer's duty to check before they hire someone. If the authorities scratch it further, they would find most of your workers are illegals, all paid cash under the table. The tax department will happily collect all the money as a back payment."

"Look, don't try to pull the wool over my eyes," D.D. snapped, with a flicker of fear in his eyes. "I know that people coming from the Communist countries with a Visitor's or Student Visa cannot get a work permit here in Canada."

"And that would be true if I were only a Hungarian citizen. However, I'm also a British Subject, with a British passport, so I don't need a work permit here in Canada."

"That's it!" D.D. roared, "You're fired. As of this minute, you are no longer working here. And if you have any of your personal belongings here, too bad, you may not return to the shop to claim them."

"And how will you stop me from claiming my belongings, DD? And why is it so important for you to get rid of me in such a hurry? Could it be that I might know too much about your dirty business practices and just found out that you could not silence me that easily?"

D.D. reached for the top drawer of his desk. Rocky jumped over the desk and slammed the drawer in D.D.'s wrists. "Whatever you have there, don't pull it out. I'm willing to come to a peaceful agreement with you. If you leave Kira alone, I'll leave you in peace. But watch it, bastard, as I'll keep my eyes and ears open, and one harmful word about the girl, and you will have the Tax department and the safety board checking on your operation. Not to mention immigration for hiring illegal workers. But I will save you the trouble. You don't need to fire me, as I'm quitting."

At the door, Rocky turned back and said, "By the way, tell Eugene that he is nothing but a dirty scumbag, willing to sell his soul for a few pennies."

**

That evening, Rocky marched into Dolly's parlor. "From now on, I'll be responsible for Kira's expenses," he said.

Dolly nodded, "Since I know you quit the Diamond Industry earlier today, how are you planning to do that?"

"By the sacred beard of Saint Nepomuk," Rocky snapped, using Dolly's favorite expression when she was under stress. "News travels fast around here, especially if it is bad. But don't worry, Dolly; I'll manage. And for now, I'll pay for both our room and board."

Dolly shrugged. "Fine with me, my boy. But I have one more question. Did you mention to DD that you're the father of Kira's baby?"

"No! I didn't. It isn't any of his business. I just told him that if he knew what Kira and her family went through the last many years, he wouldn't talk about her like that. What I don't understand is Eugene's attitude... Because he is perfectly aware of Kira's situation. So why would he be such a rat, selling out his own flesh and blood?"

Dolly said, "He might be in debt, owning DD too much money to dare to contradict him. Or DD might know something about him that could land him in trouble with the law. Associated with DD is never a good idea. Far too many of his friends turned up dead in the gutter!" she crossed herself and added, "But you didn't hear this from me, of course!"

Dolly liked how Rocky rose to accept his responsibility. It showed a strong and noble character. But she kept her financial agreement with Desmond Diamond to herself. There was no reason to let any of them know that she still demanded payment from D.D. and, of course, from Ernest Gordon himself. These people did not know about the medical and hospital bills that an endangered pregnancy like Kira's could ultimately amount to.

Chapter 24

In the early morning at the end of November, a chill hung in the air, the kind that seeps into your bones and heralds the onset of winter. The sky, a pale wash of grey, promised daylight but held back the sun's warmth, casting a subdued light over everything. Still clinging to the remnants of sleep, Danny opened the door to find an official-looking tall stranger framed against this bleak morning. The stranger's breath formed small clouds of vapor in the cold air as he spoke, further emphasizing the unexpected nature of his visit.

"Hello, can I talk to Mrs. Gordon?" the stranger asked, his voice cutting through the silence of the dawn with an unsettling formality.

"Who?" Danny mumbled, rubbing his hands together for warmth, not just from sleepiness but also from the sudden intrusion of the cold, both physical and metaphorical, into the warmth of their home.

The man, seemingly unaffected by the cold, consulted the file in his hand, his demeanor patient yet insistent, as if accustomed to dealing with confusion. "Mrs. Kira Gordon. I believe she lives here," he said, his tone softening slightly, perhaps in recognition of the early hour.

Danny stepped outside, the door closing behind him with a click that seemed too loud in the morning. He was now fully awake, the cold clarity of the situation settling in as he faced the stranger.

"Baroness Lipnitsky, the proprietor of the house, is not home presently, and I'm instructed to refer any business dealings with her tenants to her directly. If you leave your business card with me, I'll ensure she contacts you as soon as possible."

As the man reached into his pocket and produced a card, Danny noticed the stark contrast between the warmth of their home and the cold, uncertain situation now at their doorstep, underscored by the crisp, unforgiving morning air.

Danny read the card and said, "Mr. Ewan McGregor, from Immigration, Baroness Lipnitsky, will call you and sort out whatever is needed to be sorted out." He stepped back inside and closed the door.

Dolly was just arriving when McGregor was heading to the street. To avoid bumping into him, she slipped into the yard at the side, curious to find out from Danny what the man with the briefcase wanted. She hated people coming to her house uninvited, mostly trying to sell something she didn't want or harassing her or one of her borders.

Danny turned the business card over to her. "He was enquiring about Kira. I do not know what trouble she is in, but a person directly from Immigration can't be good news, right?"

"Damn right, it doesn't," Dolly muttered as she marched into her office to call the Rabbi. "I wonder which fucker reported Kira to the authorities?" As she waited for the call to connect, the weight of Kira's situation pressed upon her. The late 1960s immigration laws were a labyrinth, and Kira was caught in its most confounding maze. Dolly knew the coming conversation would not just be about legal strategies but about forging a path of hope through seemingly insurmountable barriers.

Rabbi Salamon arrived, his brow furrowed in thought, he brought a dossier of notes on similar cases, insights into immigration law, and anecdotes of the Hungarian community's experiences with Canadian immigration authorities.

"I wonder who reported Kira to Immigration?" Rabbi Salamon speculated while cleaning his glasses with his large handkerchief, "It could have been DD's wife, with her mother's support. They are a rabid bunch, capable of placing their so-called social standing above human decency," he grumbled.

"Damn the bitches! I bet the women placed the call without the prior knowledge of either DD or Earnest! We better tell Rocky about this, as he is our strongest card." Dolly fumed. "But I don't think we should mention anything to Kira yet, do you?"

"But we have no choice." Rabbi Salamon shook his bushy head. "The Immigration Officer will insist on seeing her in person. But we could insist that the meeting occur here and at our convenience."

"Good idea. And have a doctor standing by in case Kira has a panic attack. She is still very fragile, and in her current condition, any additional stress could risk her pregnancy. We just have to ensure she understands before the interview takes place that, she has our full support. Including Rocky's."

"Well, we just have to wait and see how flexible our Mr. Ewan McGregor from Immigration can be!"

**

It took the doctor's note, referring to Kira's current delicate medical condition, to finally convince Mr. McGregor of the importance of having the interview conducted on the premises of Dolly's home.

The hours leading up to Mr. McGregor's arrival were a flurry of activity and hushed conversations, each moment thick with anticipation. Dolly, Rabbi Salamon, and Rocky moved through the house purposefully, their actions underscored by a palpable tension. Amidst this, Kira was adrift in a sea of conflicting emotions, her thoughts a tumultuous mix of fear, gratitude, and a fragile thread of hope.

She watched her friends and her newfound family rally around her, each offering strength in their own way. Yet, beneath the surface of their busy preparations, a silent understanding passed between them, an acknowledgment of the gravity of the situation. In these quiet moments, as Kira observed the determined set of Dolly's jaw, the worry etched into Rabbi Salamon's brow, and the protective glint in Rocky's eyes, the full weight of what was to come settled around her like a cloak.

They were preparing for battle, not with swords and shields, but with words and wills, ready to defend one of their own from an unseen adversary. As the clock ticked away, the atmosphere in the house grew thick with a mix of dread and determination, a testament to the bond that had formed between them all. It was a bond that Kira had never expected to find, yet now clung to as her only lifeline in a world that seemed determined to sweep her away.

Dolly ushered Mr. McGregor into the living room and offered him a chair, he pulled the file out of his briefcase and introduced himself. "My name is Mr. McGregor, and as you already know, I'm from immigration. I'm here to ask Mrs. Gordon a couple of questions. I promise to be short and as gentle as possible. After looking around, I see many people here," he declared, "and I needed to know whether it was alright with her to talk in front of these people. I also need to assess whether her English is good enough to conduct the interview without an interpreter."

Kira looked at Dolly and Rabbi Salamon, then at Rocky. She shook her head. "I'm all right to talk to you in their presence. They are my friends, and I know they have the best intentions for me. And let's try this without an interpreter first. However, if we need one, Dolly, I understand, is a qualified interpreter certified by the United Nations.

"And if I need help with some words, I'm sure all the others will pitch in. They do it anyway." She laughed and sat down on the sofa. "The entire household has taken it upon themselves to correct my English. One of these days, I expect even Dolly's little white terrier will stop me in mid-sentence and correct my pronunciation."

They all laughed at the little terrier sleeping at Dolly's feet.

Dolly smiled. "It is for your benefit. We force you to speak English here most of the time. The sooner you learn, the better off you are."

After everyone introduced themselves, the officer asked Kira, "How are you, my dear? How far along are you with your pregnancy?"

She smiled. "I'm in my sixth month."

Mr. McGregor opened his file. "You arrived in Canada as Kira Chopaky, age twenty-one, on June 30th, 1967, with a three-month non-renewable visitor's visa. Correct?"

"Yes. It is."

"And you understood then that your visitor's visa was not renewable. Correct?"

"Yes."

"And six weeks later, you were married to Mr. Gordon."

"Correct."

"A day after the wedding, you ended up in a hospital severely hemorrhaging, and you claim that this was the first time you knew you were three months pregnant, obviously not by your husband."

Kira nodded.

"My job is to determine whether you lied to the authorities when you claimed to be a visitor when you arrived, already pregnant and whether you conned Mr. Gordon to marry you so you can stay here legally, without informing him about your pregnancy. Do you understand the charges against you?"

Kira felt as though she were standing at the edge of a precipice, the outcome of this conversation capable of tipping her into the unknown. Though spoken with a professional detachment, McGregor's questions seemed to Kira like probes into the most tender parts of her soul. With each inquiry, she felt more exposed, her carefully constructed defenses crumbling under the weight of her reality.

In the silence that followed each of Mr. McGregor's questions, Kira's mind raced. She thought about the life she had left behind— its challenges and its few joys—and the new life she had begun to build in Canada, a life now threatened by the specter of deportation. The fear of being sent back, of being judged not just by Mr. McGregor but by an entire system that couldn't possibly understand the complexities of her journey, was overwhelming. She feared not just for herself but for the future of the child she carried, a child who represented a new beginning but now, perhaps, a vulnerability.

As she answered Mr. McGregor's questions, Kira tried to convey the facts of her situation and the emotional truth of her experience. She wanted him to see her not as a case file but as a human being shaped by circumstances within and beyond her control. She spoke of her past, family, and hopes with a frankness that surprised even her. It was as if she had nothing to hide, faced with the possibility of losing everything.

Yet, amidst the fear and vulnerability, Kira felt a flicker of something else—a quiet strength born from her trials. She realized that no matter the outcome of this interview, she had survived far worse. This realization did not diminish her fear but lent her a certain steadiness, a resolve to face whatever came with dignity.

Kira looked into Mr. McGregor's eyes, searching for a hint of understanding, a sign that her words would transcend the barrier of officialdom to touch something human in him. At that moment, she was not just a subject of immigration law but a person with a story, a life marked by struggle and resilience.

Kira, overwhelmed, frantically looked around and said, "No, Mr. McGregor, I didn't lie to anyone. When I arrived, I was not aware I was pregnant. The first few weeks before and after my arrival were so hectic that I didn't pay much attention to my body. I assumed my morning sickness was only my usual nervous reaction to stress. I've had this condition since I was fourteen years old. And my periods were rather irregular, anyway, because of that. So, no, I did not know at all." Kira plucked a napkin from the container on the center table and began twirling it. "And it was certainly not me who enticed Mr. Gordon to marry me!"

Mr. McGregor looked at his file and frowned. "I see here that Mr. Gordon confirmed that although it took him by surprise to find out that you were already pregnant with someone else's child, he still didn't want to lay charges against you. He was more reluctant to discuss this case with us than your other relatives."

The last remark suggested disapproval, although it was unclear whether Mr. McGregor objected to the relatives' zeal or Mr. Gordon's lack of eagerness to force the issue.

"So, whose idea was for you to marry Mr. Gordon?"

"It was Mr. Gordon himself who kept pursuing me after my cousin's wedding, frequently taking me to expensive restaurants and dancing. He was very persistent, and it also seemed to make his mother happy—she was visiting from Hungary at the time. Mind you, he also had my relatives' approval. They explained that marriage to Mr. Gordon was an alternative for requesting refugee status here for me."

"Were you planning to do that, Mrs. Gordon?"

Kira swallowed and nodded. "When I arrived, a few people tried to convince me to go directly to the authorities and claim refugee status. Because of my father, a person convicted during a political trial by a Communist country, I would qualify. A friend of my father living in Hamilton has an acquaintance, a Canadian War Veteran and a great admirer of people involved in the Hungarian revolution, who offered to help me with the details."

"And what happened to that idea? Why didn't you go along with it?"

"My uncle Eugene and my aunt Paula both decided that it would be a terrible mistake. It would harm my parents back in Hungary if I claimed refugee status here. They convinced me the only way I could stay in Canada legally was to marry a Canadian citizen. And since I didn't know any better, I followed the idea. I couldn't live with myself if I had harmed my parents, even inadvertently."

"Did you have any feelings for Mr. Gordon at all?"

Kira looked at Mr. McGregor with a twisted smile. "Have you met him in person?"

He nodded and waited for Kira to continue.

"He is a good-looking bastard, isn't he? Every girl's dream: tall, slim, wavy black hair and black eyes, a charming Clark Gable incarnation. He practically swept me off my feet. And his mother, a nice little old lady, reminded me of my beloved grandmother, was delighted with my company. It was easy to say *Yes*. How would I have known that he married me only because..." Kira thought...*Because he never said no to his mother, who disapproved of his long-standing German girlfriend? Because she believed me to be a nice Jewish girl?*

Still humiliated by the whole mess, Kira wondered if the man before her could understand her complicated situation. Even she had difficulty understanding why she insisted on having the marriage consummated after her new husband admitted he only married her because it made his mother happy, and that added more insult to her injury by blatantly telling her she wasn't even his type. Was it a simple feminine pride? True, no men had ever rejected her so blatantly before! Men whistled in approval, trying to get her attention back at home, on the street, or in her high school hallway. Did she just want to prove to herself that her sexuality and femininity were intact?

Kira blurted out, "Sir, I'm absolutely certain that *the* furthest thing from my mind was to worry about my marriage annulled and, therefore, take away the only way to legitimize my immigration standing."

Mr. McGregor's final question: "What would happen to you if you were deported back to Hungary?"

Her glance at Dolly, Rabbi Salamon, and Rocky offered a fleeting moment of solace—their presence a silent testament to the support and understanding found in this unexpected family. Yet, the fear of what might come, of the possibility that she could be torn from this semblance of home and security, sent a shiver down her spine. The thought of returning to Hungary, to face an uncertain but undoubtedly grim fate, tightened the anxiety in her stomach.

Kira's thoughts raced back to her homeland, the oppressive atmosphere that suffocated her every ambition and dream. She remembered the stifling fear of living under a regime that viewed her family with suspicion, her every move scrutinized. The memory of leaving behind everything familiar, embarking on a journey fueled by desperation and the faint glimmer of hope for a better life, was as vivid as if it had happened yesterday. The sensation of being trapped between two worlds, neither fully belonging to her old home nor her new, enveloped her in a cloak of loneliness that was hard to shake off.

"I would rather commit suicide!" Kira screamed. "Do you know what it feels like to be tied to my father's fate? To be a hostage?" Her last few words were articulated in small staccatos, spitting them as if they were part of her broken soul. Overwhelmed, she stood up and, blinded by her tears, rapidly escaped without excusing herself.

Nobody moved as Kira's outburst froze everyone to their seats.

After a deep sigh, Mr. McGregor stood up and suggested, "She obviously needs time to pull herself together. Why don't I come back either tomorrow or the day after and finish this? Is everyone here in agreement?"

Rabbi Salamon nodded and pulled out his notebook. He checked the date and said, "Tomorrow, about the same time, will work for me."

Chapter 25

Rocky watched Kira as she ran out of the room. He wondered what would happen now, when the phone in the hallway rang. At first, nobody noticed it until Danny came out from the kitchen to answer it. Then he shouted, "Rocky, this is for you!"

"Take a message, Danny. This is not the right time for me to talk to anybody," Rocky said.

"No can do, my boy," Danny shouted back. "She said it is urgent, as she is only here for a few more hours. Her plane leaves close to midnight. She said she must see you right away."

"Who is it?" Rocky replied, annoyed.

Danny listened in and said, "Speedy, you idiot." Then he lifted his hand apologetically and said, "Sorry, that's what she said to tell you."

Rocky walked to the hallway to pick up the phone. "Hello there," he said, "you couldn't have chosen a worse time to call. But where are you?"

"In Toronto. Haven't you noticed in the Varsity News that our club is participating in the international track and field competition? Our return flight to Budapest leaves close to midnight, and I sneaked away from our coach—doubling as our prison guard, for a couple of hours. Can you come over to the International Student Centre right now?"

"Jesus, Speedy, I can't. Not right now. We are dealing with a very delicate matter that must be handled immediately. I'll try to meet you there in an hour. I have a lot to tell you. So, wait for me, all right?" Rocky, his determination unwavering, returned to the living room, ready to face the situation head-on but found that the meeting had adjourned.

- 189 -

**

Rocky jumped into a cab driving by the house and directed it to the corner of St. George's and College Street. He paid the driver and ran into the International Student Centre. He found Speedy on the top floor, sitting on a worn sofa, reading a Playboy magazine.

"Ah, a forbidden fruit," commented Rocky sarcastically.

Speedy looked up and smiled. "What's your problem? They have excellent articles. It is a magazine to feed the eyes and the brain simultaneously. I had a hell of a hard time getting rid of coach Wilmos. He insisted on accompanying me here. But in the end, I made him disappear. Puff!" she said and, twirling her fingers, made a snapping noise.

"Ha, ha, funny! Don't tell me you locked him in the washroom. But, no, really, I don't really want to know what you did to the unfortunate fellow. Anyway, when you called, a guy from Immigration was there to interview Kira. Her dearly beloved relatives called the authorities on her, claiming that she was here illegally. It was a few uncomfortable hours, and it is still not over. The hearing is to be resumed tomorrow afternoon. Kira is a mess, and I just hope we can get her into a better frame of mind before tomorrow's meeting."

"Good luck with that, my boy. Seriously, believe me when I wish my old friend the best. Even if she still hates my guts."

"I hope we will convince the guy from Immigration that Kira was a victim of circumstances and that she has all the qualifications to meet the standards to claim refugee status here. Otherwise, she will be deported back to Hungary."

"She could have done that as soon as she landed. Why didn't she?"

"Because Kira believes that by asking for refugee status, she will jeopardize her parents' well-being back in Hungary. Apparently, her cousin and her idiot uncle convinced her of that when she arrived. Do you think they are right? Would her parents be punished for that?"

Speedy turned serious. "You know just as well that the entire system is based on its unpredictability. Especially now, after the so-called *unfortunate and truly fucked up* mission getting your uncle back to Hungary!"

"Well, it was unfortunate and fucked up only from the Hungarians' point of view. We considered it a successful mission by preventing it from happening. As a result, all Hungarian agents directly involved with the mission, both in Washington and Toronto, were caught and arrested. All employees of the Hungarian Consulate in Toronto and the Hungarian Embassy in Ottawa had been called back in a hurry. For over a week, there was only one low-level secretary remaining in the Ottawa office, whose only job was to inform callers that both the Embassy and the Consulate in Toronto were not open for business. No explanation, just that. To add more excitement, Mr. Kovács from the Toronto office has also disappeared. No sight of him."

"What did you do to him?"

"Me? Speedy, are you out of your mind? I haven't seen him since he asked me right at this very spot whether I sent the card with the request to my uncle in Washington to meet me here! But I can tell you about the Halloween party when the two Bulgarian agents got busted! That was fun!"

"Later, my boy, later. I still have lots to tell you. Our club came to this international track and field competition on the same MALEV flight, jam-packed with the newly appointed embassy and consulate staffers. I talked to most of them—they all seemed bright and reform-minded. I guess the *Powers in Hungary* suddenly needed to demonstrate to the Canadians and the USA that they were not tied too strongly to the strings of aprons of the KGB-run Soviet System. Anyway, the way I read the current situation is that this latest international embarrassment will actually give your father a breather, enough time for him to make arrangements to leave."

"Only you can help to arrange that," Rocky replied,, with hope.

Speedy pointed at her stuffed backpack by her feet and said hesitantly, "I don't know about that."

"Speedy, what are you planning to do? You can't be serious?" Rocky looked at her, shocked by the sudden suspicion.

"That I would contemplate defecting? Can you just picture the headlines? *Truth revealed by the defecting daughter and star athlete about the ongoing physical and emotional abuse the athletes must face daily within the Soviet Block! The heroic war hero who cut his own throat so he couldn't betray his comrades during the war, falling from grace and becoming a pariah because his daughter defected to the West!*"

"Speedy! Don't talk rubbish!" Why the sudden urge now for you to jump the boat? Has anything happened that I should know about? I need you to return and deliver a letter to my father explaining about Kira and the baby."

"The truth is, Rocky, that the whole team got sick and tired of being verbally and physically abused by our trainer, Wilmos. And no matter how many times we tried to complain, nothing was done— nobody cared. As long as we were the winning team, Uncle Wilmos could literally get away with murder. So, I convinced our team members to lose this competition deliberately."

"Now, that must have hurt Uncle Wilmos' ego!"

"Never mind his ego! But his pocket and his reputation! And all the perks that come with it! They might even fire him as a coach! Or worse, accuse him of being part of the conspiracy and send him to the Gulag! So, he is busy finding the person responsible for the *deliberate sabotage by lowering the team morale.* He questioned all of us separately, and he told me I was lucky to have my father in that position, or he would be tempted to charge me along with the whole team with sabotage."

"I don't believe he would dare to do anything harmful to you or any of the others. And anyway, as I mentioned, I need you to deliver this letter to my father."

"Does that mean you accept I'm no longer the enemy?"

Rocky stared at her for a minute before he replied. "Now that you mention it! Would you be willing to come home with me and try to reconcile with Kira? I know how difficult it must be for you to face her after all these long years, and I wouldn't ask you if it were not so important for Kira's mental state! That would be the best way to boost her morale, especially tomorrow's meeting with the Immigration officer."

Speedy looked at Rocky, white as a sheet, her mouth trembling from the sudden rush of emotion. She put her hands beside her on the armchair for support. "Rocky! I can't! Really, I can't!" And she seriously doubted she could come up with any excuse for spreading all the ugly rumors, playing all the dirty tricks, and the daily torments to which she exposed Kira during their high school years. Could Kira ever forgive Speedy? And she wondered if her role in getting Kira her passport would at least amount to something.

**

Speedy tried very hard not to remember that rainy, cold day a year ago in April, the very day when one of her best friends, Johnny, was laid to rest. And the suicide note he sent to all his friends, requesting them to make up for their parents' deeds to find and help their parents' victims…

But she could hardly turn down the invitation for tea at Olga's home after the funeral and was surprised to find Frank there as well. Olga, the current secretary of Comrade Barath, the Minister of The Interior, and Frank, his chauffeur, were formerly serving Colonel Alex Chopaky in the same capacity way back before the uprising. Speedy recalled first meeting them when she was close friends with Kira Chopaky. She observed them now at the funeral, wiping away their tears, mourning Johnny more deeply than his own father did.

While Olga served Speedy tea and cake, Frank went straight to the point. "Speedy, don't you think it is time to change your attitude toward Kira Chopaky?"

Speedy could only stare and wait for whatever might follow. She didn't have to wait long.

"Johnny sent both Olga and me a copy of his farewell suicide letter, so it should not be a total surprise that we're aware of his request to you to help find and rescue some of your parents' intended victims. I suggest you begin with your old childhood friend, Kira Chopaky."

"My help? I can't even go near her; she would not trust me as far as she could throw me," Speedy sputtered.

"And, I might add, for a good reason. You humiliated her in public during your high school years more times than I could count."

"How would you know about that?"

"Girl, I had the displeasure of witnessing you publicly shaming poor Kira many times while I waited for you outside at your high school. I was truly ashamed of you then! I would have left you at the curb had it not been my official duty to pick you up then. So, I suggest you make up for it."

"But how?" Speedy stammered, tears flowing down her cheeks.

"By arranging it to get her passport. Much sooner than later, as she too is suicidal!"

"How do you know this? When was the last time you've been in contact with the Chopakys?"

Olga replied softly, "We have other means of learning about their current state." She pulled a few typewritten pages out of her purse and handed them over to Speedy.

Speedy hesitated, took them, and sat down on one of Olga's big comfortable armchairs. "What is this?"

"Go ahead, read them," Olga instructed. "You'll learn more than you had bargained for." She filled Speedy's teacup and shoved the plate filled with slices of her famous honey cakes toward her on the table. "Take your time," she said. leaving Speedy alone with the revealing documents.

Strictly confidential.

Agent reports on the Chopaky family.

Agent: codenamed Tinodi, identified as M. K. dentist. (He lived in the same cell with Alex Chopaky for two years. After his release, he often met Alex Chopaky and his family at his dental practice on Maestro Street, where he treated the family's teeth. They've been in a friendly relationship the whole time. They recruited him in early December 1963.)

Although Speedy had been aware of people being recruited to spy and report on others, this was the first time she had a document proving it. She forced herself to read on, finding it painful to learn about her former childhood friend's desperation as she revealed them to a person she believed to be a close and intimate family friend.

Judging by the thorough report, the agent met regularly with his handler from the beginning of December 1963, each time choosing a different location, whether in the handler's office, in a public place, or occasionally, directly at the Agent's home. Each time, they gave the agent a detailed task. In Tinódi's case, it was to deepen the personal connection with Chopaky, requesting him to visit them regularly at their home, to appraise when, where, and whom amongst the other former prisoners Chopaky had met with and the topics of their conversations.

The agent verbally informed later that Chopaky still owes him 1000.00Ft for the dentist fee, and they more than likely assumed that the agent was there hoping to collect. When the money didn't come up during the conversation, the Chopakys became friendlier. He assumed that the reason Chopaky had difficulty coughing up the money they owed him for their dental fee was that Chopaky, currently working at the Telephone Company, was paid very little, and they had to watch every penny they spent.

The agent's last report two weeks earlier centred mostly on Kira while he treated her at his clinic.

Kira told me her second cousin invited her to Canada for several months. She admitted that she already applied for her passport but, given their circumstances, wasn't at all sure she would get it. I asked her what her options were. Her hopes and plans for her future? She broke down and admitted that she felt hopeless. In Hungary, without higher education, she could only get low-paying menial work, and the atmosphere at her current job, as a lowly clerk at a Furniture distribution company, was so poisonous that she feared unless she got the passport in the next couple of weeks, she could no longer go on living. I tried to cheer her up by asking her, in that case, why should I spend all this time and energy fixing up her teeth just to flaunt them in the coffin? She originally came to me with a diagnosis including at least seven fillings, as it was obvious her mother could not get a job during Alex's imprisonment, which included medical and dental insurance.

The handler's comment sent chills down Speedy's spine:

1. *Determine whether Kira Chopaky's request for a passport conflicts with the interest of the State.*

2. *Being suicidal, refer Kira Chopaky ASAP to the Bureau of Youth Protection.*

The report is marked URGENT and will be sent directly to the Minister of Interior.

Signed: Colonel Sz.

Speedy stopped reading here and with tears in her eyes looked at Olga who had returned to the room. "Have you seen this one?"

"Yes, I have."

"Are there any other copies of this?"

"As far as I know, it is the only one."

"Did you present it to the Minister already?"

"No. As soon as it had arrived, I pulled it and filed it with all the others I deemed to keep in my possession."

Speedy nodded. "That will give me time to act. I'll let you know if there is any development. In the meantime, keep the fire stoking." She nervously gobbled up the slice of cake, downed the tea, and ran out of Olga's apartment as fast as she could.

The next day, she arrived on her bicycle, carrying a backpack, a good half an hour before the passport office opened for business. She knocked on the door, ignoring the sign and the middle-aged, plump, graying woman dressed in police uniform vigorously pointing at the correct opening time.

The policewoman finally lost her patience, yanked open the door, and growled at Speedy. "What's your hurry? Can't you see it is too early? Come back in half an hour!"

She attempted to shut the door on Speedy's face, but Speedy showed her left foot into the opening, forcing the woman to back up. Speedy entered, and locking the door behind her.

Still backing up between fear and confusion, the woman asked, "What do you want?"

Trying to be less intimidating, Speedy turned on her charming smile. "I'm here to find out if my good friend Kira Chopaky has already sent in her passport application."

After the woman managed to get back inside her cubicle, she sat behind her desk. "And who might you be, asking that question?"

Speedy looked around, checking for other signs of life in the office, but there were none. She reached in her backpack and pulled out a package of Chesterfield cigarettes, a bottle of French cognac, and a large box of Belgian chocolate, placing them in front of the woman.

"Oh, how clumsy I am!" Speedy claimed. "I forgot to introduce myself! I'm Mary Bogár, and my father, Croaky Colonel, is the head of the Internal Police Force. Kira was one of my best childhood friends, and she had a rare opportunity to visit relatives in the West. Getting her the expedited passport is a surprise gift from me. So, would you mind checking it to see if she applied for one recently?"

The woman, looking at the luxurious gifts in front of her, drooled but appeared hesitant to take what was obviously a bribe. She got up from her chair, walked to her office door, and shut it firmly behind them. Then she walked back to her desk, reached toward the rejected pile of applications, pulled out the top one, and apologized. "Sorry about this oversight! Just let me use the right stamp, and I promise to send it to her with my approval and compliments."

Speedy saw her gifts suddenly disappear into the deep bottom of the drawer by the woman's feet. Before she left the office, Speedy said, "In about two days, then?" She waited until the officer nodded. "Thanks a million. I'll never forget you!"

The woman replied, "I rather you did, my dear. Because nothing unusual happened here before nine am, except I came in early to make myself a cup of espresso before my shift." And she winked at Speedy and, miming, closed her mouth with an invisible zipper.

Speedy chuckled.

**

Rocky said. "Do you really hate Kira so much that you refuse to help her and me? Because by now, it is the same thing. That girl will not be happy till she gets reunited with you. At one time, she was your best friend, almost soul mate. Don't refuse me, please! She needs to trust me again. I need her to be strong and happy! I don't want my child to be raised by a miserable, broken person." Rocky was in tears by now.

Rocky would never know what it felt for Speedy to hear him say those words about Kira.

"So, how are you meeting up with your team?" Rocky asked. "Won't you get in trouble taking off, with your belongings, without a word?"

"William, our coach, will be sore but relieved when he sees me an hour before the plane takes off. Losing the competition was bad enough. He can't afford to lose me as well. So, let's go, Rocky, and make nice with Kira before I lose my nerve."

Chapter 26

Rocky grabbed Speedy's backpack and they left the International Student Centre. It was cold, wet, and dark outside. They flagged a taxi, directing it to Dolly's house. Speedy tried to lift the mood by probing Rocky about whether he experienced any emotional longings for the *old country*.

"Like what?" Rocky looked at her, wondering if she lost her mind. "Other than a few people, like my dad, old Betty, or Father Tibor?"

Speedy teased Rocky. "How about our savior, the great creator of the Gulyas Communism in Hungary, Janos Kadar?"

"Now I'm convinced that you really lost your mind, Speedy. As if you didn't know it had happened with a large amount of Western financial aid."

"You're no fun, Rocky! I'm trying to keep your mind off unpleasant things to come, and you must ruin it with reality. Don't you remember, back home, when we gathered in the local café every time the Illés group released a new record? It felt like a small rebellion, a way to breathe fresh air. Or whenever we talked about Puskás, it wasn't just football—it was about remembering our glory days, about holding onto something purely Hungarian amidst all the chaos."

Speedy remembered the uproar back home when Hungary's water polo team clinched the gold in Tokyo. It was more than just a victory; it was a testament to Hungarian spirit, a beacon of hope that even in the darkest times, they could still shine on the world stage.

Rocky wasn't in the mood to reminisce about the good old days. All he could concentrate on was how he would pull off the next half-hour, bringing Kira and Speedy together. Luckily, the cab pulled into the driveway, cutting Rocky's intended sharp remark short.

"Speedy, I'm sorry, but that matters nothing to me anymore! And just for your information, I never attended an Illes concert, as I had no time or even money to spend on tickets or get drunk in a local pub while discussing politics, sport, or music."

**

Kira awoke full of energy and hungry like a wolf. Someone rapped. She said, "Come in." Rocky opened her bedroom door and asked whether she was up and ready to have visitors. She nodded, he entered,, but not alone. Speedy was with him!

Speedy came close to her bed and sat down. Without saying a word, she bent down and hugged Kira tight, just as she used to when they were still close friends. She whispered, "Kira, I'm so very sorry!" Then she burst into tears, and cried together.

Rocky said, "Kira, please forgive her. She is not a bad person. Her father forced her to do all those awful things to you. I know she will try to make up for all the pain she has caused you. She has already helped you get your passport, and mine too…"

Before Kira could respond, Speedy gently touched her stomach and felt the baby kicking. Then she smiled through her tears and whispered, "Remember how we used to come up with names for our future children? You insisted on naming your first-born Adam. It has such a noble ring, don't you think so? I hope you'll let me see him and play with him sometime."

Then, after Speedy hugged her again, Rocky led her out of the room.

As the door closed behind them, Kira remained seated, her gaze fixed on the intricate patterns of the worn rug beneath her feet. The room, now silent, seemed to echo with the remnants of the conversation, each word heavy with implications for her future. Speedy's name ignited a flurry of emotions within her, a tumultuous blend of anger, hurt, and an unexpected flicker of hope.

Kira's mind drifted back to their school years, to the memories she had tried so hard to bury. Speedy, once her closest confidant, had become her most formidable adversary, turning those years into a relentless storm of public humiliations and private torments. However, the revelation of Speedy's involvement in securing her passport cast a new light on those dark memories. Could someone who had once caused her so much pain also be the one to offer a lifeline in her moment of desperation?

The very thought of reconciliation was fraught with complexity. Kira wrestled with her pride and the weight of past grievances, yet she couldn't ignore the part of her that longed for closure, a resolution that might never come if she remained insincere in her bitterness. It was a delicate dance between the desire to move forward and the fear of reopening old wounds.

In the solitude of the room, Kira considered the possibility of forgiveness. What would it mean to face Speedy again, hear her out, and understand the reasons behind her actions? The thought was terrifying, yet there was an undercurrent of relief at the prospect of confronting their shared past, of perhaps finding common ground amid the rubble of their fractured relationship.

The soft click of the door interrupted her contemplation. Rocky re-entered the room, his expression tentatively hopeful. Kira met his gaze, her resolve strengthening. Regardless of the outcome, she knew that this was a necessary step, not just for the sake of their shared history but also for her own peace of mind.

"I've been thinking," Kira began, her voice steady, despite the turmoil within, "about Speedy. About everything that's happened. Rocky, I'm unsure what the future holds, but I'm willing to try. For us, the baby, and maybe even myself."

Rocky's relief was palpable, and his response was a soft exhalation of breath, which he seemed to have been holding. "Thank you, Kira. That means more than you know."

Kira felt a cautious sense of optimism as she watched Rocky's relieved smile. The road ahead would be difficult, fraught with challenges and uncomfortable truths, but perhaps it was the first step toward healing, toward a future where the shadows of the past no longer held them captive.

**

The following day, Mr. McGregor arrived on the dot at 1pm. Everyone concerned with the case had duly assembled in the parlor by then. Mr. McGregor immediately noticed Kira's elevated mood from the previous afternoon and welcomed the change. He still had many questions for her and hoped to understand the situation before the day ended. So, he pulled out his files and summarized yesterday's findings:

"So, based on yesterday's session, we can safely state that Mr. Gordon pursued you at his mother's urging to get married. And that you were not aware of your pregnancy till you ended up in the hospital, heavily hemorrhaging. And you also claim your former husband is not the father of your baby."

"Correct," said Kira.

"And may I ask who the father is, then?"

Rocky stepped forward. "I am the father of Kira's baby."

Mr. McGregor looked up from his notes. "How can you be so sure about that?"

Rocky told him about their accidental meeting in early May last spring on the train on their way to Eger. Seeing her so dejected, he invited Kira for dinner at his father's home that night.

"I wasn't sure she would come until she actually did," Rocky recalled. "She appeared to have a good time at my father's place. She was lively and communicative, an instant success with my family. Then, just when we finished dinner, she suddenly got up and walked out in the middle of the conversation. Something didn't feel right, so I followed her."

He recalled the freezing rain for nearly six kilometers up the old ruins. "I stayed out of her sight as she headed up to the old ruins, witnessed her collapse by the tree, right by the cliff's edge, and grew concerned as she edged toward the precipice. I pulled her back before she jumped, but the rescue mission turned into a struggle," Rocky admitted shyly. "We ended up making love. It was such a spur of the moment that it shocked both of us. Then she got up to run away from me, shouting that just because I saved her life, she didn't owe me anything.".

Still dejected by the memory, Rocky admitted, "I did not know what happened to her after that. Life caught up with me, arranging for my trip to the West, and by the time I was ready to look her up in Budapest, she had already left for Canada."

Mr. McGregor said, "Did she tell you why she tried to attempt suicide?"

"She was not very coherent, but I recall her mentioning her grandfather's sudden death a day before her father's release from prison...after six and a half years of waiting,"

Mr. McGregor nodded. "It must have been quite a coincidence that both of you lived under the same roof in Toronto. Since you claim, Rocky, that you had no prior information about her new address in Canada? Did you know at the time of your arrival that you would meet her here?"

"That is not entirely correct, Sir. When I knew the exact day of my arrival, I went by Kira's parents' place to get her Toronto address. It was her grandmother who gave it to me. And I wrote her a long letter, telling her I wanted to see her in Toronto. However, the letter returned to me stamped that the person at that address was unknown. I didn't know what to make of that. But I was still determined that I would try my best to find her once I arrived in Toronto."

"Were you aware of Kira's condition when you arrived?"

"No, sir, I was not. I only found out after I arrived, in a rather convoluted way from her relatives, of all people. After meeting them, I'm not surprised about the Diamonds' reactions to Kira's condition. But her Uncle Eugene shocked me! He should know what life was like for Kira and her parents after Mr. Chopaky's arrest in nineteen-fifty-six. Being Mr. Chopaky's brother-in-law couldn't have made life easy for him. Why else would Uncle Eugene escape to Canada and leave his own family behind in Budapest?"

Mr. McGregor scratched his head. "So, how did both of you end up living here?"

"After I ended up at the hospital," Kira replied, "my relatives confronted me in front of the staff and other patients. The following day, Rabbi Salamon showed up and brought me here upon hearing about my trouble. Apparently, the Baroness offered me sanctuary in exchange for some minor housekeeping."

Mr. McGregor turned to Rocky. "And you? How did you end up living here?"

"It was my aunt in London who suggested for me to become one of Dolly's renters, so I came directly here from the airport. But Kira and I didn't meet until the evening when the Hungarian agents showed up for the kidnap attempt."

Mr. McGregor put his notes down and looked at both. "It must have been a very exciting time for all of you! But let's just stay on course now. I understand Kira is reluctant to apply for refugee status because of the danger she thinks it would pose to her parents. Now granted, your first marriage was not what anybody wished for, but because the baby's father is here and a British subject, what prevents you from marrying him, my girl? Wouldn't that be the most obvious solution to your problem?"

"Even if Rocky were ready to do so," Kira said, "my divorce procedure will take many months. And it still looks like an arranged marriage, isn't it?"

"Well, if you mean it to be a shotgun wedding, it is not," stated Rocky firmly. "I'll be happy and proud to be your husband and father to our child, Kira."

"And if you insist on a religious ceremony, my dear Kira," Rabbi Salamon pitched in, "some issues here must be clarified. I had married you to Mr. Gordon, based on your Canadian relatives' affiliations, believing that you're Jewish. Since they are related to your mother, it was the logical thing for me to believe that you, too, were the same. But I just learned that your mother converted and had registered you as a Presbyterian at birth. Had I known it, I couldn't have married you before a formal conversion to Judaism." Then he asked Kira the obvious question, "And by the way, why did you let me believe you were Jewish?"

Kira responded defiantly, "I reminded my aunt when Mr. Gordon asked me to marry him that I was baptized. She replied it was time for me to correct my mother's sin for leaving the religion, and she actually forbade me to tell this to anyone. It was just one of those things I was not supposed to mention to others. Like my father's imprisonment or my mother's making a living during those times by selling pretzels in the Puppet Theatre or the Zoo in the summer. I never considered that part of our life to be shameful. It wasn't our fault that my father was imprisoned and that my mother was forced to make a living by selling pretzels! It was an honest living! But given that I was at the mercy of my relatives, I had no choice but to keep my mouth shut about this part of my life as well."

"Well, my dear, if that's the case, I will start the divorce process immediately." Rabbi Salamon stated and rose from the chair, ready to leave.

Chapter 27

Two days later, Speedy sat in the armchair in André Görgey's study in Eger, recounting the situation regarding Rocky and Kira. "Sorry about delivering it verbally. I didn't want to risk getting caught with a letter in my possession. I hope I haven't forgotten anything important," she said shyly.

"You risked a lot by coming here in person to share all this with me," André said, "The last I heard about Rocky was when his aunt informed me of his safe arrival in London before leaving for Toronto. And Kira, did you see her in Toronto?"

She replied timidly, "Rocky talked me into it, and he was right: It was high time I apologized to her for all the monstrous things I had done to her in the past. Well, I feel better about it, anyway. I only hope she does, too."

André Görgey nodded. "How long did you stay in Toronto?"

"Less than a week. We participated in the international track and field competition hosted by the University of Toronto."

"And how was it?"

"Don't ask. We came in last," Speedy replied sheepishly. "Our coach was not pleased."

"I can only imagine."

"Knowing that he suspected my role in sabotaging the event, I was tempted to jump ship, but Rocky talked me out. He said I was the only person he could trust to warn you to get out of Hungary sooner rather than later. Certain people in prominent positions are mad as hell and ready to do anything to take revenge on your relative's unsuccessful kidnapping attempt. It actually became an international embarrassment for them, and they don't take that lightly."

"How about the Chopakys? Aren't they targeted as well?"

"As long as Kira does not request refugee status in Canada, her parents will be safe, at least temporarily. But for now, I believe they will focus on you because of your relationship with Rocky and Miklós."

She paused for a moment, furrowing her brow, and added, "I'll never understand the mentality of the State here! They would accept Kira marrying a Canadian citizen to legalize her status there, but if she were to request refugee status—even though she has plenty of legitimate reasons—they would consider it treason. I just hope she marries Rocky for her sake and that of her parents. Mind you, she couldn't have picked a better man to be the father of her baby."

Speedy, shamed by her outburst, swallowed hard. She was still not sure she was ready to give up her romantic dreams about Rocky, even for Kira's sake.

"That must have been difficult for you." André Görgey nodded and touched her arm. "To learn about Kira's pregnancy and to consider giving him up...I wonder if the Chopakys know anything about Kira's condition?"

Speedy shook her head. "I don't believe they do."

"So," André summed it up, "the only information her parents had about her in the last few months was from the relatives. This means we better call to update them about Kira's real situation."

Speedy nodded, her earlier resolve hardening into determination. Despite the personal turmoil, the focus shifted to the practicalities of reaching out to the Chopakys, bridging the gap from recounting past actions to taking current ones.

Andre said, "Since you met her in Toronto, wouldn't you like to call them in person?"

Speedy shook her head and whispered, "No way! I'm not ready for that yet. It would be better if it came directly from you."

Andre reached for the telephone and was ready to dial. He rapidly replaced it when he realized he did not know the number. He held up one hand and said, "Speedy, don't leave yet. Can you help me find Chopaky's phone number?"

Speedy slapped her forehead and exclaimed, "How foolish of me! I forgot that Alex's sentence included the removal of their telephone as well. I wonder if they had since got one"

It took Speedy a dozen phone calls to various unnamed agencies before she finally got her answer. "I was right. The Chopakys just recently got a new phone, mind you, only a party line to be shared with one of the Customs Offices." Her voice dripping with sarcasm, she said, "They only had to wait for it for seven long years, but, here it is," she passed the piece of paper with the number on it over to Andre.

**

The following day, André Görgey called Chopaky's number. After five rings, a pleasant baritone picked up the phone. "Hello! If you are looking for the Customs Office, this is not it."

"Is it the Chopaky residence?" André said.

"Yes, it is. The problem is that we are sharing a party line with the Customs Office, which means we have to wait for the line to be free before we talk or overhear a conversation not meant for us."

André introduced himself and said that Peter was a classmate of Kira in high school. "My son is currently living in Toronto, attending university there on a scholarship, and he has information about your daughter."

"When and where can we meet?" Alex Chopaky said rapidly, his voice choking with emotion.

"This coming weekend would be perfect for me. I live in Eger, and if you don't mind a bit of a train ride, you're more than welcome to come to my place."

"Thank you, Mr. Görgey," Alex replied, relieved that the man understood his need to meet where they can discuss delicate issues far from his home, known to have ears. "Do you mind if I bring my wife and my mother as well? They, too, want to know what happened to our daughter. The sporadic and very curt letters that we received from her in the last many months, besides the gibberish we're getting from the relatives, make us uneasy about her. So, any news is welcome, especially from an unbiased source."

"Please, come, all of you."

"We will be there on Saturday in the early afternoon. We'll take the express train that leaves at twelve. We really don't want to intrude for too long. We intend to return with the early evening express, so please don't make too much fuss over us."

"No, no, it won't do, Mr. Chopaky. You must come on the early train and stay as long as you wish. My family would be very upset with me if I didn't extend my hospitality to you. So, please come. I'll be waiting for you at the train station by ten in the morning."

**

As the train neared Eger, Alex Chopaky stared out the window, his thoughts a tumultuous mix of hope and dread; he felt the weight of the impending meeting. *What news of Kira will we receive?* he pondered, the question a heavy stone in his heart. *Can anything prepare us for the truth of her life in Toronto?* These questions haunted him, yet he clung to the hope that, despite everything, Kira was safe and finding her way.

Rozi Chopaky closed her eyes as the train rumbled on, remembering Kira as a child, her laughter filling the house. Those bright and vivid memories now seemed worlds away, overshadowed by the silence that had grown between them.

André Görgey had no trouble identifying the tall, slim man in his early forties, wearing a grey winter coat and furry hat, as he got off the train. Turning back to the door, the man reached up to help an elderly lady using a cane and then a younger woman looking strikingly familiar, clutching a large handbag. He recognized the man instantly, as he had seen his pictures in many newspapers after announcing the sentences of the secret trial in June 1958.

Görgey walked up to the little group and reached out. "Mr. Chopaky, I'm André Görgey."

Chopaky, looking straight into André Görgey's eyes, shook his hand. It was a good, firm handshake, and the grey eyes were equally open and honest. They were approximately the same height, although Chopaky seemed taller, since he was at least ten years younger and slimmer.

Görgey liked the younger man. He turned his attention to the two women standing by him. The older one, wearing black, evidently still in mourning, had the same grey, penetrating eyes as her son, and the same slightly curved, notable nose. The other one, a slim, strikingly beautiful woman, must be Kira's mother, Görgey decided. He politely took the bag from the younger woman and led the way.

Eger, a jewel in the crown of Hungarian heritage, boasted winding streets that told tales of centuries past. The city was famed for its fortress, which stood as a proud reminder of resistance against Ottoman invasion, and its thermal baths that drew visitors seeking solace in their healing waters. The main square, with its vibrant market and the majestic Eger Cathedral, pulsed with the life of the city, a testament to its enduring spirit.

As the early morning fog lifted, Eger's streets came alive with the sounds of market vendors setting up, their voices mingling with the clang of the cathedral bells. The air was filled with the aroma of freshly baked *kürtőskalács* and strong Hungarian coffee, inviting passersby to pause and indulge. The cobblestones, worn smooth by time, echoed with the footsteps of history, leading wanderers through alleyways draped in flowers and past buildings whose walls whispered stories of old.

The Görgey residence, nestled at the end of a cobblestone lane, stood as a testament to traditional Hungarian elegance. Its façade, a blend of Baroque and Neo-Classical elements, was adorned with ivy that traced the contours of its arched windows. The garden, a riot of colours even in the waning light of autumn, welcomed visitors with the scent of blooming *Rozis* and the faint whisper of leaves rustling in the breeze.

Inside, the house was a warm embrace of history and comfort. The study, where André Görgey spent much of his time, was lined with bookshelves reaching to the ceiling, filled with volumes of history, literature, and philosophy. A grand oak desk sat squarely in front of a large window looking over the garden, and the walls were adorned with family portraits and mementos from travels abroad, each telling its own story.

Andre noticed Chopaky's hesitation and his quick glances around the room, gesturing towards the walls and then at his ears.

"No, Mr. Chopaky, our walls have no ears," he reassured him. "We can be certain that no stranger has entered our home without our prior approval for a very long time." He smiled, "We have our

Betty to chase away any intruders. Once you meet her, you'll agree with me. She's up for the challenge."

The shadowed corners of the Görgey study, illuminated only by the soft glow of a desk lamp, mirrored the tension and uncertainty that Alex Chopaky felt as he awaited news of his daughter. The weight of silence in the room was almost tangible, punctuated only by the occasional crackle of the fireplace, a stark contrast to the turmoil brewing within him.

André Görgey finally spoke of Kira. Alex's relief was palpable; it was as though the tension that had held him in a vice was slowly unwinding. He found himself leaning forward, eager for every word, his hands clasped together to still their trembling.

When Andre finished conveying the detailed message about Kira, her grandmother burst into tears, "My Kira! Oh, the poor soul! She must be terribly lonely and homesick!" Then she sobered up quickly, and her sympathy turned into anger. Lifting her cane threateningly, she shouted, "Just wait till I arrive. I'll give them a piece of my mind."

"So," Alex finally gathered enough strength and commented, "Finally, we know the truth. The letters we received from the relatives and from the husband made no sense."

His wife, Rozi, was also overwhelmed. She kept looking down at her fingers, twirling the edges of her handkerchief, and could only whisper, "And we thought she would be out of harm's way there."

André Görgey felt he had to intervene. "But she is. She is in a good place now and well taken care of. And my son will do what is right. I met Kira late last spring, and I will be proud to have her and you in the family, Mr. Chopaky. We have a lot in common. So, why don't we make this a family celebration? Forget the bad stuff and welcome the good. Betty, can we have the brandy?"

Rozi Chopaky, thinking it over, announced, "Well, by the sound of it, Mr. Görgey, your son not only saved our Kira's life but provided us with a grandchild. You're right! We have something to celebrate."

André Görgey raised his glass again and suggested, "Why don't we call them in Toronto? Let them know we are on their side and trust them to do what is best for them. Then we can discuss who will visit them first."

**

Considering the six-hour difference, the phone call to Toronto happened conveniently at lunchtime.

It was Dolly who picked it up and, hearing the voice of the elder Görgey, said, "Well, old Fox, it's about time you called. Seems you can catch more than one relative this time. But I assume you first want to talk to your son. Let me call him for you." She turned toward the stairways and shouted, "Rocky, my boy, telephone. And hurry, it is a long distance."

Rocky, getting ready for the communal meal, popped out of his room and still toweling his wet hair, leaned over the barrier and asked, "Who is it, Dolly?"

"Don't ask questions. You'll find out soon enough. Now hurry before we get disconnected. You know how unpredictable the lines are from Hungary."

Rocky dropped the towel in the hallway and took the stairs down to the main floor.

"Hello," he shouted after grabbing the phone. Then, hearing his father's voice, he swallowed hard, not knowing what to say next.

"Can you hear me, son?" the elder Görgey asked.

But Rocky, overcome by emotions, could only nod.

Dolly poked Rocky in the ribs and whispered, "Speak up, you fool. He can't see you."

"Yes, father," Rocky finally stammered, clutching the receiver, his knuckles turning white.

"Listen, son, I just wanted to let you know I'm thrilled to be a grandfather. Please assure Kira that we welcome her into the family. By the way, Kira's parents are here with me, and they send their love to all of you. Is she there, by any chance?"

Rocky took a deep breath and said, "Wait a minute. Let's see if we can locate her in a hurry." He turned to Dolly. "Is Kira around? Her parents want to speak to her."

Kira, as if psychic, walked in from the kitchen, carrying a cup of aromatic herbal tea. Rocky placed the phone in her hand and said, "It is for you, Honey."

Kira, making a face at him, took the phone from his hand and placing it to her ear, said, "Hello, who am I talking to?" When she heard her father's voice, she dropped the teacup. She needed to grab the phone with both hands to hear correctly. The world was spinning around her, and she stood there listening to the voice she had heard so long ago.

"Kira, it is Dad. It is all right, my dear. We know everything. And no matter what, we love and trust you, just as we always have. You hear me?"

She heard through the fog, and all she could do was whisper, "Yes, Papa, I hear you. Thank you." And then, dropping the phone, she fainted.

Rocky and Dolly ran towards her, while Miklós, walking into the scene, grabbed the phone and said, "Please forgive us, but there is a bit of a mishap. Kira just fainted. We'll call you back as soon as things settle down." He placed the phone down before he turned to the people hovering over Kira, trying to revive her.

"Figures," Dolly muttered through her teeth after observing that Kira fell right into the puddle of tea. She grabbed Kira's housecoat and yanked her up into a sitting position.

"Kira! Can you hear me?" she shouted. When Kira opened her eyes, trying to focus Dolly said, "Don't faint on me, girl! Not when things turn around for the better for you!"

Dolly walked to the liquor cabinet, opened it, and, grabbing a bottle of Courvoisier, poured a good portion into a glass. She went back to Kira and, with two fingers holding her nose, poured the drink down Kira's throat. Kira had no choice but to swallow the brandy. Then she shook herself and slowly stood up. But her legs were still shaking so badly that she needed to sit down.

Rocky helped her to the sofa and, after comfortably seated, she asked, "Was that my father on the phone?"

"Yeah, it was your dad and mine. They called from Eger."

Kira straightened her shoulders. "You mean my parents are visiting yours? In Eger? But why, and how?"

Rocky began dialing the international operator, requesting to make a call to his father's home. It took over an hour before the connection was established. He heard the operator asking his father whether they could talk with the party from Toronto, and he heard his father's eager voice responding with a heartfelt agreement.

"Hello, father. It's me, Rocky. Kira is feeling better. Can you put her father on the phone?"

"Yes, of course. I'm so glad she's feeling better. Let me get Mr. Chop...I mean Alex, on the phone. Just a second."

Rocky took the phone to Kira and gently put it into her hand. "Here, talk to your dad."

She put the phone to her ear and eagerly said, "Papa, it is so good to hear your voice. Is Mom and Grandma all right?"

"Knowing the truth helps. We wish we could have been aware of it before and reassure you of our love and trust."

"Oh, Papa, I was so afraid I disappointed you."

"Hush, girl, you can never disappoint me. I know you. You'd hurt no one and could do nothing that could dishonor us. But I'll give the phone to your mom now before she grabs it out of my hands. She needs to hear your voice, too. Love you, girl."

Kira's mother wanted to know how her pregnancy was developing—did she have support during these trying days. She said, "I wish I could be there for you when the baby comes."

Then she passed the phone to Grandma, who could only cry and repeat, "Kira, my dear girl, how I miss you. I wish you were home."

It did not surprise Kira to hear her mother's stern voice in the background, contradicting her grandmother. She knew that no matter what, her parents had not wanted her to be back in Hungary, even if her grandmother had wished her so. But it was so good to hear their voices, know they still loved her, and get their support in her decision to keep the baby.

Chapter 28

André Görgey was the only family member with a shot at the coveted passport. Alex Chopaky, still shackled by a decade-long probation from his 1963 amnesty, had half a decade waiting ahead—barred from even dreaming of the West. Rozi, his wife, though legally eligible for travel, couldn't bear the thought of leaving Alex behind, fearing the unpredictable whims of the Hungarian secret service. The family, aware of Grandma's fiery spirit and protective instincts, gently declined her offer to visit Kira, fearing more for her safety than theirs.

A week after André submitted his passport application, an enigmatic letter arrived, summoning him to a clandestine meeting in Budapest. Expecting the Secret Service's standard welcome, André skipped the usual map consultation to find the exact meeting location. He wasn't surprised when, before he called a taxi at the railway station in Budapest, a black sedan appeared, and two imposing men demanded he identify himself, blindfolded and shoved him into the car.

Memories of his 1950s prison stint flooded back—of how he'd whimsically implicated *Walt Whitman* and *Edgar Allan Poe* in his alleged spy ring, a desperate ploy to expose the trial's absurdity. Yet, the trial's preordained verdicts rendered his clever ruse futile. Fortuitously, a bizarre incident involving a Chesterfield cigarette saved him from the gallows, relegating him instead to solitary confinement—a twist of fate that spared his life until Stalin's death prompted a wave of releases.

Although the Secret Service as a uniformed identity was officially disbanded during the Hungarian Revolution, by the early days of 1968, although they no longer wore a military uniform, they still existed under a different name. Only to alternate brutal force with masterful persuasion, always with a veiled threat that it could change back in a moment of need. The Force became a mass of nameless and faceless objects penetrating every level of life, spying on everyone, collecting information that could coerce people to cooperate with the whim of the state. André had hoped he was up to facing them directly.

Once the blindfold fell away, André found himself in a luxuriously appointed office, the setting oddly familiar. The grandeur of the antique desk, throne-like chair, and lavish decor sparked a sense of déjà vu. His escort swiftly thwarted his attempt to peek outside, but not before he recognized the iconic boulevard outside and the mansion that was built for and used by Count István Széchenyi, one of the most outstanding Hungarian state leaders a century ago, hinting at the power and history embedded within these walls.

As André settled into the office's opulent yet familiar surroundings, the door swung open to reveal a figure from his past, one whose presence evoked a flood of memories. Tibor Kerekes, with his distinctive white hair and eyes twinkling with good humor, was not just any old acquaintance. Their bond had been forged in the crucible of war and hardened through the trials of post-war survival in a country scarred by occupation and oppression.

"Tibor, my dear old friend!" André greeted, his voice tinged with a mixture of surprise and warmth.

When they first met, the world was a different place. They had been young men then, idealistic and brave, navigating the perilous landscapes of Nazi-occupied France. Together, they had undertaken daring missions to rescue downed British pilots, relying on nothing but their wits and an unspoken trust that had made them an indomitable team.

After the war, their paths diverged as they returned to Hungary under the shadow of a new oppressor. Tibor's brilliance as a linguist and translator had quickly caught the eye of the emerging regime, a fact that had initially placed a wedge between them. André, ever the skeptic of political machinations, had found himself ensnared in the government's purges, his name tarnished by false accusations of espionage.

Yet, Tibor had come to his aid in those dark times, leveraging his newfound position to mitigate the harshness of André's sentence. It was an act of bravery and loyalty that André had never forgotten, a debt of gratitude that lay unspoken between them but had forever sealed their friendship.

André leaned forward, lowering his voice, a habit ingrained from years of cautious living. "Tibor, do you remember the nights in Paris when our biggest worry was finding our way back from the Resistance meetings without getting caught?"

Tibor chuckled, the sound a mixture of nostalgia and bitterness. "I remember thinking we were invincible. And now, look at us, whispering in shadowed corners like thieves."

André's eyes met Tibor's, a spark of the old defiance flickering in them. "Perhaps, but thieves with a cause, my friend. We've traded dark alleys for these gilded cages, but the fight, it seems, remains much the same."

Tibor sighed, leaning back in his chair, the weight of decades visible in his posture. "Indeed, André. But back then, we knew who our enemies were. Today, the lines are blurred. Allies become foes, and foes become allies. It's a treacherous path we tread."

A silence fell between them, filled with the unsaid. Memories of a past filled with clarity and purpose contrasted sharply with the murky waters of their current endeavors.

"André, the world has changed since we last roamed the streets of Paris, but some bonds remain unbreakable," Tibor began, his voice low and earnest. "Our country faces new challenges, and once again, we find ourselves at a crossroads. I need your help, not just as a patriot but as a friend."

The following request—securing a loan from the IMF—was a testament to the trust Tibor placed in André's capabilities. It was a mission fraught with risk yet imbued with the potential to alter the course of their nation's future. As André pondered Tibor's proposal, he realized that this was more than a diplomatic endeavor; it was a continuation of their shared legacy, a new chapter in their lifelong commitment to the survival and prosperity of their homeland.

As André processed Tibor's straightforward request, skepticism and responsibility churned within him. The task was monumental in securing financial aid and navigating the murky waters of international diplomacy and the ethical dilemmas it presented.

André pondered the irony of seeking assistance from the very institutions that, in another life, he might have critiqued. Yet, the weight of Hungary's needs and the opportunity to influence a positive outcome for his country compelled him forward. This mission, fraught with both risk and necessity, underscored a pivotal moment in his life—one where his past experiences and skills could either pave the way for a brighter future or entangle him further in the complex web of political maneuvering.

"Oh, so the coffers are empty, and, in desperation, the leaders require my services?" André laughed. "Well, we both know that hungry Hungarians are restless Hungarians, and seeing what's brewing directly to the north of us, many people expect major changes in the same direction."

Tibor nodded. Sobering up, he replied, "If you refer to the Czechs and Mr. Dubcek, you're right on track. The Old Man so far sympathizes with the dynamic new chap, but he is very careful about openly backing him. I believe that his sympathy at this moment comes from more of his hatred of Comrade Novotny, Dubcek's predecessor." Tibor chuckled. "The hair-splitting morose bastard had the gall to remind and rub in the favors the Old Man received from him in Nineteen-fifty-six so he could stay in power. But he is watching carefully how far this so-called Socialism with a Human Face may be allowed to develop by the Big Bear."

André made a mental note that his friend must be in an influential position to be so frank with him or just too brave or stupid to believe he could get away talking so openly about the highest-ranking person in the country. For his friend's sake, he sincerely hoped for the first.

But at the end of the conversation, Tibor presented André Görgey with a diplomatic passport, several letters of recommendation, and names of people in the West to get in touch with and lay the ground for further discussion leading to international business cooperation and a large loan from the IMF.

André Görgey was allowed to leave the meeting without the guards following him. He paused at the edge of Kodaly Circle, one of the bustling squares of Budapest, the cold January breeze tugging at his coat. Around him, the city thrummed with the life of a nation under the Soviet Union's shadow, yet his mind was not on the imposing statues or the whispering agents that dotted the crowd. He was thinking of Riocky in Toronto, of the letters hidden away in his drawer, each word a testament to the distance between them. Fueled by a father's longing, this personal mission sharpened his resolve.

As he turned away from the square, André's steps were determined. His journey to secure an IMF loan was not just about navigating political tumult; it was a quest to bridge the vast emotional distances imposed by iron curtains and ideological divides.

Once a revered figure for his valiant efforts in the resistance during World War II, André's post-war years had been marred by betrayal and imprisonment. Accused of espionage in a regime quick to quash dissent, he endured years of solitary confinement, a punishment for his unyielding spirit and the international acclaim his literary works garnered.

1968 had opened a new chapter in André's life, promising a glimmer of hope amidst the shadows of past ordeals. Hungary, though still under the watchful eye of the Soviet Union, began to experience the subtle thawing of the Cold War's icy facade. It was a time of cautious optimism, potential change, and, for André, a chance to reconnect with a world beyond the Iron Curtain.

As he prepared to enter the international stage, André was not just a man seeking to visit his son in Toronto; he symbolized Hungary's complexities, hopes, and desperate bid for economic salvation. The offer from Mr. Kerekes, a former jail comrade turned government official, was a testament to the intricate dance of power, loyalty, and survival. André's journey was more than a quest for financial aid; it was a foray into the delicate art of diplomacy, where every word and gesture could tip the scales of fate.

**

André's departure was laden with emotion as he bid farewell to his closest allies. Mr. Varga, Rocky's mentor during high school, presented him with a touching farewell gift, a book of George Faludy's poetry, which was a stark reminder of the connections that transcended borders, offering a semblance of solace as he stepped into the unknown.

"So that you'll not forget me," Mr. Varga said, gently shoveling him toward the door to avoid a prolonged farewell. But not before he said, pointing at his gift to André, "Look him up if you can. He, too, lives in Toronto nowadays."

André slipped the book into his coat pocket and smiled as he recalled the times when sitting around the bonfires in Madrid in 1938 reading George Faludy's notable translations of his Hungarian rendition of poems by François Villon, the 15th-century French poet known for his raw, emotional, and often defiant works.

It was not an accident that Mr. Varga gave one of George Faludy's poetry books to André as a farewell gift. George Faludi, a renowned Hungarian poet, writer, and translator whose life and work spanned much of the 20th century, reflected the tumultuous historical events of his time. He was celebrated and marred by political upheavals, including World War II, the rise of totalitarian regimes, and the Cold War.

Throughout his life, Faludy lived in various countries, including France, England, the United States, and Canada, as he fled from Nazi and later Communist persecution. His experience of exile and his unyielding commitment to freedom and democracy were recurrent themes in his poetry and essays.

He was definitely one person André wished to meet while in Toronto.

André also dropped in to see the Chopakys before departing for the Airport. The increasing emotional toll was evident on them. Their conversations with André, often veiled in coded language to evade the ever-present threat of surveillance, revealed their complex blend of hope and apprehension. André could not help but admire Alex trying to overcome his frustration over his own limitations. Bound by the conditions of his amnesty, Alex was sidelined, a spectator in a game where he yearned to contribute but was helpless.

André took solace in Grandma's fiery spirit and protective instincts. Though rejected, her offer to visit Kira underscored her willingness to fight for her family's happiness at any cost. In her eyes, André saw not just the fierce matriarch he had always admired but a symbol of the enduring strength that had carried their family through generations of turmoil.

As André made his way to the airport, the tapestry of Budapest's streets unfurled memories at every turn. Each landmark whispered tales of his youth, revolutions quelled, and dreams deferred. Yet, amidst this reflective journey, a spark of anticipation flickered within him. The West held the promise of reunion and the allure of freedom, a stark contrast to the shadows that had lengthened over his homeland. André found himself at a crossroads, not just geographically but in the essence of his being—poised between the past's grip and the future's call.

The prospect of meeting Lady Anna and immersing himself in her colorful household offered a respite from the heaviness that had settled over André. He anticipated the lively exchanges, the warmth of old friendships, and the vibrancy of a world untouched by the shadows that lingered over Hungary. It was a much-needed interlude—a chance to breathe freely and gather strength for the awaited challenges. André looked forward to catching up on news and gossip, to moments of laughter and lightness that seemed all too rare in his recent past.

Chapter 29

André Görgey arrived in Toronto in the last week of February 1968, just in time for the birth of his grandson. The waiting room in the hospital was filled with Dolly's crew, supporting the expectant father and anxious grandfather. Dolly and Yvonne kept Kira company, holding her hands and wiping the sweat from her face. But everything went well, and by early evening, the exhausted Kira, all smiles, looked at her new screeching baby boy who let everyone know he was hungry. With a satisfied grin, the nurse placed the baby beside her on the bed. Kira sat up and, baring her breast, placed the little one on her side. She looked down in wonder. Her son. Her precious little baby. Her very demanding and hungry baby.

As André Görgey stood silently in the corner of the crowded room, his eyes lingered on Kira, cradling her newborn son with a tenderness that pierced his heart. Amidst the laughter and chatter, a profound sense of displacement washed over him. Here, in this foreign land, far from the cobblestone streets of Eger, he was a grandfather. The title carried a weight he had not anticipated, stirring a mixture of pride, worry, and haunting nostalgia.

He thought back to when he was a young father, full of dreams and aspirations for his family when the world seemed vast but conquerable. Watching Kira with her child, he realized that those dreams had morphed into a fervent hope for his grandson and mother's safety, happiness, and stability.

Turning his gaze away from the intimate mother-and-child scene, André allowed himself a moment of introspection. He wondered about the legacy he was passing on, the stories of resilience and struggle that seemed to be the family's inheritance. He wished he could shield them from the pain and challenges that seemed to shadow the Görgey name, yet he knew this was not within his power.

Six days later, Kira and the baby returned to Dolly's house, where the tenants were all outside, waiting for their arrival. They shouted and clapped, causing the new baby to protest.

"Here," Rocky said, gently taking the squealing baby from her at the door, "Let me introduce him to our friends."

Kira reluctantly released the squirming bundle to Rocky, who proudly held the little boy up.

Then he asked her, "But what is his name? You named him, didn't you?"

"Adam," Kira whispered, looking back hesitantly, waiting for approval.

Rocky nodded and turned to his friends. "I'm proud to present our son, Adam Chopaky Görgey."

Kira reached out to grab the little boy away from Rocky, but then she changed her mind. The announcement rocked her to her core. Throughout her pregnancy, not for a moment did she think the baby to be anything but her own. She wasn't at all sure she could share him with anyone, including Rocky. But she also knew she could not deny him his son. And she could definitely not keep him from André, who ensured Kira that it thrilled him to be a grandfather.

**

The new baby's arrival caused upheaval in Dolly's house. Some changes were inevitable, as Rocky insisted on being there for his son, diapering, bathing, and, if needed, even bottle-feeding. And that meant being physically close to them in the third-floor apartment.

Wilma loved the apartment's skylights and used the large room as her studio. She was reluctant to give it up but understood the new family's needs. So, she moved down to Rocky's room till Danny could complete a studio with a skylight for her on the top of the garage. He could hardly wait to get started, as he was afraid they would run out of ideas for improvement, thus forcing him to go outside the home to find a new project.

"I'll stock up on more bandages," Dolly muttered, crossing her fingers behind her. If Danny got into a new building project, it guaranteed a few more injuries.

People in Dolly's house moved around, playing musical rooms, to everyone's satisfaction. Even André Görgey found a room on his own there, although he originally offered to find another accommodation that everyone vetoed. So, André stayed, even though he knew nothing could replace his home and family back in Eger.

As soon as Kira settled in with the baby in the apartment, reluctantly having Rocky move into the other bedroom, she went downstairs to the main hall to call her parents. Her nightmares had intensified since she got back from the hospital, and it became urgent for her to hear her parents' voice. It was early afternoon in Toronto, which meant early evening in Budapest. She asked the international operator to place the call and, with shaking hands, waited for her father to pick up the phone at the other end.

Recognizing her voice, her father asked, "Kira? Is everything alright?"

"I just needed to hear your voice," she replied nervously.

"How are you and the baby? And what is his name?"

"O Papa, he is wonderful. And Rocky insisted we call him Adam Chopaky Görgey."

"Adam, the first man. Good name for the little tyke," Alex replied.

**

A week later, Kira woke up with a tremendous headache. Feeling nauseous, she got up and, after slowly maneuvering herself to the bathroom, kneeled down, hugged the toilet, and threw up last night's supper. Her upchucking woke Rocky, who rushed to her side with a wet towel to wipe her face.

He kept fussing over her. "Kira, what did you eat last night? As far as I remember, there was nothing heavy on the menu."

Kira mumbled, "No, I only had some tea and a toast."

"Can you get up?"

Kira nodded and tried to push herself up from the floor. Her arms were shaking so much that she could not get up. Instead, she turned toward the toilet bowl and threw up again. Then, she passed out.

Rocky panicked. He ran to the door and yanked it wide open, shouting, "Help! Somebody, please, help! It's Kira!"

Within seconds, Dolly was upstairs, jumping two stairs all at once. "What happened? Where is she?"

Rocky pointed to the bathroom, and Dolly followed his lead. She bent down, trying to shake Kira, calling her name. "Kira, Kira, wake up, it's Dolly…"

By then, the door had flung wide open, and people from downstairs kept piling in. Wilma was still wearing her housecoat, and most others were in their pajamas. "What happened? How can I help?"

Dolly pointed at Kira's unconscious body on the washroom floor. "Did she fall?"

Rocky said, "No, she was kneeling, throwing up, then she fainted. And I can't seem to wake her."

Suddenly, they heard Adam crying. It was time to feed and change him, but everyone had forgotten about the little one in the chaos. Dolly made a quick decision. "Rocky, you call the ambulance. Wilma, you take the baby. The rest of you clear out. I will try to make Kira as comfortable as possible."

By then, André Görgey was upstairs and informed everyone that he had already called and the ambulance was coming. Indeed, it had already arrived, and the two attendants, carrying the equipment, were climbing the stairs to the second floor.

Rocky went with Kira in the ambulance. The attendants rolled Kira inside, and Rocky followed her in the hallway to the examination room. Sometime later, a doctor came out to talk to the worried relatives.

"What's the prognosis, doctor?" Rocky said, his hands shaking.

The young doctor replied, "We don't really know yet. We would like to keep her here for observation. We know she developed a temperature and has difficulty keeping anything in her stomach. We put her on an IV to stop her from dehydration. And just in case, start her on a set of antibiotics as well."

"You know she is a nursing mother, don't you?" Rocky said.

"No, I didn't, but obviously, she cannot nurse under the circumstances. Is there anybody to take care of the infant while the mother is in the hospital?" the doctor said.

"Yes, of course. My son will be well taken care of. Just make sure his mother will get better."

**

After a fortnight, Kira's health had not improved. Her appetite was low, and she kept tearing up at the least sign of provocation.

"It sounds like severe depression to me," the doctor said. "It happens after giving birth. If you are agreeable, I'll call in a psychiatrist. It can't hurt."

Dolly asked for Dr. Isobel Seraph, an excellent specialist and a close friend. "Kira will be more comfortable with her, and knowing her background, it is very important to have someone she knows well, probing her mental state."

Isobel was more than pleased to treat Kira. The feeling must have been mutual because Isobel talked Kira into returning to the house within a few days. She came by twice a week and they spent several hours together, chatting away about the state of the world, reminiscing about their childhood, family, parents, and grandparents, and even exchanging favorite Christmas cake recipes.

Then, one day, Isobel asked Kira directly, "How did you react when your mother, after being released from prison, told you that in case they executed your father, she was planning to commit suicide?"

Kira was slow to respond. "Well, knowing my parents' close relationship, it wasn't a total surprise. By then, I had a taste of being an orphan, as I spent almost two months away from them with strangers. So, I said I'd not want to be left behind."

Isobel grabbed Kira's hand and asked, rather shaken, "You mean you wanted to commit suicide along with your mother?"

Kira looked at Isobel defiantly. "What choice did I have then? To become the ward of the very state responsible for my parents' death? As I was sure that my paternal grandparents wouldn't want to outlive their only son if the very same regime executed him, they spent their youth fighting for!"

Isobel forced the issue further. "So, how about now? How would you react if anything happened to your parents in Hungary?"

Kira pulled her hand away and replied, "I don't think I could survive!"

"Even though you're a mother to a newborn child, who totally depends on you?"

Kira couldn't look Isobel in her eyes. She just nodded and whispered stubbornly, "That pledge still binds my fate to my father!"

"But it was the pledge of a ten-year-old child!" Isobel pleaded, truly frightened by Kira's ferocity of attachment to her father. Kira just turned toward the wall, closing all communication channels between them.

Isobel was in a serious bind. Knowing full well that the probability of the Chopakys leaving Hungary safely was almost zero, how would she deal with the situation? She knew about the sacred oath to keep patients' disclosures secret, but this was one piece of information she knew she could not keep to herself. She must reach out to her friends and request an emergency consultation.

**

Rabbi Salamon rushed to Isobel's office. "Where is the fire?"

"It concerns Kira, but wait till the others arrive. Besides you, I called Dolly. the Reverend, the Priest, and the Görgeys. It is a very delicate problem, and frankly, I need everyone's support."

Isobel's advisory board listened with a grave face. In the end, Dolly summarized the situation: "So, you're saying Kira is suffering from severe anxiety and, in her case, the only cure is to get her parents to safety?"

"Through the years, Kira must have developed an acute and direct psychic connection with her father. She thinks she can actually feel when he is in distress. She is also convinced that this connection is so strong that if anything bad happened to him—an accident or fatal illness—she would immediately feel the same pain and die along with him, even if thousands of miles separated them."

"Have you come across such a problem before? And if so, how do you treat it?" André asked.

"We are just beginning to identify this symptom as a post-traumatic disorder, hitting people who had survived great upheavals like war, revolution, and natural disasters, and until recently, the only cure was electrical shock therapy. Which is extremely painful and causes a memory loss for the patient, albeit not a permanent one."

Worried, Rocky inquired, "What's the alternative

Isobel explained, "I can only see Kira's condition improving when her parents would be out of danger. But we know the chances of her parents' escape from Hungary are about one in a million. My experiences with other patients believing this strongly—that their well-being solely relies on other people's welfare, usually means that they no longer feel in control over their own fate, and they give up entirely. And I would be the last doctor subjecting her to shock therapy."

"Are you sure about the low chances of Chopakys' escape?" Rabbi Salamon said.

André answered. "Alex and I talked about this before I left. He told me he can't apply for a passport until Nineteen-seventy-three, five years from now. So, it means there is no chance for him to leave the country legally until then."

"And illegally?" Rocky said.

"That would take a few dedicated individuals with enough imagination, money, and connections—and, of course, courage and time," replied André.

"And who is going to tell Kira that?" Isobel said sharply.

"We must somehow reassure her. We can't risk her falling deeper into a depression. Adam needs her mother, and frankly, I need her too!" Rocky said.

Father Ordogh, placing his hands under his chin, leaned forward in his chair and said softly, "I understand that the current political situations are pretty grave, and the likelihood of rescuing the Chopakys is just a dream, but isn't there a saying that as long as there is life, there is hope? Our faith is based on believing in the Divine

Intervention and knowing the Chopakys, they must have already experienced a few in their lifetime."

André nodded. "True enough, Alex has so far escaped the hangman's noose against all odds, in addition to some other hair-raising life-threatening situations. Let's hope his luck will hold out a bit longer."

"In the meantime," Miklós said, "We should tread around Kira lightly. We don't want to upset her with the reality just yet."

When they arrived home, Dolly marched into the room. She spotted Kira standing by the fireplace, waiting for them to attend their usual late afternoon chat in the parlor.

Dolly planted her hands firmly on her hips and declared, "Listen, girl, life's thrown you another curveball, but you're not one to lie down and let it roll over you. Remember, you're tougher than you think. We've got a mountain to climb, but we'll do it one step at a time." Dolly pulled a clean hanky from her pants pocket, shoved it toward Kira, and said firmly, "Kira, you've got a whole troop behind you, ready to march. It's time to dry those tears and start planning our next move. We're in this fight together."

Kira smiled, and all the others laughed as if they had just broken the evil spell.

Miklos walked up to Dolly and wrapped her in his arms, kissing her soundly and whispering into her ears as soon as they left for their bedroom, "And what happened to the soft approach?" he asked, with a twinkle in his eyes.

Dolly pulled her hands from behind, showing her fingers crossed for luck. "That *was* the soft approach!"

THE END

ABOUT THE AUTHOR

Judith Kopácsi Gelberger is an accomplished author renowned for her compelling storytelling and deep historical insights.

Born in Hungary, she witnessed firsthand the tumultuous events of the mid-20th century, experiences that profoundly shaped her literary voice. After fleeing the oppressive regime in Hungary, Judith settled in Canada, where she pursued her passion for writing.

Her work vividly captures the human spirit's resilience, often set against the backdrop of significant historical events. Judith's latest project, a historical fiction trilogy titled "The Price of Freedom," showcases her ability to weave intricate narratives that resonate with readers. The first book in the series, "Unlikely Allies," delves into the lives of Rocky Görgey and Kira Chopaky, two former high school classmates who escape a dictatorship and navigate the challenges of finding acceptance in 1967 Toronto. Through their journey, Judith explores themes of freedom, identity, and the enduring power of hope.

Judith's writing is characterized by meticulous research and a profound empathy for her characters. She brings history to life, allowing readers to experience the struggles and triumphs of her protagonists. Her dedication to authenticity and detail has earned her a loyal readership and critical acclaim.

Beyond her literary achievements, Judith is also a passionate advocate for human rights and social justice. Her personal experiences as a refugee have fueled her commitment to raising awareness about the plight of displaced individuals worldwide. Through her work and advocacy, Judith Kopácsi Gelberger continues to inspire and enlighten, leaving an indelible mark on the literary world and beyond.

CIRCE'S DANCE AND OTHER STORIES (2023)

By Heather Laltoo Ferguson

Circe's Dance comprise thought provoking narratives that delve into the complexities of human perception and prejudice. Her stories will resonate with the reader long after the last page is turned.

Franklin Mohan—author Love Has Two Moons And Other Stories

AMAZON

A TIME TO LOVE AN A TIME TO DIE (2020)

By Michael Joll

Finely drawn characters. Visually dramatic, tense and emotionally satisfying, this is one of the finest novels of the Great War. In this poignant story, the writing stands in stark contrast with the unvarnished brutality of trench warfare.

AMAZON

DANCING MY WAY TO 80 (2019)

By Doris Naraine

Biography published privately and not available for sale.

ATTITUDE (2020)

By Dave Moores

Fresh, gritty and laced with dry humour, Attitude is a fast-paced story readers of all ages won't want to put down. It's dead of winter and an outbreak of weird stuff, random acts of vandalism are unsettling the citizens of Southmead.

AMAZON

DOWN INDEPENDENCE BOULEVARD AND OTHER STORIES (2023)

[WINNER 2022 GUYANA PRIZE FOR LITERATURE: FICTION]

by Ken Puddicombe

"A brilliant collection of stories telling the tales of people forced to leave their homes...craving the past, escaping from racial

- 232 -

conflicts and dictatorship..."—Judith Kopacsi Gelberger, author of *Heroes Don't Cry*.

AMAZON

FROM MY WINDOW (2023)

By Rena Flannigan

"A fitting epitaph to a life well lived."— Raymond Holmes, Author: *Witnesses And Other Stories.*

AMAZON

GABRIELLE (2021)

By Michael Joll

Gabrielle transcends time and space, taking the reader on a journey to Poland, France, Holland and Israel as she searches for her identity.

AMAZON

GENERATIONS (2020)

Biography published privately and not available for sale.

HACKER (2024)

By MICHAEL JOLL

Detective Sergeant Richard Williams joins teenage hacker Penny McBride to solve her father's murder and they come up against the mob. Wil they succeed?

AMAZON

I WENT TO THE END OF THE RAINBOW (2020)

by Pramita Chakraborty

A beautifully illustrated, captivating tale about a young child who can't sleep and embarks on a adventure through the colours of the rainbow.

AMAZON

JUNTA (2014)

By Ken Puddicombe

"A gripping story (of) an imperfect democracy…the tension…builds increasingly from page to page."—Rico Downer, author of *There Once Was a Little England*

AMAZON

LOVE HAS TWO MOONS (2021)

By Franklin Mohan

With humour, insight and sensitivity, Franklin Mohan peels back the subtle layers of prejudice and racism in North American and Caribbean society—Raymond Holmes, author of *Witnesses and other short stories*

AMAZON

MEET ME AT THE FOUR CORNERS (2021)

Anthology

Twenty-six stories, fiction and non-Fiction, some of them prize winning submissions from the writers of the Brampton Writers' Guild, are featured in this collection.

AMAZON

PEOPLE OF GUYANA (2018)

By Ian McDonald and Peter Jailall

"These beautifully crafted poems are shaped by their generosity of spirit and abundant capacity for empathy and fun…" —Clem Seecharan

AMAZON

PERFECT EXECUTION AND OTHER STORIES (2017)

by Michael Joll

"Michael Joll is a master of surprise endings, but they never seem forced. He always stays true to his characters and their worlds." — Nancy Kay Clark, author and editor, *CommuterLit.com*

AMAZON

PERSONS OF INTEREST (2019)

By Michael Joll

"Exotic and intriguing! Joll brilliantly captures the reader's interest with vivid imagery and a relentless sleuth." —Phyllis Humby, short story writer, poet and novelist.

AMAZON

POEMS FOR MARY (2020)

By Ian Mc Donald

"The garden which my wife has created, it is as much a work of art as a painting by a master spirit or a piece of perfect music by a composer."—Ian Mc Donald, author, poet.

AMAZON

RACING WITH THE RAIN

(2nd Ed 2023)

By Ken Puddicombe

"Puddicombe's brilliant novel...an historic political conflict in Guyana, during the Cold War and the cold cynicism and tragic irony of a state sacrificed to super-power hegemony." -Frank Birbalsingh, author of *Novels and The Nation: Essays in Canadian*

AMAZON

RUTHLESS RHYTHMS (2022)

By Judith Gelberger

If poetry is a window into the soul of the author, Judith Gelberger has opened one which illuminates some of the most painful emotions and experiences of human existence...—Raymond Holmes – Author of *Witnesses And Other Short Stories*

AMAZON

SCALING NEW HEIGHTS (2022)

Anthology

Forty-two pieces from the members of Pakaraima Writers Group are featured in this their first collection of poetry and non-fiction travel articles.

AMAZON

TASTE MY WORDS (2022)

By Lisa Freemantle

Freemantle's compositions are imbued with a highly poetic energy instilling in the reader a subtle, penetrating fever of contentment...." —Dr. Franklin Mohan, author *Love Has Two Moons and Other Stories*

AMAZON

THE DARKEST HOURS

By Michael Joll (2023)

The Darkest Hours takes the reader from London slums to the war-torn skies of England and France as characters plot and struggle to survive in a world caught up in the conflict of WWII.

AMAZON

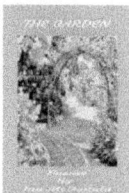

THE GARDEN (2021)

By Ian McDonald

Ian McDonald's poems are full of light and love. His easy style about the beauty of nature connects with his readers.

AMAZON

TOWARDS THE PEBBLED SHORE (2022)

By Peter Jailall

"...thoughtfully conceived, expressed movingly and written with great clarity. I think this may be Peter's best book yet. It lifts the heart."

Ian McDonald, author The Garden and other works

TROPICAL SCENES

(2023)

By Ken Puddicombe

"Each poem covers more ground than lengthy chapters." —Cherry Narula, author: *Nona and Daniel, Goldfinch Sunshine Project.*

AMAZON

UNFATHOMABLE AND OTHER POEMS (2020)

by Ken Puddicombe

These poems cover a variety of themes, all connected to a childhood growing up in British Guiana, the rise of nationalism and the pre- and post-independence eras.

AMAZON

WEALTH THROUGH REAL ESTATE INVESTING (2021)

By Jay Brijpaul

Jay Brijpaul has tapped his vast experience and expertise in the Real Estate industry. This book provides comprehensive coverage of What, How, When, Where to invest in real estate.

AMAZON

WINDWARD LEGS (2021)

By Dave Moores

A pungent cocktail of choppy romance, corporate larceny and the thrills and spills of sailboat racing, Windward Legs is the rousing and captivating story of a woman's journey to rediscover who she is.

AMAZON

WITHOUT A WURDUVA LIE (2024)

By GARRY FERGUSON

An entertaining and humourous compendium of short stories and poetry that reflect a now-vanished way of life in small communities.

AMAZON

**WITNESSES AND OTHER STORIES
(2020)**

By Raymond Holmes

"Suspenseful, historical, futuristic and riveting...stories and characters who will stay with you." —Bruce A. Hanson, Award winning author of adult and children's fiction.

AMAZON

www.ingramcontent.com/pod-product-compliance
Lightning Source LLC
Chambersburg PA
CBHW072222170626
46813CB00003B/1064